WEED KILLERS

(CHRISTMAS MOURNING)

JUDY FORD

Bernie Fazakerley
Publications

Weed Killers

(Christmas Mourning)

Published by Bernie Fazakerley Publications

Copyright © 2020 Judy Ford.

Madonna and Child image © 2018 Catherine Young

ISBN13: 978-1-911083-66-5

ISBN10: 1-91-108366-X

DEDICATION

This book is dedicated to the memory of Luke
Rotherham 13/8/1983 to 5/1/2011.

He was quiet and reserved but became an
animated extrovert in front of an audience.

An actor, writer and director, a deep thinker,
loved by people of all ages.

"Because I knew you I have been changed for good."

CONTENTS

MAP OF OXFORD

For details of the licence governing distribution of data contained in this map, see www.openstreetmap.org/copyright

1. THE NINTH DAY BEFORE CHRISTMAS

'What's up? Are you OK?' Peter stepped back to allow his unexpected visitor to enter.

'Yes. I'm fine.' Trainee Police Constable Stella Gilbert nodded perfunctorily and looked up at Peter with a weak smile. Then she bowed her head and shielded her face from his gaze by putting up her hand to remove her uniform hat. 'It's just, Inspector Burton told me to go home, but if I'm back before the end of my shift Gran will want to know why and I …,' she sniffed and wiped her arm across her face. 'I don't want her to …'

Peter stared in dismay as she seemed to be about to break down in tears. He put out his arm towards her, shepherding her past the old-fashioned oak hall stand, gaily decorated with tinsel and fairy lights in recognition of the season, and down the passage towards the kitchen.

'Come in here and sit down and-'

'Granddad!' A small child emerged from a room on the left, ran down the hall and took hold of Peter round one leg. 'Come back and play!'

'Not now, Ricky,' Peter told him gently. 'We've got a visitor. Go and get Abigail and come into the kitchen. We're all going to have a drink and a biscuit. How's that?'

'A *chocolate* biscuit?' asked Ricky, hopefully.

'That's right,' Peter nodded, 'a chocolate biscuit. But don't let on to Mummy,' he added conspiratorially, putting his fingers to his lips to signify silence. 'She told me you eat too much chocolate.'

Ricky stared back with a glare of disapproval on his small brown face. Stella smiled in spite of her distress.

'I agree with you Ricky,' she told him. 'I don't see how anyone can have too much chocolate!'

Peter led the way into the kitchen. He filled the kettle at the sink and left it to boil while he searched in a wall cupboard for the biscuits. Stella sat down at the large wooden table and put her hat down in front of her. A scuffling at the door announced the arrival of Ricky and his younger sister Abigail.

Stella turned to look at them. They made an odd pair. Ricky's dark skin, brown eyes and frizzy black hair contrasted starkly with his sister's ginger mop and pale pink cheeks. She stood in the doorway watching the newcomer with wondering green eyes. In her experience, guests often brought presents, especially at this time of the year.

Ricky climbed up on to the chair next to Stella's and sat watching his grandfather expectantly, with his elbows planted firmly on the table and his hands ready for the promised treat. Abigail toddled in after him and came to a stop holding on to Stella's chair, looking up hopefully into her face. Stella, smiling kindly, bent down and lifted her on to her lap.

Peter handed a chocolate-covered biscuit to each of the children and then put down the packet on the table, within Stella's reach but far enough from Ricky that he would not be able to help himself to more. He poured water into a large brown teapot and set it down on the table along with two mugs and a jug of milk. Then he took a seat opposite Stella and looked her in the eye. 'Now tell me what this is all about,' he urged gently.

'It – it was horrible,' Stella began. Then she stopped and took a bite out of her biscuit. Peter poured the tea without speaking and pushed one of the mugs towards her.

'It's PC Hughes,' Stella resumed. 'This car just ran him down.'

'Gavin?' Peter exclaimed in alarm, dropping his biscuit in

his tea and hastily fishing it out with a spoon.

'No,' Stella shook her head vigorously, 'not Gavin. I meant Kenny. You know – Kenny Hughes. Gavin's his dad. I never thought before; I suppose they're both PC Hughes. I'm paired with him at the moment. He's been really good at letting me get more experience.'

'Does Gavin know about it?' Peter demanded, leaning anxiously across the table towards Stella. 'How badly hurt is Kenny?'

'I don't know,' Stella replied miserably. 'The ambulance took him off to A and E. He was still breathing, but he looked bad – sort of the wrong colour, if you know what I mean. I suppose Inspector Burton will have told Gavin – I never thought of that. She said I looked shaken up and I ought to go home and rest, but I want to know how Kenny is and I don't want Gran to know about it.' Then, seeing Peter looking at her, she added, 'at least not yet.'

'OK.' Peter sat back again and picked up his mug. 'Drink your tea and tell me about it from the beginning.'

Stella swallowed a mouthful of tea, took a deep breath and began her story.

'Inspector Burton asked us to help with a raid on this big house in Kidlington. Someone had reported there was something wrong about it, I'm not sure what. I think it was drugs being stored there or something. Anyway, Inspector Burton asked me and Kenny to wait round the back in case anyone came out that way. It's an old-ish house and they've built more houses behind it and another road, and it's got a garage in the back garden. They didn't think anyone was in the house, but just in case, they sent us round the back to catch them if they tried to get out that way.'

'I see,' Peter nodded encouragingly. 'And Tracy – Inspector Burton – went in at the front, did she?'

'That's right. She had about six officers with her, so I know it must've been something big. We heard them shouting for them to open up, and then we heard them breaking the door down. Then, all of a sudden, the garage door opened and this guy came out of it. When he saw us, he tried to make a run for it, but Kenny caught him and told me to put the handcuffs on him. He said …,' Stella gulped and took a sip of tea. 'He said to me this would be my first real arrest. He told me to caution him, so I started saying the words, but then there was this awful noise of a car coming towards us and Kenny – Kenny pushed us back into the garage.'

'And the car hit Kenny?' prompted Peter gently as Stella fell silent.

'Mm-mm,' Stella nodded, her eyes wide and frightened. 'It hit him an awful whack and smashed him against the wall, and then it raced off up the road. I didn't think to try to get the number until it was too far away and I couldn't read it. The guy I'd arrested pulled away from me – I couldn't stop him – and ran after it.'

'Did he get away?'

'No. I forgot to say, PC Stanton was there as well, with PD Q. She let Q go and she chased him and caught him by the arm. You should have heard the way he swore when PC Stanton arrested him again! I think Q probably left some tooth marks on him where he tried to get away from her.' Stella smiled briefly and then her face fell again. 'Kenny was just lying there at the bottom of the wall. I tried to help him, but I couldn't remember all the things I was supposed to do. I just held him and told him the ambulance would be there soon. PC Stanton took the man off round to the front of the house and then we were on our own. It seemed like ages before the ambulance came.'

'You were there with him, that's the main thing,' Peter said earnestly. 'Don't think about all the things you didn't do. Everyone feels like that when something like that happens. We always think we could have done more, but all anyone can do is to do their best.'

He glanced down at his watch.

'The kids' mum will be here any minute,' he told her. 'She's on an early shift this week. As soon as they're off my hands, I'll take you over to the hospital to see Kenny. How's that?'

'Would you really? That would be great,' Stella smiled back. 'I want to know he's alright before I go home and have to tell Gran … She worries about me, you see. She thinks policing is a dangerous job and … I'm afraid she'll want me to give it up.'

'Well, she's not wrong that you could have picked a safer career,' Peter remarked cautiously, 'and of course she worries about you, but I'm sure she understands that it's what you want to do.'

'But what if I'm no good at it?' faltered Stella, self-doubt resurging as she remembered how she had missed taking the number of the car and fumbled in caring for her injured colleague.

'You *are* good at it,' Peter assured her firmly. 'Even Jonah says so, and he's never one to admit that anyone measures up to his high standards when it comes to policing!'

'That's not fair!' Stella giggled in spite of her anxieties. She was well aware of the friendly rivalry that there had been between the two detectives, before Peter's retirement from Thames Valley CID. 'DCI Porter never criticises other officers. You're just being mean to him to make me feel better.'

'And we certainly can't afford to lose you,' Peter continued, relieved to see her smiling. 'We need more black officers in the force, and especially women. You're doing a great job and don't let anyone tell you otherwise.'

The doorbell rang. Ricky was immediately off his seat and pulling at the kitchen door. Abigail too, wriggled on Stella's lap and struggled to get down.

'That'll be Crystal,' Peter said, getting to his feet. 'Alright, Ricky, I'm coming!'

He hurried through the hall, impeded by Ricky pushing past his legs, and opened the door to admit his daughter-in-law. She stood smiling on the doorstep for a moment, her blue coat hanging open over her nurse's uniform, before stepping forward and sweeping her son off his feet as Ricky hurled himself towards her.

'Get your coat, it's time to go home, young man!' she

declared, hugging him to her and then setting him back down on his feet. 'Have you been a good boy for Granddad?'

'Yes,' Ricky assured her confidently. Then he turned and headed off to a row of hooks attached at child-height to the wall next to the hall stand. He selected a blue duffle coat and put one arm into it. Peter helped him to put it on while Crystal kneeled down to greet her daughter, who had followed Peter and Ricky out of the kitchen.

Abigail smiled and threw her small arms around her mother. Crystal hugged her tight and then exclaimed in dismay as she looked down and saw the brown chocolatey smears that had appeared on her uniform. She gently turned Abigail's hands over so that she could see the palms.

'Oh Abby!' she sighed. 'What have you got on these hands of yours? I think we'd better clean you up before we go home, don't you?'

'Sorry,' Peter apologised. 'It's my fault, I'm afraid. I gave them chocolate biscuits just a few minutes before you got here. I should have-'

'You said not to tell!' Ricky interrupted indignantly. '*I* didn't say about the chocolate. Why did you-?'

'When you're caught red-handed it's better to plead guilty,' Peter told him with a smile. 'Now let's see your hands too. I don't want to be responsible for any more damage.'

'My hands aren't red,' Ricky insisted, hiding them behind his back, 'and Abby's aren't either – they're pink! And yours are pink with brown spots,' he added as an afterthought, bringing his right hand back out in order to point at Peter's freckles.

'I can see you're practising to be a lawyer when you grow up,' Stella intervened, coming out of the kitchen with a pack of wet-wipes which she had spotted on the working surface there. 'You could convince people that black was white with all your arguments!' She turned to Crystal. 'I'm sorry, I think I'm the guilty one. I turned up unannounced and Peter gave us all a drink and a biscuit.'

While the two young women cleaned the children's hands

and faces and helped them into coats and gloves, Peter busied himself wandering round the house collecting together items for them to take home: books, toys, plastic drinking cups and Abby's favourite blanket, without which she could not sleep. Soon they were all ready to go.

'I'm off duty tomorrow,' Crystal reminded Peter, as she fastened Ricky into his safety seat in the back of her car. 'And Eddie's on leave from Thursday, because he's got days he has to use up before the end of the year, so you'll only have the kids for Wednesday and then a nice long holiday until the New Year.'

'Don't forget, I'm always happy to have them for a few hours, if you and Eddie need some time to yourselves. It doesn't have to be just when you're both working.'

'I won't forget, but you do plenty already. I don't know how we'd manage without you to be honest.'

Crystal got into the car and prepared to drive off. Then she wound the window down and added, 'and you've got Jonah to care for as well, remember. And Lucy will be home soon, too!'

'Lucy will want her turn with the kids,' Peter responded, 'so don't be backward in come forward if you need any help with them over Christmas. I know what it's like for nurses when everyone else is off and you still have to work.'

He watched as the car moved off down the drive and turned out into the road, waving at Ricky's face, pressed up against the window, until it disappeared out of sight behind the tall copper beech hedge. Then he turned back to Stella.

'OK. Shall we go to the hospital now?'

* * *

'There he is!'

Peter looked across the waiting area, following Stella's pointing finger, and immediately identified the blue bulk of PC Gavin Hughes, still in his police uniform, resting on a rather inadequate-looking seat fixed to the wall. His size 13 shoes were planted firmly on the floor and his long legs were splayed allowing his huge hands to dangle between them. He sat staring straight ahead, unseeing as if in a trance.

Two seats along from Gavin, Peter saw a plump woman in a full skirt and a hand-knitted jumper. That must be Gavin's wife. He had met her once or twice, but not for some time. She was busy knitting, the wool trailing down from the needles into a large carrier bag lying at her feet.

Feeling Stella hesitating beside him, Peter strode across the room and stood in front of Gavin, who gave a start and looked up.

'Gavin?' Peter said tentatively. 'Stella told me what happened. We came to see …'

'Stella?' Gavin replied in a puzzled tone.

'Stella Gilbert,' Peter repeated. 'She was with Kenny when it happened.'

Gavin looked round and seemed to see Stella for the first time.

'You were there?' he asked, still sounding bewildered. 'I'm sorry, they didn't tell me. It must have been … Are you alright?'

'Yes,' Stella nodded, stepping forward and putting her hand tentatively on Gavin's broad shoulder. 'The car didn't touch me. Kenny pushed me out of the way.'

'They told us at reception you were waiting here,' Peter explained. 'Is there any news?'

'He's in theatre,' Christine answered when her husband did not reply. 'They said it might be some time.' She pushed the wool firmly on to the needles and stowed her knitting away in the carrier bag. 'Would you like some ginger cake?'

She picked up a large square cake tin, which was lying on the unoccupied seat between her and Gavin, opened it and held it out towards Peter and Stella. 'Go on – help yourselves. I made it last night. It's good, though I say it myself!'

They both took a piece of the sticky confection. Christine offered the tin to Gavin, who shook his head morosely. She put it back down and closed the lid firmly. Then she bent down and fished her knitting back out of her bag.

'Excuse me getting on with this,' she said, looking up at Peter and Stella. 'I promised Mr Bannister I'd have twenty pairs of these gloves done by Friday.'

Peter nodded his acquiescence and silently waved away her apology. He sat down next to her, wishing that the seats were arranged more conveniently for conversation. To speak to Gavin, he would have to lean over Christine and the tin of gingerbread.

'They're for the homeless shelter,' Christine continued. 'It's only open at night, so the guests are out on the streets during the day. So we're aiming to see that they each have a warm hat, scarf and gloves before the coldest weather sets in.'

Stella sat down next to Peter, who turned to her and smiled reassuringly.

'We always go down there on Christmas morning, don't we Gav?' Christine went on. 'There's a church lets us use their hall to give them Christmas dinner. I've got ten Christmas puddings all lined up ready, haven't I Gav?'

Gavin nodded absently and continued to stare into the distance.

Peter glanced down at his watch, wondering how long they ought to stay. Having come, he did not like to leave his ex-colleague in this state of shock, but the note that he had left for his wife, Bernie, had suggested that he was simply enquiring after Kenny's condition and then coming back to get their evening meal. And there was Stella to consider. A lengthy wait and an uncertain outcome was not calculated to improve her state of anxiety.

'What time does your shift end?' he whispered to her. 'When does your Gran expect you home?'

Stella consulted her own watch. 'Forty minutes,' she whispered back.

'In that case, I suggest we stay for half an hour and if he's not out of surgery by then I'll take you home. We don't want your gran worrying.'

He had hardly finished speaking when a door opened and two women dressed in surgical scrubs came through. They looked round the waiting area as if searching for something. Then the younger of the two led the way across to Gavin and his wife.

'Mr and Mrs Hughes?' the older woman asked, looking down first at Gavin and then at Christine.

'Yes?' Christine immediately looked up hopefully and pushed her knitting further on to the needles as if preparing to go somewhere. Gavin also looked up, more alert than he had seemed since Peter and Stella has arrived.

'I'm Davina Greenslade,' she told them. 'I'm a consultant surgeon. I operated on your son, Kenneth.' She paused and looked from Gavin to Christine again and then round at the others. 'I – I wonder – shall we go somewhere a bit more private?'

She looked towards the door, but neither Christine nor Gavin moved from their seats.

'How is he?' Christine demanded at once. Then, seeing the doctor looking dubiously towards Peter, she added, 'It's OK. These are friends of ours. Please! Tell us at once!'

'Well, if you're sure …?'

'Yes – yes!' Christine's face became more anxious and her eyes flashed across to the other woman, who gave her a little half-smile of compassion, and then back to Davina Greenslade. 'There's something wrong, isn't there?'

'I'm very sorry.' The surgeon put out her hand and rested it gently on Christine's shoulder. 'We did our best, but we couldn't save him, I'm afraid.'

Gavin's mouth fell open. He leaned across and took Christine's hand in his.

'Kenny's dead?' gasped Christine. 'You're saying he's dead?'

'Yes. I'm afraid I am,' the doctor confirmed. 'His internal injuries were too extensive. We did our best, but that wasn't enough. I am truly sorry.'

'Of course,' Gavin spoke robotically without any feeling in his voice. 'It's not your fault. Thank you for trying.'

'That's right,' Christine agreed fervently. 'You're not to

blame. It's that – that – that scumbag who ran over him who ought to be sorry!' she added, suddenly raising her voice and gripping the knitting in clenched fists. Then she looked down at her hands and uncurled her fingers. Shaking her head as if astonished at her own outburst, she methodically put away her knitting and picked up the bag. 'Can we see him?' she asked. 'We'd like to say good bye – wouldn't we Gav?'

Peter tapped Stella gently on her hand and mouthed silently to her, 'I think we'd better go.'

Stella nodded. She stood up and went over to Gavin. 'Sir?' she said nervously. 'I just wanted to say how sorry I am and – and what a great mentor Kenny was. I – I – well, that's it, really.'

'Thanks.' Gavin got to his feet and patted Stella on the shoulder. 'And thanks for telling me about how it happened. I'm sorry you had to be there to see it. Don't let it put you off … I mean, you're going to make a good officer.'

Apparently exhausted by this sudden burst of eloquence, he collapsed back into his seat and put his head in his hands. Stella stood hesitating for a moment. Then, on a sudden impulse, she bent forward, put her hands on his shoulders and kissed him on the crown of his head. Then she turned round abruptly and headed for the door. Peter nodded briefly towards Gavin and Christine and then ran to catch her up.

They walked down the corridor in silence, neither of them able to think of anything to say.

'Peter! What brings you here?'

Peter looked towards the voice and saw a familiar figure in black suit and clerical collar coming out of a side corridor.

'Father Damien! It's good to see you. I suppose you must be on your rounds, visiting the sick.'

'Not exactly, the priest replied. 'Don't forget, I do one day a week hospital chaplaincy now – a little side line to keep St Cyprian's from the bankruptcy that always seems to be just around the corner. I'd love to chat, but I can't stop – I'm on my way to see a bereaved family. A road traffic accident I believe. They –' he faltered as he took in Stella's uniform and remembered Peter's long association with the police '– They told me it was a police officer. Please tell me it's not–'

'No, no,' Peter assured him hastily. 'It's no one you know … or at least … I think you have met Gavin Hughes. He does a lot of work with the homeless community. He came round and collected Brendan Connolly that night he confessed to–'

'Oh yes, Brendan!' the priest's face lit up as he remembered the incident. 'Yes, of course I remember PC Hughes, but I got the impression they were talking about someone younger.'

'His son, Kenneth,' Peter told him succinctly. 'Or Kenny, as he liked to be known. He followed his dad into the police service.'

'Are they Catholics, do you know?' Damien asked. 'Or …,' he hesitated, 'if they'd rather have one of my colleagues …? We have a humanist chaplain if they aren't …'

'I can't honestly say,' Peter answered, 'but I'm sure Gavin won't give you a hard time whatever. He's very easy-going. My guess is they're "Church of England, I suppose", he added, making quotation marks in the air with his fingers. 'Gavin isn't one of your deep thinkers. He probably got taken to Sunday School when he was a kid and never got round to questioning what he was taught there.'

'And how are they taking it? You've seen them since they found out, I take it?'

'Pole-axed,' Peter replied concisely. 'At least, that goes for Gavin. Christine, I'm not sure about – in denial I think – still knitting and handing round ginger cake.'

'She's angry too,' Stella added. '*I* think it's PC Hughes who's in denial. He looked like he couldn't believe it was happening.'

'That's not unusual,' Damien agreed. 'This sort of thing can take a long time to sink in. Did you know the dead officer well?'

'PC Gilbert was with Kenny when it happened,' Peter answered for her, seeing Stella hesitating over how to reply to this.

'Were you?' Father Damien looked towards Stella with

compassion in his eyes. 'It must have been … Look, I can't stop now, but …' He fished in his pocket and pulled out a card, which he handed to Stella. 'If you ever decide you'd like to talk to someone about it, just ring this number – it's for the chaplaincy here. Or if you'd prefer, you can get me on my mobile any time. That's on the back. Now, I'm sorry, but I must rush.'

He headed off the way they had come, while Peter and Stella continued along the corridor and out into the car park. As they approached Peter's car, his phone started to ring. He hastily unlocked the door to allow Stella to get in and then took the call.

'Bernie!' he greeted his wife, 'Are you home? I'm sorry I wasn't there when you got back, but–'

'How's Stella?' Bernie interrupted, 'and what about Kenny Hughes?'

'I'm just taking Stella home now,' Peter told her, mindful that Stella could hear his end of the conversation if not Bernie's. 'Kenny didn't make it, I'm afraid. They did emergency surgery, but he had internal injuries, or so the doctor said. Anyway, we'd better get going or Stella's gran will be wondering where she is.'

He ended the call and hurried to get into the car and drive off. It was not many minutes before they were pulling up outside the terraced house in East Oxford where Stella lived with her grandmother and one of her half-brothers.

As Peter got out and prepared to escort Stella to the front door, he glanced across at the similar house opposite, which has once been his own home. In that cramped two-up-two-down, he and Angie had brought up Hannah and Eddie. And in the small kitchen, Angie had been killed by a gang of youths who objected to a black Jamaican marrying a police officer. The latest owners had painted the brickwork white and replaced the old wooden window frames with plastic.

Celeste Gilbert had evidently been looking out for her granddaughter's return and had the door open before they reached it. She smiled when she saw Peter, but her eyes were anxious, suspecting that his unplanned presence signified that all was not well.

'Peter! How lovely to see you,' she called out in her musical West Indian accent. 'How're you doing? Come in and have a cup of tea. It's been too long since we had a chat.'

'Thanks, but I'm afraid I can't,' Peter smiled back. 'Bernie's expecting me home. I just bumped into Stella and thought I might as well drop her off on the way,' he added, trying to sound casual as if nothing out of the ordinary had taken place. 'Some other time maybe. It'd be good to catch up.'

'And to talk about old times,' Celeste nodded her agreement. 'There's not so many of us left from when you lived in the street. Old Mrs Patel has gone into a home. Your house has been sold again. There's a young Asian couple there now, with a baby and an old man – her father, I think, or maybe grandfather – who seems to spend all day at the mosque.'

'I suppose that's why they chose this road,' Peter suggested, 'to be near it.'

'And Peggy James has gone to live with her daughter,' Celeste continued, 'and the Galbraiths, who used to live next to you, they've moved back to Scotland. Like I said, me and the kids are almost all that's left of the old guard now. And talking of kids, how's Lucy getting on at uni? Is she back for Christmas yet?'

'She comes back on Saturday,' Peter told her. 'They keep the medics hard at it – none of these eight-week terms like the Oxford undergraduates!'

'I'll just nip up to my room and change out of my uniform,' Stella put in, glad that Peter's presence had deflected her grandmother from her usual questions about how her day at work had gone.

'That's right,' Celeste moved to one side to allow her to pass. 'You do that. Dinner's all ready and keeping warm in the oven.' She turned back to Peter. 'I suppose I'd better let you get off home. Don't forget to come round for that chat sometime.' Then, once Stella was safely on her way upstairs, she stepped outside and pulled the door closed behind her. 'Now Peter,' she said in a lower voice, 'how about you tell me the real reason you're here.'

'No flies on you, eh?' Peter grinned. 'OK. I'll come clean. You'll probably hear on the news that a police officer was killed on duty today.'

Celeste's eyes opened wide and she took in a breath as if preparing to speak, but Peter did not allow her time to interrupt.

'His name's Kenny Hughes,' he continued. 'Stella was with him when it happened. She's worried that it'll make you anxious about her safety, so when she tells you about it, try to keep it low-key. If you let on you're worried it'll upset her and it's bad enough for her as it is.'

'What happened?' demanded Celeste as soon as Peter finished speaking. 'Is Stella alright?' Then without waiting for a reply, she went on, 'I just *knew* something like this would happen. I said to her, "you're a bright girl, Stella, there's plenty of jobs you could do. Why you want to become a police officer, with all them lads with knives on the street – and guns, even, these days?" But would she listen to her old Grandma? – Oh no! Kids these days, they think they know it all!'

'I understand how you feel, but incidents like the one today only happen once in a blue moon. They get lots of publicity precisely *because* they're rare,' Peter argued. 'And the police service isn't the only job that has risks. Crystal was telling me only the other day about one of her nursing friends who got a black eye from a drunk in A and E.'

'But police officers deliberately put themselves in danger,' Celeste argued. 'That's the difference.'

'And it's what Stella's always wanted,' Peter coaxed gently. 'Don't you remember how proud she was when she got her first cadet uniform? And she's good at it. We need more officers like her.'

'You mean you want more black officers so you can't be accused of institutional racism,' Celeste retorted.

'Well yes, we do need more black officers, but not just to

make us look good. We need more ethnic minority officers because we need people who can identify with the disaffected youngsters who are in danger of drifting into crime – people like your Leroy was,' he added, risking a slightly more combative approach. 'He saw me as the enemy when he was a teenager. Things might have been different if there'd been officers like Stella around that he could have identified with.'

'He turned himself round though, didn't he?' Celeste said defensively.

'Yes, and all credit to him for doing it,' Peter agreed, 'but it would've been a whole lot easier for him if he'd never got that criminal record or been involved with that gang he was mixed up in. Seeing Stella out there patrolling the streets may just prevent other kids getting caught up in all that. And besides, it'll break her heart if she feels she has to give it all up to save you fretting.'

'Alright,' Celeste sighed. 'I'll play it cool, but you'd better be right about it not being as dangerous as it looks. Well, I'd better get the dinner on the table.' She turned to go back inside and then looked back at Peter. 'Will you be at the carol service on Sunday?'

'Yes,' Peter confirmed. 'We'll all be there.'

* * *

When he let himself in through the front door of their house in Headington, Peter smelled cooking coming from the kitchen. Usually it was his job to prepare the family meals, but on this occasion Bernie had responded to finding his note by taking it upon herself to make a dish of cauliflower cheese and an apple crumble, which were now safely keeping warm in the oven.

'What exactly happened?' Peter's second wife appeared in the hall before Peter had time to take off his coat. 'And how's Stella – really?' she added, having deduced that Peter had said as little as possible on the phone for fear of the young police officer overhearing.

'And who's in charge of the case?' demanded an authoritative voice from behind Bernie. 'Do they have any suspects?'

Peter smiled to himself as he saw their permanent guest, DCI Porter, emerging from the kitchen in his electric wheelchair. Trust Jonah to want chapter and verse on the investigation even before it was properly begun.

'Stella seems OK,' he replied, addressing what he saw as the most pressing point first. 'But it may mainly be that it hasn't really sunk in yet. Anyway, she's safe with her gran now. I expect they'll give her some leave to recuperate – maybe 'til the New Year.'

'In her place, I'd rather be at work,' Bernie said decidedly. 'When something like this happens, there's nothing worse than being stuck at home with nothing to do except brood on it.'

'Anyway, she'll be needed as a witness,' added Jonah brightly. He manoeuvred his chair past Bernie in order to address Peter more easily. 'Did anyone else see what happened? Have they made any arrests?'

'Look,' Peter protested, 'all I know is what Stella told me. They were assisting with a drugs raid on a house, and someone drove a car at Kenny and crushed him against a wall – that's all I can tell you. And I don't think they've assigned anyone to lead the investigation yet,' he added, giving Jonah a knowing look, 'so you may be able to muscle in and take over, like we all know you want to!'

'And suspects?' repeated Jonah insistently.

'They've got a man in custody,' Peter told him, 'but that was before the incident. Poor Stella! It was supposed to be her big moment – her first proper arrest – and now …' He sighed. 'It's a mad world where police officers get randomly killed just for doing their jobs.'

'Let's all just have our tea,' suggested Bernie, giving Jonah a warning look. 'It's all ready. I'm sure the inquisition can wait until after we've eaten.'

Peter hung his coat up on a hook on the wall and followed

Bernie back into the kitchen.

'Tell me about your day,' he said, sitting down at the large table in the centre of the room in front of a plate piled high with cauliflower cheese. 'How did the test drive go?'

'It was brilliant, wasn't it Jonah?' Bernie answered at once, grateful for the change of topic. 'They've ironed out a lot of the bugs in the software. I'm really starting to believe in the idea that this could be the future for mobility for disabled people.'

She and Jonah had spent the afternoon at a disused airfield test-driving a new driverless car that could be controlled entirely by voice commands. Although it was unlikely that it would benefit Jonah, since there were a good number of years of development still needed, he felt a sense of purpose in contributing towards a venture that might enable people with spinal injuries similar to his to travel independently in the future.

'They got me helping to simulate driving in traffic,' Bernie continued. 'I drove our car and the boys drove theirs and Jonah had to keep a safe distance and respond when we changed speed or direction.'

'I'm glad I'm usually stuck in the back where I can't see the road,' Jonah interjected with a grin. 'I had no idea you were such an erratic driver!'

'They asked me to test how the car coped when other drivers did unexpected things!' Bernie protested indignantly. 'I am a very safe driver – unlike you in that wheelchair of yours when you're on a case and in a hurry to get somewhere!'

* * *

They were just starting to wonder if it was time to begin making preparations for bed when there was a ring on the doorbell.

'Who can that be at this time of night?' wondered Jonah, looking up from the screen attached to his wheelchair where he had been scanning the news websites for more information about the attack on Kenny Hughes.

'I'll get it,' said Peter, putting down the book he was reading and getting to his feet.

Bernie and Jonah sat listening to voices in the hall, trying to work out who the visitor might be. Then the lounge door opened and Father Damien entered followed by Peter.

'I know it's late,' Damien apologised, 'but I was hoping you might be able to help me eat some of this.' He held out the cake tin that Christine Hughes had had with her at the hospital that afternoon. 'When she realised that I was single, Mrs Hughes insisted in giving me the rest of the ginger cake. She seems to think that no man could possibly eat properly if he doesn't have a woman around to look after him. I didn't like to say "no" but I've still got a mountain of shortbread that Deirdre Carr gave me yesterday.'

'Of course we'll help,' Bernie smiled. She knew that Damien often suffered from over-solicitous female members of his flock. 'Come in the kitchen and I'll make us a brew, and we'll all have some now – while you tell us how you got on with Gavin and his wife.'

'As you rightly deduced,' Damien began when they were settled round the kitchen table with cups of tea and plates of gingerbread in front of them, 'what I really came for was to give you the heads up about PC Hughes. I'm rather worried about him.'

'Me too,' Peter agreed, 'but I was hoping you might have been able to …'

'I said a prayer with them,' Damien told them, 'which they seemed grateful for, but … Well, there's Mrs Hughes busy with her knitting and talking nineteen to the dozen about the school Christmas party, and there's Gavin just sitting there staring into the distance as if he doesn't know what's hit him. I wasn't sure he was hearing me half the time.'

'Where are they now?' asked Jonah. 'Not still at the hospital, I assume?'

'Oh no! A constable drove them home. I gave them my number and some leaflets from the bereavement team and told them they were welcome to ring any time. That was about all I could do. I was wondering if he might … I don't know … feel more at ease with someone he knows, maybe with a similar background?' Damien looked meaningfully towards Peter.

'Of course. I'll go over and see him in the morning,' Peter agreed at once. 'I've known Gavin for years. He's a real salt-of-the-earth copper, but things do often take a while to sink in with him. He must have broken this sort of news to lots of people over the years. He'd know exactly what to do when it's someone else's son, but when it's his own…!' Peter sighed. 'He must be quite lost, but maybe after a night's sleep …'

'If he can get any sleep' Bernie observed drily. 'I don't think I would.'

'And if he happens to mention anyone who might have had it in for Kenny-' Jonah began, but Bernie cut him off short.

'You can stop right there,' she said with more anger in her voice than she had intended. 'Peter's going over there to support Gavin, not to cross-examine him for you! If those questions need to be asked, it'll be up to the SIO – when they're appointed – to decide when to ask them.'

'I only thought-,' Jonah tried to defend himself.

'No, you didn't,' Peter backed Bernie up with unusual vigour. 'You didn't think. That's your trouble. *If* you get put in charge of this case *then* you can start thinking about questioning Gavin and Christine. Until then just back off, can't you?'

'I thought you were retired,' Damien said to Jonah in the silence that followed, hoping to turn the conversation on to a less contentious topic. 'Is there really a chance that you'll be called on to investigate this awful business?'

'Jonah's been allowed back part-time,' Bernie told him, forcing herself to speak calmly. 'There's a shortage of experienced detectives and the government has committed to increasing police numbers, so it sort of suits everyone.'

'I work Tuesday to Thursday each week,' Jonah added. 'So I'll be back on duty tomorrow, with no currently outstanding cases in my in-tray.'

'And we all know what you'll be doing the moment you get in in the morning,' Bernie grinned, her anger evaporating as quickly as it had come. 'You'll be hammering on the Chief Super's door demanding to be given this murder to sort out.'

'Well, somebody's got to do it,' Jonah grinned back.

'Just so long as you don't go harassing Gavin,' Peter conceded ungraciously. He secretly hoped that Jonah would be the Senior Investigating Officer and that he would be allowed to assist from the side lines, but he was not going to give his friend the satisfaction of knowing this. He turned back to Damien. 'Thanks for giving us the heads-up. Poor Gavin's a lot more sensitive than people think. Just because he's built like a rhinoceros, it doesn't mean he's got a skin like one.'

'Well, I'd better be off,' the priest said, getting to his feet. 'Will I see you at Mass on Sunday?' he asked, looking towards Peter.

'We'll be there,' Jonah answered for him. 'We need all the help we can get with this mess. Better say a few hail Marys for Gavin and Christine while you're about it too!'

2. THE EIGHTH DAY BEFORE CHRISTMAS

'Hang on! Just let me move that out of your way.' Gavin bent down and picked up the large cardboard box that was blocking Peter's route past the tall Christmas tree which stood just inside the door of the small front room. He stood holding it while Peter squeezed past and sat down in one of three large armchairs upholstered in serviceable brown velvet.

'I'm putting all this stuff away,' he went on, putting the box back down on the floor and waving his arm towards the Christmas tree, covered with baubles and tinsel on one side and bare on the other. 'We can't face all the ... I mean, it'd feel so strange without Kenny to ... I'll put the kettle on,' he finished, pushing past the box and disappearing out of the door.

Peter sat staring round and wondering what he was going to say to Gavin when he returned. Any words would feel inadequate and banal. The room was decorated with crepe paper streamers. Clusters of balloons hung at the corners of the ceiling. The bay window had fairy lights attached around each pane and a large gold-coloured star surrounded by spray-on snow in its centre. All round the picture rail Christmas cards hung on multi-coloured ribbons.

Peter lowered his eyes and noticed the much smaller array of sympathy cards ranged along the mantelpiece over where there had once been a hearth. He should have brought one he supposed, but it was always so difficult to choose such things and even harder to know what to write inside them. Whoever had sent these had been quick off the mark – neighbours, perhaps? Or colleagues who had heard the news on the police grapevine.

'Here you are!' Gavin returned with a tray, which he put down on top of the cardboard box while he pulled out a small table from under the television set. 'I hope tea's OK, I forgot to ask if you'd prefer coffee.'

'Tea's fine,' Peter assured him, leaning forward to help with moving two mugs and a plate of chocolate brownies from the tray on to the table.

'And I haven't brought the sugar,' Gavin continued anxiously. 'Shall I-?'

'No. That's fine. I don't take it.'

'Good.' Gavin sounded relieved. Probably his wife always took care of entertaining guests and he was nervous about getting something wrong. 'Help yourself,' he added, picking up the plate and holding it out towards Peter.

'Thanks.' Peter took one of the brownies and sat contemplating it for a few moments, conscious that he should say something but unsure how to begin.

'Chrissie's gone into work,' Gavin told him when the silence started to become uncomfortable. 'She says she can't let the children down. They've been practising so hard for their nativity play tomorrow and she's in charge. And … she doesn't want them to know … I mean, she's afraid it would upset them … and it might spoil their Christmas.'

Peter remembered that Gavin's wife taught at a Special School for children with profound physical and learning disabilities. Yes, perhaps it would be difficult to explain her sudden absence to them. But surely she could have used a little white lie? Mrs Hughes isn't well today – almost certainly not a lie in any case. More likely, she didn't want to be left at home with Gavin, putting Christmas away before it had even started and brooding on what had happened to their son. Or maybe she was subconsciously hoping that if she ignored Kenny's death it would magically go away.

'I don't blame her,' Gavin was continuing. 'I'd much rather be at work myself, only I wouldn't be much use. I don't seem to be able to concentrate on anything for five minutes.'

'You're on compassionate leave then? How long've they given you?'

'The Chief Super says "as long as it takes". I don't know if that's a hint that it's time I jacked the job in. I've done my thirty years.'

His friend sounded so despondent that Peter hastened to reassure him. 'I'm sure she didn't mean it like that. The last thing she needs is to lose a good experienced officer. That's what she means – don't come back too soon and end up going off on long-term sick.'

'Chrissie says the great thing is to keep busy,' Gavin resumed. 'So I'm going to try to get some of the jobs done around the house that I never get time for – once I've got this lot out of the way,' he added looking round at the Christmas tree and decorations. He sighed. 'I started making a list, but I just don't seem to be able to think straight today.'

'That's not surprising,' Peter assured him gently. 'I remember when Angie was killed the simplest things just seemed impossible to get right. If I hadn't known that I had to keep the show on the road for the sake of the kids I'd probably have completely fallen apart. But even so, I don't know where I'd have been if Bernie hadn't stepped in and helped.'

'We always thought we'd have a string of kids,' Gavin said unexpectedly. 'But Chrissie had a haemorrhage after Kenny was born and they had to operate to save her life. They patched her up, but after that we couldn't have any more.'

'I'm sorry,' Peter mumbled lamely, the full extent of his friend's loss suddenly hitting home. He ought to say something, but what could you say to a man who had just lost his only child – and in such a brutal way? He was still struggling to find the right words when the doorbell rang.

'Excuse me,' Gavin said, getting to his feet and making his way out of the room, stumbling over the box of Christmas decorations as he did so.

Peter listened to the sounds from the hall: Gavin's heavy footsteps, followed by the latch turning and a faint murmur of traffic once the door was open.

'PC Hughes?' came a bright, young voice. 'Toby Hitchin. I don't think we've met, but Ken told me a lot about you. We did our basic training together. I just wanted to come round and – you know – give my condolences.'

'You'd better come in.'

The door snapped shut and there were more sounds of footsteps on the tiles. Then a fresh-faced young man in police uniform appeared in the room. He looked across at Peter with a puzzled expression. Peter got up and held out his hand.

'This is Peter Johns,' Gavin explained from behind the youth. 'He was a DI back in the day.'

'Oh. Right. I get it.' The young man accepted Peter's proffered hand and shook it briefly. 'PC Toby Hitchin. I think you must've been before my time.'

'I expect so,' Peter agreed, sitting down again. 'It's a while back now.'

'But he still takes an interest,' Gavin put in. 'He lives with DCI Porter. You must know him.'

'The wheelchair cop!' Toby exclaimed. 'Yes, of course I've heard of him – never met him though. So you're mates with the great Jonah Porter? That must be exciting. Did you work with him on any of his cases?'

'Not since he became famous,' Peter told him shortly.

'Tea?' enquired Gavin, 'and please, do sit down.'

'No thanks,' Toby shook his head. 'I don't want to be any trouble. I just wanted to tell you what a great guy Ken was and how much he'll be missed.'

'Well at least take one of my wife's brownies,' Gavin urged. 'She'll be disappointed to know you came round and didn't try them.'

'Thanks.' The constable took one of the cakes and sat down next to Peter. Then he seemed to remember something, stood up again and started fumbling in his pocket. He took out a large mauve envelope and handed it to Gavin. 'This is from me and some of the others on the night shift,' he told him before subsiding back into his chair.

'Thanks.' Gavin put down the plate of brownies and opened the envelope. The card that it contained had a garland of flowers and the words "With Deepest Sympathy" on the front. He opened it and scanned down the list of names inside. 'Tell them all, thank you very much.' He walked over to the mantelpiece and added the card to the row.

'In fact,' Gavin turned to face Toby again. 'Take them back some of the brownies. I'll get a box for them.'

Peter thought he detected an expression of relief on his friend's face as Gavin bustled out of the room. He turned to speak to Toby.

'So you're one of Kenny's mates?'

'Well,' Toby admitted through a mouthful of chocolate brownie, 'we *were*, but I haven't seen much of him since I was transferred to Banbury.'

'Ah!' Peter nodded, wondering to himself whether he was being unfair in suspecting that the young man was revelling in the role he had cast for himself as best buddy of the deceased. 'It was good of you to come all the way from Banbury – especially after working a night shift.'

'Actually,' Toby admitted, 'it was a good excuse for getting a morning in Oxford to do some Christmas shopping.'

Well, at least he was honest enough to admit that the visit suited his own ends, and he hadn't taken time out of his shift to pay his respects – even if he had failed to change out of his uniform before going off on his shopping trip. His sergeant might have a few words to say to him about that.

Gavin returned with an empty margarine tub, which he proceeded to pack full of the sticky chocolate treats. 'Will that be enough to go round?'

'Yeah, thanks. The guys will really appreciate that.' Toby took the box and stood up again. 'I suppose I'd better be getting off. I don't want to be any trouble, I just wanted you to know what a great guy Ken was and how much we all liked and respected him. We had a lot of good laughs too, while we were training. He'll be missed.'

'Thanks,' Gavin muttered, 'I appreciate you coming.' He opened the door and Toby, still repeating ritual platitudes, followed him out. Peter heard the front door closing and Gavin's footsteps returning along the hall.

'How about I give you a hand with putting these things away?' he suggested, putting down his empty mug and heading over to the Christmas tree. 'Do the decorations all go in this box?'

'Yes, that's right. The tinsel and baubles just go in the bottom and then there's this other box for these to stop them getting squashed.' Gavin plucked a stylised angel from the tree and held it up for Peter to see. It was constructed from a cone of shiny card with a ball of cotton wool for a head, and wings cut from a paper doily. 'Kenny made these when he was in Junior School. We've put them on the tree every year since. There should be ten of them. I've only found four so far, so that leaves six more still on the tree.'

Peter nodded sympathetically as he started methodically stripping the tree of its adornments, lining the box with tinsel and then placing the baubles carefully on top.

'We bought these for Kenny's first Christmas,' Gavin told him, fingering a collection of brightly-painted wooden figures: Mary, Joseph, a donkey and various other animals, and a manger with baby Jesus lying in it. 'My mum said it was disrespectful hanging them on the tree, but I couldn't see the harm in it.'

'I can't either,' Peter agreed, 'but I suppose it's more usual to have them in a crib.'

He carried on lifting items off the branches and stowing them carefully in the box. A few minutes later it seemed that all that was left were the fairy lights and a large silver star on the very top of the tree. Peter stretched up to reach this down.

'There are only nine!' Gavin murmured, gazing down at the box of paper angels. 'Where's the other one got to?'

Peter walked round the tree examining every branch,

conscious of the importance of finding the missing ornament.

'Perhaps if we take the lights off we'll spot it while we're doing it,' he suggested. 'Sometimes the more you look for a thing, the more difficult it is to find it.'

'It's a green one,' Gavin informed him, following Peter's advice and unplugging the lights. 'There were three red ones, three gold ones and four green ones.'

They carefully unwound the chain of lights from the branches and Peter wound up the flex and added the lights to the top of the cardboard box. Gavin continued to peer at the tree in search of the missing angel. 'It's not here,' he concluded at last. 'Maybe it dropped down the back.'

He reached under the branches and felt around behind the large pot in which the tree was planted. No luck.

'Let's pull the tree out so we can get behind it,' suggested Peter. Still no sign of the missing angel. Peter wondered if he dared suggest that Gavin could have been mistaken in thinking that there were ten. Wouldn't an equal number of each colour have been more likely? But he had evidently counted the angels every Christmas for perhaps the last twenty years. It was inconceivable that he had got it wrong.

Gavin scrambled to his feet and stretched his back. 'Oh well!' he sighed. 'I guess it's just one of those things. Better get this tree outside, I suppose. Do you mind going ahead and opening the doors?'

He picked up the pot with surprising ease and followed Peter with it down the hall and out through the front door.

'Steady on!' came a startled voice from outside, which Peter recognised, with some surprise, as Jonah's.

He was waiting outside for Bernie to ring the bell. He backed his wheelchair away from the door as the tree appeared through it threatening to collide with him.

'Sorry!' Gavin apologised, aghast at his near miss. 'I didn't know you were there.'

'It's my fault,' Peter added. 'I should have looked out and checked there was no one about when I opened the door.'

'No harm done!' Bernie declared heartily, keen to alleviate

Gavin's anxiety. 'Now, if you can just put that tree down somewhere out of the way so I can get Jonah's ramp in place …?'

Gavin deposited the tree on a gravel area at the side of the drive before turning to greet Jonah and Bernie.

'Come in both of you,' he called to them, following behind Jonah as he drove his chair up the ramp and in through the front door. 'The sitting room's on the left!'

Jonah led the way into the front room, which seemed much larger now that it was no longer dominated by the big Christmas tree, and parked his chair facing the group of armchairs. Bernie followed carrying a laptop computer. Gavin closed the front door and then joined them.

'Sit down,' he urged Bernie. 'Would you like some tea?'

'We won't, thanks,' Jonah replied in a business-like manner. 'This isn't a social call, I'm afraid. I've been put in charge of investigating who ran Kenny down and why. We're here to bring you up to date with progress and to ask you some questions – if that's OK?'

'Yes, of course.' Gavin hurried across the room and sat down opposite Jonah. 'But I don't see what I can tell you. I mean, surely he was just in the wrong place at the wrong time?'

'You're probably right,' Jonah agreed, 'but we can't just assume that. The chances are it was a member of the drugs gang trying to stop him arresting his mate – or maybe just out to get a police officer – but you never know, it could have been more personal. Can you think of anyone who could have had a grudge against Kenny?'

'No.' Gavin shook his head.

'Stella says he was very popular,' Peter added.

'No criminals who blamed him for getting them put away?' Jonah suggested.

'No.' Gavin shook his head again. 'He didn't get involved in that sort of thing – organised crime and stuff. He was like me – just an ordinary bobby on the beat. I can't see any of the drunks and shoplifters that he arrested being out to kill him.'

'Did he have a girlfriend?' queried Jonah, abruptly changing tack, 'or any ex-girlfriends?'

Gavin's mouth dropped open. For several seconds he did not speak. Jonah sat in silence watching and waiting.

'Bella!' Gavin gasped at last. 'We should've told her! I suppose she'll have heard on the news. Have they released his name yet?'

'Yes,' Bernie confirmed. 'It was on the breakfast show this morning – just his name and rank, nothing about you or your family.'

'Who is Bella?' asked Jonah gently.

'Kenny's girlfriend – or she was until a few weeks ago. They stopped seeing each other back in October.'

'Did she break it off or did he dump her or was it mutual?' Jonah enquired.

'I'm not sure,' Gavin shook his head slowly with a rather vacant expression on his face. He seemed to be thinking. 'I can't remember exactly what he said about it – just not to invite her over for drinks at Christmas. That's all I remember. Chrissie might know more about it.'

'And how long had they been together?'

'Nine months – a year maybe. She came over on Boxing Day last year, so they must have met before that. They weren't living together. Kenny still had his room here with us and she lives with her parents too. But they used to go out together most evenings when he wasn't on duty, and they went to Ibiza together in the summer.'

'And you've no idea what made them fall out?' Jonah persisted.

'I think she was finding it hard to come to terms with him being in the force,' Gavin replied after another long pause. 'I remember a couple of times her ringing us wanting to know where he was when he got called out unexpectedly or couldn't get away at the end of his shift – you know how it is.'

'She'd have preferred him to have a nine-to-five job?' suggested Jonah.

'Yes,' Gavin agreed, 'and I think it got worse after she lost her own job. She was with Thomas Cook[1]. But we still ought to have told her,' he repeated regretfully. 'She shouldn't have had to hear it on the news.'

'We can get someone to do that for you,' Jonah offered. 'If you just give me her name and address, I'll get someone to go out to her. She may not have got to hear about it yet. Not everyone listens to the breakfast news.'

'Her name's Bella Kennedy,' Gavin told him gratefully. 'She lives in Kidlington, but I don't have the address. Kenny will have it written down somewhere. Shall I have a look in his room?'

'We'll do that,' Jonah said, forestalling Gavin who was in the act of getting to his feet. 'We'd better check his room anyway.'

Gavin slumped back into his chair.

'Just routine,' Jonah assured him, noticing a hint of alarm on his face. 'I'm sure it *is* just a random incident, but we have to consider all the possibilities, just in case.'

Peter detected the slight touch of annoyance in his voice as he added, 'I suppose Kenny's room is upstairs?'

'That's right,' Gavin nodded. 'The bathroom's straight ahead of you when you go up. Kenny's room is next to it to the left.'

'Peter?' Jonah looked towards his friend. 'Do you mind going up and having a look around? You know the sort of thing we're after, don't you?'

Peter nodded, getting to his feet and heading off on his errand. Jonah smiled at him gratefully as he passed. He did not often allow himself to become frustrated with his disability, and on this occasion his irritation was caused not so much by his inability to climb the stairs as by his own lack of forethought in not having brought another officer with him to perform a task that he ought to have anticipated.

Following Gavin's directions, Peter found Kenny's room easily. It was a little smaller than the lounge and was at the

---

[1] This famous British travel company collapsed in September 2019.

back of the house, overlooking the garden. He had kept it remarkably tidy for a young man in his twenties – quite unlike Peter's experience with his own son, Eddie. A tribute to police discipline and order, perhaps? Or maybe his mother had a hand in it.

There was a small desk in a corner near the window with a computer on it and two drawers at the side. Peter advanced across the room and opened the upper drawer, feeling a pang of guilt at the intrusion but knowing that it was a necessary part of the investigation. Nothing of interest here – just a collection of pens and a pocket calculator.

The second drawer was more promising. It contained a diary and a small notebook. Peter took them out and flicked through the pages. The diary was blank – but then who used a paper diary these days? It was probably a present from an older relative who did not realise that young people kept all their appointments in their phones. Where was Kenny's phone? Probably taken from him in the hospital with the rest of his personal effects and now handed over to Jonah's team.

He turned his attention to the notebook. The first page had a list of apparently random words and phrases, some with letters replaced by numbers or other characters – probably passwords, Peter deduced. They might come in handy when it came to investigating Kenny's phone and computer. The following pages had names – some with addresses, others with only telephone numbers. They were in no particular order, presumably added consecutively as Kenny acquired a need for them. Peter sat down at the desk and thumbed methodically through the book.

Eventually he struck gold. The name "Bella" appeared at the top of a page, with a mobile phone number beneath it, followed by a date: 6th June 1992. Then, lower down, "Belinda and John" and an address in Kidlington. This must surely be Bella Kennedy, and the other two names were presumably her parents.

Peter debated whether to go straight back down with this information, but then decided that, once downstairs, it might be difficult to justify to Gavin the need to search his son's room further. He had better check around for any evidence that might suggest a reason for him having been targeted for an attack.

He slid open the door of a fitted wardrobe, which filled the alcove next to the chimney breast, and looked inside. The rail held a police tunic and uniform trousers, several pairs of jeans, three uniform shirts and a smart dress-shirt. Nothing remarkable here – apart from the spotless and crease-free appearance of the clothes, most likely Chrissie's doing.

At the far end of the rail hung a scout leader's uniform (long trousers for winter and shorts for summer). Had anything been done to inform the troop about what had happened to Kenny? How would those youngsters react to hearing of his violent death? Here were more people whose Christmas was set to be blighted by that mindless act.

The chest of drawers and bedside cabinet proved equally unrewarding. Kenny Hughes did not seem to have any dark secrets or skeletons in his cupboard. There was no secret cache of drugs, no threatening letters, no unexplained stash of cash, not even so much as a locked drawer where private things could be kept away from the eyes of his parents.

Peter picked up the notebook and returned to the sitting room. He held it up for Jonah to see and then handed it to Bernie.

'The address is in there,' he told them, 'along with various other names and addresses. I suppose you may want to follow up on some of them.'

'Yes. Good. I'll get Andy Lepage on to it as soon as we get back,' Jonah said briskly. 'Now, I think that's everything, so-'

'You said you were going to update Gavin on the investigation,' Peter reminded him quickly, seeing that Jonah was preparing to leave.

'Yes. I'm sorry – got the bit between my teeth a bit too much,' Jonah apologised, grinning round contritely at Gavin. 'Let's see …'

'First, tell me how Stella is,' Gavin pleaded anxiously.

'She's upset, naturally,' Jonah told him, 'but bearing up remarkably well.'

'She's determined not to let it worry her gran,' Peter added. 'She's a real trooper and no mistake!'

'She's got a counselling session booked for tomorrow,' Jonah went on, 'which reminds me: the Chief Super asked me to let you know that you're entitled too.'

'Tell her thanks, but no thanks,' Gavin responded gruffly. 'I'm not one for bearing my soul to a complete stranger.'

'I think Stella feels a bit like that,' Jonah grinned, 'but it was a condition of her being allowed back on duty, and she wants to help catch the guy who did it – and by doing more than just being our main witness to the assault.'

He paused and seemed to be thinking.

'OK,' he resumed after a few seconds, 'I suppose I'd better start with a bit of background. The owners of the house are living abroad for a couple of years – the States, I think – and they've let their house while they're away. They put their furniture into store and used a reputable agency to manage it all. As far as they were concerned, it was being occupied by a Mr and Mrs McLeod from Dundee.'

'But I take it Mr and Mrs McLeod don't exist?' suggested Peter.

'Well it seems they do, but it's not clear that they are the people who rented the house,' Jonah replied. 'But I'll come on to that in a minute. The reason the police got called in was that some of the neighbours started to get suspicious and they contacted the agent, who came over to have a look. They got no reply when they knocked on the door, and the tenants weren't answering their texts and voicemails either, so in the end they tried using their key to access the property – which was when they discovered that the locks had been changed!'

'The windows had all been covered from inside,' Bernie joined in, 'and there was a funny smell when they tried looking through the letterbox.'

'Cannabis?' asked Peter.

'That's right,' Jonah nodded. 'It turned out the whole

house had been put down to cannabis production. The upstairs rooms had been converted into hothouses, with heat lamps and automatic watering systems and all sorts, and downstairs they had all the facilities for processing the crop after harvesting. The windows were all blacked out to prevent anyone seeing the bright lights from outside and they'd rigged up some sort of ventilation shaft through the chimney.'

'And the man Stella and Kenny arrested was one of the gang trying to escape out the back way?' asked Peter. 'Did they catch any of the others?'

'No.' Jonah shook his head. 'It looks as if he was the only one in there at the time. He tried to do a bunk when Tracy and her team broke in at the front, and got neatly apprehended by Kenny. Unfortunately, he's not talking, so we've no idea where the rest of the gang are or who the driver of the car may have been.'

'He won't even tell us his name,' Bernie added.

'Too frightened to talk,' Jonah confirmed. 'He's only a young lad – more of a boy than a man – and I reckon the big boys have given him a graphic description of what will happen to him if he grasses on them. We're keeping him in custody while we work on finding out who he is and try to convince him that, since he's clearly guilty of involvement in the manufacture of a Class B drug, he might as well try to mitigate his offence by shopping his mates.'

'Do the owners of the house know about all this?' asked Peter. 'It'll be a bit of a shock for them.'

'More than a bit,' Bernie agreed. 'The whole place has been gutted. It's a real mess! It'll cost thousands to put back into a liveable condition.'

'Don't they have any comeback from the agents?' asked Gavin anxiously. 'I mean – it's not the owners' fault, is it?'

'Not the agents' either, according to them,' Jonah replied. 'They showed Tracy all the paperwork. "Mr and Mrs McLeod" went round the house, told a plausible story about needing to move down to Oxford and wanting to rent until they'd sold their house in Dundee and found somewhere down here to buy, showed them their passports and bank statements and everything, and signed a one-year secure shorthold tenancy agreement. Their names are on the electoral roll at their Dundee address and they had references from their employers. Everything was completely in order. The Dundee police are checking them out, but my guess is that it's a case of identity theft and they'll turn out to know nothing at all about any of this. I'm meeting the agent this afternoon, so I may know more after that.'

'And the car that hit Kenny?' asked Gavin in a bemused voice. 'Where did it come from? I mean …'

'It must have been waiting in the road at the back of the house,' Jonah told him, 'or else maybe the driver just happened to arrive back at the moment Kenny arrested the other member of the gang. The SOCOs[2] have taken casts of tyre tracks from the grass opposite, but we've no way of knowing if they're from that car or another one.'

'They've picked up a whole load of other things from that side of the house,' Bernie added. 'The evidence bags looked like the harvest from an exceptionally thorough litter-pick! The local residents ought to be grateful to them for cleaning up the street so well.'

'Yes,' Jonah grinned wryly, 'they've got a lot to go through there and most of it's bound to be irrelevant, but you just never know – maybe one of the cigarette butts or lumps of chewing gum will turn out to have been thrown away by the driver of the car and have his DNA on it, or an old newspaper will have his address scrawled on the front for the delivery boy.'

'But most likely it's all nothing to do with the incident,' Peter warned. 'It's a public road. Anyone could have dropped things there.'

'More promisingly, they've got some scrapings of paint from where the car grazed along the wall,' Jonah continued, 'and a car abandoned not far from the crime scene. We can't

---

[2] Scenes of Crime Officers are specialist staff who collect forensic evidence from a crime scene.

be sure, but it fits the description Stella gave of the one that hit Kenny. We've got forensics working on it to see if the paint matches or if there's anything else to prove it *is* the one.'

'It's registered to a man who lives in Bicester and works at the university,' Bernie added. 'He left it at the Pear Tree Park and Ride yesterday morning and only knew it was stolen when he got the police on the phone to him at the lab to say it was suspected of involvement in a crime.'

'That's right,' Jonah took up the story again. 'We've got CCTV from the Park and Ride which shows the car arriving at about eight and leaving again at about ten thirty, but so far nothing to help us identify whoever took it.' He turned to Gavin and addressed him earnestly. 'Don't worry. We'll do whatever it takes to find the brute who did this.'

'And Kenny?' Gavin asked absently. 'When can we …? I mean, I suppose there'll be a post mortem and an inquest?'

'He's with Mike Carson now,' Jonah told him. 'He said it wouldn't need to be an extensive PM, because the doctors who operated made a record of all his injuries. It'll just be a check to see that there's no evidence of medical negligence, I think. I'll let you know when the coroner's office gives us a date for the inquest, but you ought to hear direct from them as well.'

'And when will we …?' Gavin appeared to be struggling to find the right words. 'I mean … what about … the funeral? How long …?'

'I'll ask Mike to talk to the coroner about releasing the body,' Jonah promised. 'I can't see why they'd need to delay. It's not as if it can tell us anything about what happened.'

'Thanks.' Gavin looked a little less apprehensive. 'I know everything has to be done right; it's just, with Christmas coming up …'

'I'm sure–,' Peter began, but he was cut short by the strident ringing of Bernie's phone. She fished it out of her pocket and looked down at the screen.

'It's Lucy,' she told them. 'I'd better take it.'

She swiped the screen to answer the call and then held the device up to her ear. The others fells silent, listening to the one-sided conversation.

'Hi Lucy! How're you doing? ... Yes, that's right. ... 'Yes, he is. He's his son. ... No, I didn't know he was in the force either. ... We're at his house now. Our Jonah's the SIO. ... He managed to convince them that he's the perfect choice, now that he's only employed in a sort of advisory capacity – close enough to know what's what, but far enough removed to bring some objectivity to the case. ... You might well think that; I couldn't possibly comment! ... Yes, I will. ... Now there's something else you need to know: Stella Gilbert was there with him when it happened. ... No, she's not hurt at all. According to her, he pushed her out of the way just in time. ... Yes, I'm sure she'd appreciate that. She's on duty today, so better wait until the evening. ... Of course they did, but she said she'd rather. I think she sees it like getting back on the horse after you've fallen off – do it before you have time to think too much about it and lose your nerve. ... Don't worry – there are plenty of people keeping an eye on her. Anyway, I'd better go – we're on duty too, remember!'

She put her phone away and turned to address Gavin.

'That was my daughter, Lucy,' she told him. 'As you probably gathered, she heard about Kenny on the news and was ringing to find out if it was anyone we know. She and Stella were in the same class at school. She sends her deepest sympathy.'

'Thanks.' Gavin sounded rather uncomfortable, as if he was uncertain how to respond to such condolences. Then, with renewed effort, 'She's not back from uni yet then?'

'No. Most of the students have gone home, but they keep the medics hard at it until the end of the week,' Bernie smiled. 'Practice for when they're working long shifts in understaffed hospitals after they qualify, I suppose!'

'And talking of work,' Jonah broke in, 'it's time we were going. Maybe, now he's had a few more hours in the cells, that young idiot will have come to his senses and be ready to talk.'

3. THE SEVENTH DAY BEFORE CHRISTMAS

'OK, let's see what we've got so far,' Jonah said briskly, dispensing with any greetings and gliding swiftly to the front of the briefing room. Bernie closed the door behind him and took a seat near the back. As his personal assistant, she had no official role in his work, but nevertheless took a keen interest in each investigation. 'Andrews! How have your lot got on with checking out the usual suspects?'

'Nothing so far, sir,' DI Rupert Andrews reported promptly. 'We haven't found anything to link any known drug dealers with that house in Kidlington.'

'And what about that youth we've got in custody?' Jonah turned to DS Andy Lepage. 'Has he come to his senses yet?'

'Nope!' Andy replied. 'He still isn't talking – won't even give his name. Even charging him with obstructing the police hasn't persuaded him to open up. The duty solicitor has told him that refusing to co-operate will only make things worse for him, but …,' he sighed. 'I don't know. Nobody seems to be able to get through to him.'

'Neither his fingerprints nor his DNA match anything on the database,' Andrews added. 'It looks to me like he's a youngster who's got caught up in things he doesn't understand and is out of his depth. The trouble is he's more scared of his controllers – whoever they are – than he is of us!'

'And he doesn't trust us,' Andy agreed. 'I had a chat with him on my own, hoping he might open up to me better than to a white officer, but ….' He shook his head and pulled a face indicative of exasperation.

'OK,' Jonah sighed. 'I'll have another chat with him later – try and make him see he can't hold out for ever. Now what else were we looking into yesterday?'

'We've heard from the Dundee police,' a voice called out from halfway down the room. 'Mr and Mrs McLeod check out OK.'

'Oh?' Jonah craned his neck to make eye contact with DC Joshua Pitchfork. 'Tell me more.'

'He's a postal worker and she works for a typing agency,' the young officer told him. 'They're both living apparently blameless lives in a suburb of Dundee. According to the police officer who went to see them, they don't look remotely like the pictures in the passports the people who rented the house showed to the agent. They told him that they've no idea how their names and address came to be used to take out the tenancy and they don't even know where Kidlington is.'

'So the crooks were using fake passports with real names on them, 'Jonah mused. He looked round the room again. 'OK, now who's been checking out the employers' references for the fake Mr and Mrs McLeod?'

'I have,' Andy came back at once. 'Neither of the employing companies in Dundee actually exist. The references were done over the phone, so all they needed were a couple of their mates willing to pretend to be their bosses and give them a character reference. The letter offering Mr McLeod a job in Oxford, which he used to prove that they'd be able to afford the rent, is also a forgery from a bogus company. The same goes for the bank statements.'

'So, I think we can forget the McLeods and assume that Dundee is irrelevant,' Jonah decided. 'One thing though – we do have an idea what two of the gang must look like, because the fake passports must have pictures that convinced the agent who showed them round that they were the right people. Can we have those passport photos up on the screen?'

One of the civilian staff came forward and started fiddling

with a laptop computer. Everyone waited, watching the large screen at the front of the room. Images flicked past as Jennifer Moorhouse searched for the right file. Soon they were all looking at pictures of two passports, open at the photograph page. "Mr John Alexander McLeod" was clean-shaven and pale-skinned, with dark hair and brown eyes beneath thick black brows, which met above his prominent nose. "Mrs Fiona Morag McLeod" had straight blond hair hanging down to her shoulders. Her eyebrows were thin and gracefully arched above eyes that could be almost any colour.

'Do those ring any bells with anyone?' asked Jonah, looking round the room once more. Heads shook. Neither of these faces belonged to known criminals, or at least none known in the Oxford area.

'OK.' Jonah looked towards Andrews again. 'Can you get someone to have a go at these with facial recognition software and see if they match anyone on the national database? With a slick operation like this, it seems likely that they'll have some sort of criminal record already.'

'I'll get on to it right away!' Andrews nodded.

'And keep chasing forensics to get their finger out and examine that car,' Jonah continued, 'and remind them we're also waiting for reports on those tyre marks and paint scrapes. It's urgent that we know whether we've got the right car or if we still need to be looking for it.'

'Will do,' Andrews replied, smiling to himself at Jonah's impatience. DCI Porter was notorious for wanting everything done yesterday – or preferably sooner.

'Now, let's see …,' Jonah began again, but he was interrupted by the arrival of Stella Gilbert, who had slipped in through the door and was now standing nervously at the back of the room trying to catch his eye.

'Excuse me, sir,' she called out at last. 'Sergeant Appleton asked me to tell you there are some people in Reception you may want to meet.'

'Oh?' Jonah looked back at her with interest.

'They came in to report a missing person,' Stella went on.

'The description they gave sounds rather like the man we arrested in Kidlington.'

'The lad in custody who won't tell us his name, you mean?' asked Jonah excitedly.

'Yes, sir.'

'I'll be right down,' Jonah declared at once. 'Andrews! You're in charge. See to it that everyone is gainfully employed while I check this out. It could be the breakthrough we need.'

Bernie held the door open to allow Jonah to drive his wheelchair out into the corridor. Then she and Stella hurried to keep up as he headed at maximum speed for the lift. In a matter of minutes, they were down in the reception area talking to Sergeant Malcolm Appleton, who was the desk sergeant on duty that morning.

'DCI Porter! These are Trevor and Yvonne Whittle,' Malcolm told Jonah, glancing towards an Afro-Caribbean couple in their thirties or early forties, sitting huddled together on two of the uncomfortable plastic seats attached to the wall. 'Their son, Harry, has been missing since Monday.'

'The sergeant said you may know where Harry is,' the woman gabbled, getting up and standing a little too close for comfort, looking down on Jonah in his chair. 'What's happened to him? When can we see him?'

Her husband, a tall man with anxious eyes, a high forehead and close-cropped hair going thin on top, came across and put his hand on her shoulder, pulling her back a little. He looked towards Jonah apologetically.

'Do you have a picture of your son you can show me?' Jonah asked calmly.

'Yes, yes of course.' Mrs Whittle fumbled in her handbag and brought out a crumpled photograph of a teenage boy in school uniform. 'It's not very recent I'm afraid. He doesn't like having his picture taken. This was last year or was it the year before?' she prattled on, turning to her husband for confirmation but not waiting for him to respond. 'He's left school now and got a job. Not that he tells us anything about it. Market gardening, I think he said – is that right, Trev? His teachers wanted him to stay on and do A' levels, but he didn't want to and we don't really have the money, so we said it was up to him. He's sixteen, after all. We were both working at that age, so …'

'Is this your son?' Jonah asked, as soon as she paused for breath. With a small movement of the index finger of his left hand, he made the screen attached to his chair rotate so that Mr and Mrs Whittle could see a photograph of a black youth displayed on it. 'This is a young man whom we have here in custody. He won't tell us his name.'

The couple stared down at the screen, then glanced at each other, and finally back at Jonah.

'Yes!' Yvonne Whittle gasped. 'That's Harry. What's happened? Why have you arrested him?'

'It's a long story,' Jonah told her. 'Why don't we all go somewhere more comfortable and I'll explain.'

'Can't we see Harry first?' his mother pleaded. 'I want to know he's OK. He's not hurt, is he?' she added anxiously.

'No, he's not hurt,' Jonah assured her, 'but he is in quite a lot of trouble and I'd like you to know how the land lies before you speak to him.'

'Come on, love,' her husband urged, taking hold of her elbow. 'Let's do as the man says. It'll save time in the long run.'

* * *

'Mum!' the boy stared in disbelief as his parents entered the interview room followed by Jonah, Bernie, Malcolm Appleton and the duty solicitor.

'Harry! What have you been doing?' his mother replied, hurrying towards him.

'Mr and Mrs Whittle,' Jonah said quickly. 'If you could both sit down please?'

Bernie and Malcolm rearranged chairs so that the Whittles and the solicitor could all sit on the far side of the table that stood in the centre of the room. Then Bernie sat down opposite Trevor Whittle and Jonah moved his chair into position next to her.

'I'll leave you now, sir,' Malcolm said, making for the door. 'Give me a buzz if you need anything.'

'Thank you sergeant.' Jonah fixed his eyes on Harry Whittle, studying his brown face, frizzy black hair and tired, bloodshot eyes. It did not look as if his two nights in the police cells had been very restful. 'Now young man,' he began, speaking quietly but with a hint of menace, 'please can we stop playing games? Your name is Harry Whittle. Is that correct?'

The youth nodded. Then, seeing Jonah's raised eyebrows indicating that more was required, he mumbled, 'yes. That's right.'

'Good. Now Mr Whittle – or is it OK for me to call you Harry?'

The boy nodded again. 'Yes. Harry's fine.'

'Harry then. You've already been charged with involvement in the manufacture of cannabis and with obstructing the police. Do you understand what that means?'

'But he didn't know what he was doing!' his mother broke in. 'He was just helping to grow them plants. He didn't know what they were. He told me it was market gardening. Isn't that what you thought, Harry?'

'That's something that your lawyer can bring up in court,' Jonah said firmly. 'At the moment we just want Harry to answer some questions. He was a witness to a serious assault on a police officer, resulting in death.' He turned his head to look directly at Harry, who looked down to avoid eye contact. 'If you co-operate with us from now on, we may well decide to drop the obstruction charge,' he told him. 'And we're not nearly as interested in getting you put away for growing cannabis as we are in finding out who killed our officer. Do you understand?'

'Go on Harry!' his mother urged. 'You heard what he said. Answer his questions and maybe they'll let you come home with us.'

'Your mum's right,' confirmed the solicitor. 'With this being a first offence, you'll probably get away with just a caution – provided you co-operate from now on.'

'OK.' Jonah looked towards Bernie, who reached forwards and put her hand over an inconspicuous button built in to the surface of the table. 'I'm now going to ask Dr Fazakerley to start the video recording of this interview. There are microphones and a video camera in this room to provide a permanent record of our conversation. Mr and Mrs Whittle: as a minor, your son is entitled to have one of you present with him, but you don't both need to stay if you don't want to.'

'We'd both like to be here,' Mrs Whittle said at once. 'Wouldn't we, Trev?'

'Harry?' Jonah looked towards the boy.

'Er … yes, OK.'

'Good. OK Bernie, start the tape.' Jonah fixed his eyes on Harry and began the formal interview. 'Harry Whittle, you are charged with production of a controlled drug in contravention of the Misuse of Drugs Act 1971. You do not have to say anything. But, it may harm your defence if you do not mention when questioned something which you later rely on in court. Anything you do say may be given in evidence. Do you understand?'

Harry nodded.

'Come on, Harry, speak up,' his mother intervened. 'Answer the Inspector's question.'

'Yes,' Harry mumbled. 'I understand.'

'Good.' Jonah smiled encouragingly. 'Now we're getting somewhere. First, for the record I need your date of birth and your address.'

'Oh! OK.' Harry sounded surprised to be asked something so simple. 'It's the twentieth of March two thousand and three, and I live with my mum and dad at Seven, Chichester Road, Rose Hill.'

'Good,' Jonah repeated. 'Now, tell me about this job of yours.'

'What about it?' Harry asked suspiciously.

'What exactly did it involve?'

'Nothing much,' Harry shrugged. 'Just keeping them

watered proper, checking the lights was working and turning on the ventilation in the morning. I never knew what they was!' he added defensively, his voice rising above a mumble for the first time. 'They just said, "Look after the plants"; so I did as I was told.'

'They?' Jonah pounced on the word. 'And who exactly are "they"?'

Harry bowed his head again and sat in sulky silence. After a short pause, Jonah repeated his question.

'*Who* told you to look after the plants? I want some names.'

'Come on, Harry,' his mother urged anxiously. 'You heard what they said. Answer their questions and maybe you'll get off with a caution.'

'Harry?' Jonah said again, trying unsuccessfully to catch the lad's eye.

'I strongly advise you to answer the question,' the solicitor said impassively.

'I don't know their names,' Harry growled at last.

'You must've called them something,' Jonah reasoned. 'You can't work for someone for three months – if your Mum got that right – without ever speaking to them.'

'No,' Harry insisted in an undertone. 'They told me what to do and I did it. That's all.'

'OK,' Jonah said equably. 'Describe them to me. How many of them are there?'

'Dunno. Lots sometimes. I didn't notice. I just got on with my job.'

'Then let's start with your boss,' Jonah persisted calmly. 'Tell me about the person who gave you the job. Where did you meet them?'

'Can't remember,' Harry answered sulkily, keeping his head bowed as if he were addressing the surface of the table.

'And was it a man or a woman?'

Harry remained silent, still staring at the table.

'Come on, Harry,' his mother urged impatiently. 'Answer the inspector's question.'

'It was a man,' Harry conceded reluctantly.

'Good,' Jonah said again. 'Now tell me more. What does this man look like?'

'Can't remember.'

'Try,' Jonah urged succinctly. Then, when Harry did not reply, 'Let me help you. Was he taller than you or shorter?'

'Can't remember.'

'How about this then,' Jonah tried again. 'Was he white?'

'He may have been.'

'Harry!' exclaimed Mrs Whittle. 'You must be able to remember that. Answer the inspector's questions or you'll end up in jail. Don't you understand? You tell him, Trev!'

'Your mum's right,' her husband agreed, speaking slowly and deliberately. 'I understand you don't want to grass up your mates, but you heard what he said. A policeman's been killed and they want you to help them find who did it. You do that, and there's a chance they'll drop the charges against you. If you carry on like this, I can't say I'd blame them for throwing the book at you.'

His father's intervention seemed to bring about a change in Harry's frame of mind. He looked up at last, and Jonah saw terror in his eyes and dampness on his cheeks. His whole body was shaking.

'You don't understand!' he wailed. 'I can't! They'll kill me!'

'Who?' demanded his mother at once. 'Who said they'd kill you?'

The boy threw himself forward on to the table and buried his head in his arms. His shoulders shook as he gulped in air in short sobs.

'We can protect you,' Jonah told him. 'We have a witness protection scheme. And once they're in custody, they won't be given bail if there's any chance they'll try to intimidate you. Trust me.'

'No!' Harry raised his head again and stared round wildly. 'I can't help you. I don't know *anything*! I just came in and watered the plants and got paid and went home. That's *all* I know.'

'I'm sorry, Harry,' Jonah sighed, shaking his head slowly.

'That just won't wash. There must be-'

He was interrupted by a knock on the door. Stella Gilbert's face appeared round it.

'I'm sorry Sir, but there's a man in Reception wants to see you. He won't talk to anyone else. Sergeant Appleton says can you come right away because he's making a disturbance.'

'Alright.' Jonah moved his chair away from the table. 'We don't seem to be getting anywhere here. We'll take a break and have another go later. Stay here constable. I'll send Sergeant Lepage in to sort out the video and take Mr Whittle back to the cells.'

* * *

'No, I do *not* want a cup of tea!' Bernie and Jonah heard the angry voice before they reached the reception area and saw its owner. He was dressed in camouflage fatigues and muddy military-style boots. He thumped his fist on the reception desk to emphasise his words. 'I want to speak to the officer in charge, and I want to do it *now!*'

'Are you talking about me?' asked Jonah, gliding silently through the double doors that led from the corridor.

The man spun round and the large rucksack that was propped up at his feet fell over. An enamel mug and bowl hanging from it clattered noisily as they hit the floor. Jonah studied his face. It was tanned – perhaps weathered would have been a better description – and streaked with mud, but clean-shaven, and the man's brown hair was cut short in military fashion. Jonah knew who he was, but could not recall his name.

'Are you in charge of finding the rat who ran down that police officer in Kidlington?' the man demanded aggressively.

'That's right,' Jonah admitted, smiling, still trying to remember the man's name. 'What can I do for you?'

'Is it true he's Gavin's boy?'

'Yes. That's right,' Jonah replied calmly. 'PC Kenneth Hughes. Why do you ask?'

'Have you found his killer yet?' the man snapped, ignoring Jonah's question.

'Not yet. Do you have any information that might help us?'

'Can't tell. What d'you need to know?'

'Basically, who the driver of the car was,' Jonah told him drily, 'and if you weren't there, it's unlikely you can tell us.'

'Have you found the car yet?'

'We have a vehicle under forensic examination,' Jonah replied with deliberate ambiguity.

'Is it true the police were after drugs?' Again, the man seemed to ignore what Jonah had said, intent on his own agenda.

Jonah hesitated, undecided how much to reveal. Then he answered cautiously, 'Yes, there were drugs involved in the operation.'

'So the chances are it was a drug-dealer driving the car?'

'We can't be certain of that.' Jonah replied evenly.

'But it's got to be likely, hasn't it?' the man persisted; then, suddenly changing tack, 'Where's Gavin? I haven't seen him around.'

'He's on compassionate leave,' Jonah told him. 'I expect it'll be a while before he's back in circulation.'

'Well tell him-,' the man broke off abruptly. 'Tell him … Well, if you see him just say I dropped by.'

He bent down, grasped the rucksack and threw it on to his back. Then, nodding briefly to Jonah and Bernie as he went, he strode out of the door and into the street, almost colliding with a uniformed officer who was on his way in.

'Whew!' Toby Hitchin whistled, holding the pile of manila folders that he was carrying tight to his chest. 'Who does he think he is?'

'He's a friend of PC Hughes,' Jonah told him curtly. 'He's an ex-serviceman who hasn't managed to settle into civilian life after being out in Afghanistan. The last time I met him he was living on the streets.'

'His name's Craig,' Bernie added. 'He helped us with a case last summer.'

'Did he really?' the young constable exclaimed. 'Fancy that! PC Toby Hitchin, Sir,' he added, remembering that he was speaking to a senior officer. 'I'm honoured to meet you. Pete Johns told me you're in charge of investigating Ken's murder. Have you made any progress?'

'When we have anything to tell you about it, we'll issue a press release,' Jonah told him coldly. 'I assume you haven't met Peter's wife,' he added, inclining his head towards Bernie. 'Dr Bernadette Fazakerley, who is also my personal assistant. Now, you'll have to excuse us: as you remarked, we have an investigation to conduct.'

'Yes sir. Sorry sir. I didn't mean …'

'Can I help you?' Malcolm Appleton intervened, leaning across the desk. Jonah headed back towards the interview room, followed closely by Bernie.

'Yes,' Hitchin replied. He put the folders down on the desk. 'Could you give these to DCI Davenport? She said she needs them urgently, which is why I came down from Banbury to bring them personally.'

'Thanks.' Malcolm pulled the files towards him and picked up the telephone to ring Anna Davenport's office.

'It's a bad business Ken getting killed like that,' Toby burbled on. 'Him and me did our basic training together. He was one of my best mates. I can't believe he's gone!'

* * *

'Come in Peter – all of you – I won't be a moment!' Gavin smiled down at Peter and his two grandchildren and beckoned them inside. 'Go and sit down. I'll be with you just as soon as I've put on a tie.'

Peter shepherded the children into the living room, which seemed very bare now that the Christmas decorations were gone. The afternoon sunlight slanted in through the window – crystal clear with no trace of artificial snow remaining – and made the carpet sparkle as it struck remnants of glitter that had evaded the vacuum cleaner. The mantelpiece was now full of sympathy cards and there were more on the windowsill and crowded on to a small table beneath the television set. Peter sat down and pulled Abigail up on to his lap.

'Why has he got his Christmas tree outside?' demanded Ricky, running across to the window and pointing out at the front garden. 'Is he going to bring it in later?'

'No Ricky,' Peter answered. 'Mr and Mrs Hughes aren't doing Christmas this year.'

'Why not?' asked Ricky at once.

'Because …,' Peter sighed. 'Well, you see, Ricky, when something happens to make you really sad, you don't feel like putting up decorations and pulling crackers and that sort of thing.'

'Oh.' Ricky put his elbows on the windowsill, staring out apparently deep in thought. 'Not even at Christmas?' he added eventually.

'Not even at Christmas,' Peter confirmed.

'It's good of you to offer to drive me,' Gavin said, coming back in, tightening his tie as he did so. 'I like to support Chrissie, but I could have got the bus.'

'Two busses,' Peter corrected him, 'and it's no bother. The kids will enjoy it. I'm always looking for new things to keep them entertained.'

'I was Joseph at Nursery,' Ricky told Gavin earnestly. 'Abby's too little. She doesn't go yet.'

'Yes,' Peter laughed, 'I'm afraid you may have a theatre critic in the audience this afternoon. Ricky used to be shy, but he's really come out of himself since he started going to nursery school in the mornings. Now – is it time we were off?'

They drove for some distance without speaking. Ricky, in the back, entertained them with a medley of Christmas carols, which he had learnt at nursery school. He was part way through the chorus of "Little Donkey" for the third time when Gavin broke the silence.

'Have they made any progress?' he asked tentatively. 'With the case I mean?'

'I rang Bernie at lunchtime,' Peter answered. 'She says

they've found out who the lad is that Kenny and Stella arrested, but he's still not talking. It turns out he's only sixteen, which means they've broken all sorts of rules by questioning him without an appropriate adult present, but I don't see how they could be expected to know, if he looked eighteen and wouldn't tell them his age.'

'Do you think they'll ever find out who was driving?'

'I don't honestly know,' Peter admitted. 'There's no point pretending: you know as well as I do that there are a lot of unsolved crimes – particularly when you've got organised gangs involved.'

There was another long silence. "We will rock you, rock you, rock you,' sang Ricky loudly from behind them.

'How – how does it feel?' Gavin asked at last in a low voice. 'Not knowing,' he added. Then, apparently with a great effort, 'I mean – when your wife was killed, they didn't find who did it, or not for years, anyway.'

'Seven years,' Peter agreed.

'And what was it like – for you – not knowing?'

'Pretty grim,' Peter confessed in a low voice. 'The worst was, because it happened at home, I couldn't look at any of the neighbours without wondering if it could have been one of them that did it. At least–,' he stopped abruptly. He had been intending to say that at least Gavin would not have that particular concern, but it suddenly occurred to him that this might imply that he was belittling Gavin's grief compared with his own. 'But we just had to learn to live with it,' he concluded after a long pause. 'It wasn't easy, but we got through.'

'You and your kids?'

'And Bernie. I think some people still believe that she was waiting in the wings, ready to step in and snap me up as soon as I was a free man, but it wasn't like that at all. Bernie was Angie's best friend. She was devastated at losing her too.'

'I'm worried about Chrissie,' Gavin confided. 'At the moment she's too busy with school to have time to think about things much. I don't know how she's going to cope when school breaks up and it's just the two of us at home together. She isn't good at doing nothing.'

Unlike her husband, Peter reflected. Gavin reminded him of a cart horse, calm and reliable, plodding slowly along well-worn tracks – a good man to have with you in a tight situation, but no good at strategic thinking or innovation. Chrissie was more like a hyperactive puppy, always eager to help, pushing her nose into every new thing, generous to a fault.

'Everyone grieves differently,' he said at last, conscious that this platitude was unlikely to help his friend. 'She'll find her own way in time.'

'I suppose so,' Gavin sounded dissatisfied. 'I just wish I could do something to help her. I'm afraid she hasn't taken it in yet, and when she does …'

More silence. Ricky clapped his hands together as he sang "The Little Drummer Boy". Abigail joined in with enthusiastic *pa rum pum pum pum*s.

'We usually help out with Christmas dinner at the homeless shelter,' Gavin murmured as they turned in at the school gate, 'but I don't think I can face any parties this year.'

'Maybe give it a miss for once then,' Peter suggested. 'Everyone will understand.'

'But maybe Chrissie will want to. We always do it together – it's a family thing.'

'I'd wait and see how you feel,' Peter said, feeling increasingly powerless to help his friend. What do you say to a man whose only child has been savagely killed and who is worrying that he may be losing his wife too?

The school where Christine Hughes taught was set in extensive grounds in the countryside to the north of Kidlington. When they arrived, the visitors' car park was already well populated. Peter took care to strap Abigail securely in her pushchair before releasing Ricky from his car seat.

'Now Ricky, he told him firmly, 'I want you to hold on tight to Mr Hughes' hand until we're inside. There are lots of cars moving around and we don't want you getting-' He broke off suddenly and tried to think of a way of re-wording his warning to avoid reminding Gavin of his son's fate. 'I mean, it would be easy for you to get lost amongst all the people,' he finished lamely.

'It's OK. No need for *Mr*,' Gavin said, apparently oblivious of Peter's clumsy correction. 'Chrissie and I are fine with the kids using our first names. After all, we're mates, aren't we, Ricky?'

'Are we?' Ricky smiled up at the big man's face and happily slipped his small brown hand into Gavin's massive pink one.

'Of course we are! Now come with me and I'll show you where we have to go.'

A tall woman in tweed jacket and skirt greeted them heartily as they entered the building.

'Mr Hughes! How good of you to come! We were afraid you wouldn't make it this year, in view of … your family tragedy. We were all so sorry to hear about your son.'

'Good afternoon, Mrs Beddoes,' Gavin responded. 'I couldn't let Chrissie down. She and the kids have worked so hard on the play.'

'Yes,' Mrs Beddoes agreed, 'I told her she ought to take some time off, but she insisted that the children came first. She's a real hero! And you've brought some friends with you I see,' she added, turning to look at Peter and the children.

'Yes. This is Peter Johns. We worked together until he retired. And these are his grandkids Ricky and Abigail.' Gavin turned to address Peter. 'Mrs Beddoes is the head of the lower school – Chrissie's boss.'

'Pleased to meet you, Mrs Beddoes,' Peter said politely. 'The kids are looking forward to seeing the play.'

Mrs Beddoes shook hands with Peter and then knelt down to speak to Ricky and Abigail.

'We've got some small chairs at the front for little people like you, so you can see better. Would you like someone to show you where they are?'

'Yes please,' Ricky nodded, on his best behaviour in a strange place.

Mrs Beddoes stood up and turned towards a fair-haired girl

of about seven who was standing in the entrance hall holding a pile of folded sheets of paper.

'Just a minute!' Gavin interrupted urgently. He turned and pointed at the large Christmas tree that stood just inside the door through which they had entered the building. 'Could you tell me where these angels came from?'

Peter looked round and saw that the tree was decorated with several dozen paper angels, similar to the ones that he had helped Gavin to pack away the previous day.

'The children made them,' Mrs Beddoes replied, sounding a little puzzled. 'Do you like them? Your wife brought one in and showed them how to do it.'

'Oh! Good. That's all right then. I just wondered; that's all,' Gavin said incoherently. Then he pointed up at a green angel near the top of the tree. 'Is that the one Chrissie brought in? Would you mind awfully if I took it? It's one of a set and I wouldn't want to lose it.'

Mrs Beddoes stared at him briefly and then nodded. 'Yes, of course. Go ahead.'

Then, as Gavin reached up and carefully took down the paper figure, she turned back to speak to the fair-haired girl.

'Vicky,' she said, speaking slowly and making signs with her hands. 'Please show Mr Johns and his grandchildren to the front of the hall.'

'Yes, Mrs Beddoes,' the girl nodded, putting down the papers on the shelf over a radiator and making some hand gestures of her own. Then she picked up one of the leaflets and held it out towards Peter. 'Have a programme please,' she said carefully. Then, after Peter had accepted it, she added, 'This way!' and turned round to lead them through swing doors into a wide room with chairs ranged in curved rows around a central space.

'Why did they wave their hands around like that?' asked Ricky as the girl marched to the front of the room and stood waiting for them to join her.

'She can't hear or speak very well,' Gavin explained. 'She uses her hands to talk to people.'

He placed himself in front of Vicky and looked down into her face. 'Thank you,' he said, raising his hand to his chin and then moving it away from his face in a short outward gesture.

'You're welcome!' Victoria replied slowly with slightly exaggerated movements of her lips suggesting that she was concentrating hard. She lifted her own hand to her chin and brought it down and out in a similar movement.

Then she gave Peter a nervous smile and hurried back towards the foyer.

Peter positioned Abigail's pushchair out of the way at the side of the room, between the wall and a piano. He lifted her out and peeled off her pink fur-lined jacket. He placed her on one of the child-sized chairs that stood in a row at the front of the room and then turned to Ricky. 'Let's take your coat off too. It's hot in here.'

Ricky allowed Peter to remove his gloves and duffle coat but insisted on keeping on the red woolly hat decorated with a pattern of green holly leaves, which a friend of his mother's had recently knitted for him.

'It's my *Christmas* hat!' he insisted loudly.

Peter folded the coats and pushed them into the storage space at the back of the buggy.

'Now sit down, Ricky,' he urged, pointing towards the seat next to Abigail. 'The show will be starting soon.' He turned to Gavin. 'We'd better sit behind the kids. We won't fit on those chairs and nobody will be able to see if we do.'

They took off their own coats and hung them over the backs of two of the adult chairs on the second row before sitting down immediately behind Ricky and Abigail.

'Don't worry, Abby,' Peter reassured his granddaughter, seeing her looking round anxiously. 'I'm right behind you.'

The hall was starting to fill up now. Most members of the audience were women – mothers of the children who were performing, Peter assumed – some with young children accompanying them. The few men all seemed to be with their wives. It appeared that Peter and Gavin were the only unattached males. Peter smiled to himself as the thought occurred to him that people might suspect them of being a couple – except that Gavin seemed to know some of the parents who were coming in and hurrying to their seats. Several of them smiled and waved towards him and one or two came across to express sympathy at Kenny's death. It seemed that his ex-colleague must be a regularly visitor to the school.

There was a sound of children's voices outside a pair of doors at the side of the room. Then they opened and a woman wearing a long black dress came in and walked across the space in front of the rows of chairs to take up her position at the piano. She was followed by Christine Hughes, wearing a red cable-knit sweater and a green skirt over black boots.

'*She* hasn't taken *her* hat off!' Ricky remarked loudly, pointing at her red hat topped with a white pom-pom.

She was followed by a line of children. They filled the front row of seats. Some sat on the floor in front. Several children in wheelchairs took up positions on either side of the rows of chairs. Two more members of staff came in and helped the children to settle in their places. Then Mrs Hughes stood up at the front of the room facing the audience. She looked round, first at the front row and then at those further back. Everyone fell silent as each felt her eyes resting on them. When she was sure that she had their full attention, she spoke in a clear commanding voice.

'Ladies and Gentlemen! Welcome to our Nativity Play! The children have all been practising very hard and I'm sure you will enjoy it. Before we start, I just have to run through the usual housekeeping notices. The toilets are in the foyer, where you came in. The fire exits are the doors which you came through and the doors at the front.' She indicated the doors through which the children had entered. 'In the unlikely event that the fire alarm goes off, please make your way to the assembly point, which is in the visitors' car park. We will be serving refreshments after the play, so please stay for a cup of tea or coffee. After that, if you have children in the school you may take them home, but please make sure that their teacher knows that you've done so. We don't want to think we've lost anyone!'

She scanned the room again, checking that her message had been received. Then she signalled to someone at the back before sitting down in a chair near the piano. The lights dimmed. For a few moments there was silence. Then came the familiar sound of coconut shells being tapped together to simulate a donkey's hooves. The doors from the foyer opened and heads turned to see a little procession entering.

The piano struck up the introduction to "Little Donkey". Ricky wriggled in his seat with delight and he joined in as the children sitting at the front began to sing his favourite carol. Then his mouth dropped open and he fell silent, as Mary and Joseph reached the front of the room and crossed the "stage" in front of him.

'Mary's got a chair like Jonah's!' he called out in tones of awe, turning round to speak to Peter and then turning back to stare as a boy dressed in a long tunic and the traditional tea towel headdress walked slowly from left to right across the room leaning on a sturdy wooden staff, one foot dragging slightly. In his other hand he held a rope, which was attached to the neck of a surprisingly realistic stuffed fabric donkey's head strapped ingeniously to the front of an electric wheelchair.

Its occupant was a small girl with brown skin, wearing a long blue dress and a white headscarf. Behind thick glasses, her face had an expression of deep concentration as she steered the chair round in a wide circle and brought it to a stop outside a gaily-painted plywood Wendy house, which for the purposes of the play had a cardboard sign "INN" attached over the door. The music stopped and a small boy emerged.

'No room!' he announced in a loud voice.

'It's got a tail too!' exclaimed Ricky, suddenly noticing the length of grey plaited wool ending in a black tuft, which was attached to the back of the girl's wheelchair.

Peter felt the colour rising to his cheeks as all eyes turned towards his grandson. He leaned forward and whispered in

Ricky's ear, 'Yes, but don't talk. You'll put the kids off.'

'No room!' the boy repeated, a little impatiently now.

'But we have travelled all the way from Nazareth,' protested Joseph, picking up his cue after the interruption, 'and my wife is going to have a baby.'

'The inn is full,' insisted the innkeeper, 'but there is a stable round the back. You can sleep there.'

'Thank you!' responded Joseph thankfully (whether with gratitude for the accommodation or relief that his speaking part was over, Peter could not be sure).

He moved off again, the wheelchair donkey following behind. The lights dimmed and, under cover of darkness, two teachers stepped forward to rearrange the walls of the Wendy house and bring on a wooden box containing straw. The piano struck up "Once in Royal David's City" and the children began singing again.

When the carol was over, the lights came up to reveal the interior of the Stable. Mary (her chair now without its donkey head and tail) and Joseph were sitting on either side of the manger gazing self-consciously down at a doll lying in the straw, wrapped in a white shawl. They were surrounded by children dressed in animal costumes: a donkey, two bovine creatures with fearsome looking horns, and a camel. The pianist played the introduction to "Away in a Manger" and the singing began again, with Ricky joining in enthusiastically.

The play continued predictably, if not quite conventionally. Tea-towel adorned shepherds gasped in astonishment at the appearance of angels wrapped in white sheets with tinsel wings and halos, before hurrying off, round the back of the audience and down the other aisle to reach the stable to present the infant Jesus with a knitted lamb (one of Chrissie Hughes' creations, perhaps?), all to the accompaniment of "While Shepherds Watched". The wise men all made their appearance riding wheelchair camels, and one of them used an electronic voice machine to announce that he brought frankincense to give to the baby. Finally, the children who were sitting on the front row and the floor got up and joined the cast at the front of the room to sing "We wish you a Merry Christmas!" at the tops of their voices.

Everybody applauded and several parents stood up to take photographs. Ricky also slipped off his seat and stood clapping enthusiastically until Mrs Beddoes stepped forward and held up her hand for silence.

'Thank you. Thank you!' she said, smiling round at them all. 'And I know you'll all join me in thanking the children for putting on such a splendid show. And thank you Mrs Perkins for playing the piano. And a very special thank you to Mrs Hughes who wrote and directed and organised everything.'

Mrs Hughes joined her in the centre of the stage and Mrs Beddoes led the audience in another round of applause, while nodding urgently towards a point at the side of the room hidden from view by the piano. As the clapping began to die away, she walked briskly across and shepherded out a small girl carrying a large bouquet of flowers, guiding her across the stage to present them to the producer of the play, accompanied by a resurgence of applause.

Mrs Hughes smiled down as she received the flowers. 'Thank you, Rosie. These are lovely.' She looked up to address the audience. 'And thank you all for coming. The children really do appreciate it. They've worked so hard these last few weeks.'

'Now, I'm afraid we can't offer you figgy pudding,' Mrs Beddoes intervened. (A titter of laughter went round the room at this reference to the final carol.) 'But we do have tea and coffee and nibbles coming, which I hope you'll all stay to help us eat. I'd specially like to recommend the cheese straws, which Mrs Hughes made with her class this morning – as if she didn't have enough to do rehearsing the play and getting everyone into their costumes! So if you can all stay in your seats for a few more minutes while we bring them in …'

The audience relaxed and sat back to wait for the refreshments to appear. Mrs Beddoes moved aside to allow Mrs Hughes to take the floor again.

'Children!' she announced, standing centre stage with her

bouquet clasped to her chest and addressing the rows of young faces at the front of the room. 'I want you all to follow me quietly back to your classrooms to get changed out of your costumes and to collect your things, ready to go home.'

Mrs Beddoes remained standing at the front, watching until the door closed behind the troop of sheep, oxen, kings, camels, angels and choristers. Then she clapped her hands to silence the murmur of conversation, which had started up as soon as the speeches appeared to be over.

'Just one more thing,' she announced in a sombre voice. 'On a much sadder note, I expect most of you have seen the news that a police officer was killed a few days ago in Kidlington. What you may not be aware of is that he was Mrs Hughes' son.'

An audible gasp went around the room. Peter looked towards Gavin and saw that he had his head bowed low in an effort to hide the colour rising to his cheeks. He hated being the centre of attention. Fortunately, only a minority of the parents were aware of his connection with the popular teacher.

'She wouldn't hear of taking time off, because she didn't want to spoil the children's Christmas,' the head teacher continued, 'which is a sign of the dedication that she has always had to this school and its students. I know that many of you will want to express your sympathy to her and her family at this extremely sad time, so I've left a card in the foyer which I invite you all to sign and to write your own personal messages.'

Peter made his escape as soon as he reasonably could. Unlike most of those present, he did not know anyone apart from Gavin, who had quickly been swooped upon by Mrs Perkins, the pianist and deputy head, and taken backstage to join Chrissie. He carefully steered the pushchair through clusters of parents, variously comparing Christmas plans, commenting on the play or speaking in shocked whispers about the tragedy of Kenny's death.

Out in the foyer, a queue had formed by a table where a

large card lay, now more than half-full of inscriptions from parents and friends. Peter guided Ricky past it and towards the glass exit doors. As he reached out to press the large button to open them, a young woman stepped forward from the right holding out a red Santa hat in both hands. He looked down and saw that it contained five and ten pound notes.

'We're collecting for Mrs Hughes,' she told him. 'Would you like to contribute?'

'We were so shocked to hear about her son,' another woman chipped in from his left. 'We wanted to do something to show we care.'

Peter turned and saw that she too was holding a fur-trimmed conical red hat containing money. His first instinct was to throw in a few coins and head off as quickly as he could. Then his forty years in the police service kicked in and he felt obliged to intervene.

'What exactly are you planning to do with the money you collect?' he asked, trying to sound interested rather than suspicious.

'Give it to Mrs Hughes, of course!' the first woman replied promptly. 'She's been so good with my Billy, and this is such a horrible thing to have happened, we wanted to …'

'I'm not sure she'll want to accept it,' Peter said tentatively.

'Why on earth not?' demanded the second woman.

'Well because …,' Peter began to wish he had walked past and left them to it. 'Because she might think … It would feel a bit like … like … I mean, I don't think she'd know what to do with it.'

'And what makes you an expert on what Mrs Hughes thinks?'

'Sshh, Jodie,' the other woman hissed, taking her by the elbow and steering her away from the door. 'Let the man go if he doesn't want to contribute.'

'But I'd like to know,' the woman called Jodie insisted. 'What makes him think he knows how she feels?'

'I don't,' Peter answered quietly. 'I'm just going on how I felt when my wife was murdered. And I'm concerned about what you'll do with the money if she won't take it. Are you taking down people's names so you can give it back?'

The two women looked at one another open-mouthed. Ricky started pulling at Peter's hand, keen to be off.

'We never thought of that,' Jodie said at last. 'I suppose we could always give it to charity. What do you think, Toni?'

'And what if someone accuses you of embezzling some of the money?' Peter added, pressing his advantage, while at the same time hating himself for spoiling their well-meaning gesture. 'You haven't got any records, have you, of how much you've collected?'

'So-o-o,' began Toni slowly, evidently thinking hard, 'what do you think we ought to do?'

'If I were you, I'd have a word with Mrs Beddoes,' Peter told her, relieved that the atmosphere appeared to have calmed somewhat. 'The school is bound to have some sort of charitable fund that you could ask people to contribute to. And then you could use the money to buy something for the kids – some new equipment or something – in memory of Kenny Hughes.'

'Is that his name?' asked Toni. 'Did you know him then?'

'Not really, but I worked with his dad for more than thirty years. He's in the police service too.'

'You're a policeman?' gasped Jodie, suddenly grasping the idea that they could be in trouble. 'You're not going to prosecute us for collecting are you?'

'I'm retired now,' Peter assured her. 'Too busy looking after the grandkids to hold down a job as well. Don't worry, everybody knows you're only trying to help. Talk to Mrs Beddoes. I'm sure Gavin and Chrissie would rather you got something for the school than giving them anything.'

'Thanks,' Toni nodded. 'We'll do that.'

'Come on, Granddad!' Ricky shouted, sensing that the conversation was ending and wanting to get away before the grownups thought of anything else to say.

'Alright Ricky, we're going.' Peter smiled round at Toni and Jodie. 'We'd better make tracks. Good luck with the Kenny

Hughes memorial fund.'

* * *

Driving back through Kidlington, Peter made a detour to view the place where Kenny had been killed. It was not hard to identify the spot because of the large mound of floral tributes piled up against the high brick wall that ran along the backs of the houses on the north side of the road. He did not recognise the uniformed officer who stood guard over them. New since his time, he supposed.

He drove past and parked further on, where the road widened a little. Then he got the children out of the car and walked back with them to look closer at the impromptu shrine. In several places, the pavement was blocked by parked vehicles and he had to take the pushchair out into the road to get past. Was it possible that Kenny's death had been nothing more than a tragic accident caused by the narrowness of the road and a reckless driver?

As they approached the pile of flowers, Ricky immediately homed in on a large teddy bear dressed in police uniform.

'Look Granddad!' he called out excitedly. 'There's a police bear!'

'Teddy!' agreed Abigail, leaning forward in her buggy to get a better view.

'So there is!' agreed Peter. Keeping tight hold of Ricky's hand, he bent down to read the accompanying card: "So sorry the thin blue line just got a bit thinner" and a squiggle for a signature.

Peter wondered who had left this tribute. The uniform looked home-made. It was the sort of sewing project that Chrissie Hughes might have done. Perhaps she belonged to a sewing group or a craft club and this was from a friend who also attended.

He raised his eyes and looked round, assessing the crime scene. The wall was high enough to prevent him seeing into the back garden of the house that had been the subject of the fateful police raid, but he could catch glimpses of the upper storey of the building through the bare branches of a tall silver birch tree. It was a large detached property, probably built in the 1930s.

The houses on the other side of the road were much more recent – a new development squeezed in between two existing roads, on land taken from the back gardens of each. There was a pavement on that side, separating the road from the tiny lawns in front of the new houses. Peter scanned the grass for tyre marks. Jonah had said something about the SOCOs having taken prints from opposite the house. He could see nothing, but of course, the car must have been further away, out of sight of the waiting police – probably beyond that sharp bend in the road. If there had been someone waiting in a car within sight of the house when Kenny and Stella arrived they would have been sure to have spoken to them and asked them to move away from the police operation.

He spun round on his heel again and studied the wall. Yes! The garage stuck out a few inches in front of the wall. Suppose there was a car parked opposite, half on the pavement like that one there now. Someone coming at speed round that blind corner would have to swerve to pass it and might easily not be able to steer back again before hitting anyone who was standing in front of the garage door.

But Stella had been certain that it had been a deliberate attack, and the whole police investigation seemed to be predicated on that assumption. So perhaps there was more evidence of which he was unaware.

'Were you looking for something, sir?' The young police officer broke his train of thought.

'No, no. I was just trying to picture what happened, that's all,' Peter replied, smiling sheepishly. 'Force of habit, I'm afraid. I used to be a DI.'

'Did you know him then?'

'Not really, but I used to work with his dad – PC Gavin Hughes.'

'Oh! I see.'

There was an awkward silence. Peter was just about to say that he supposed it was time to be getting the children back home when there came a call from behind him.

'Peter!' he turned to see Stella approaching. 'I wasn't expecting to see you here.'

'We were passing through,' he explained. He looked down at the pile of blooms. 'Lots of people seem to have left flowers.'

'Someone's left a bear,' Ricky contributed. 'He's a police bear. P'rhaps he's guarding them.'

'Yes,' agreed Stella, smiling down at the little boy. 'I expect he is.'

She walked along the heap, bending down to examine the cards attached to some of the bouquets. Peter followed a little behind. Who were these people who had taken the trouble to buy flowers and leave them here in the road to mark the place where a man had been killed? How many of them had known Kenny in life, and how many were just well-wishers who wanted to express dismay at a police officer losing his life while doing his job? Was it mean-spirited of him to suspect that some simply craved a sense of being part of an event that had made the national news headlines?

'PC Ken Hughes,' Stella read aloud from one of the cards. 'Cruelly killed while keeping our streets safe. Gone but not forgotten.' She turned to look at Peter. 'He hated it when people shortened his name to Ken. Anyone who really knew him wouldn't do it.'

'I don't suppose they did know him,' Peter observed. 'They're probably just well-wishers.'

'Then why couldn't they put "Kenneth"?' demanded Stella. 'That's what the news report said. What right have they to-?'

'I suppose they didn't think about it,' Peter said, trying to calm her. 'Some people just do that to everyone. I used to get annoyed when people called me Pete, but now I just try not to take any notice of it.'

'I couldn't ever think of you as "Pete",' Stella said forcefully. 'Why can't people just-?'

'I like those purple flowers best!' Ricky informed them, pointing at a bunch of chrysanthemums, 'and those yellow ones over there, and those red ones and-'

'They're all very nice,' Peter agreed, 'but I think it's time we went home. We don't want to keep Mummy waiting, do we?'

He turned back to Stella. 'Can we give you a lift?'

'If you're sure,' she said hesitantly. 'I was going to get the bus.'

'It's no bother,' Peter assured her. 'You're going home, I presume? You've finished your shift?'

'Yes – at least, I saw the counsellor this afternoon and Malcolm said to go home as soon as I'd finished with her.'

'How was it?' Peter asked.

'Alright, I suppose.'

'Are you Stella Gilbert?' the young policeman intervened. 'The trainee constable who was with him when he was killed? I'm sorry. I didn't realise. I'm Callum McLaughlin. I did a spell with Kenny when I was a trainee.'

'Hi,' Stella replied unsure what response to give.

'I'm surprised to see you're still … I mean I'd've thought they'd have given you sick leave or something.'

'They tried to,' Stella grinned, 'but I'm too stubborn for that – ask my Gran! I want to help find whoever did this.'

'Me too!' Callum agreed emphatically. 'Kenny was a great guy. He didn't deserve this.'

'Well, we'd better be getting off,' Peter murmured, breaking the uncomfortable silence that ensued. Are you ready, Stella?'

Stella nodded. Then she took Ricky's hand and together they followed Peter and the pushchair back to the car.

'Do you know if the lad you arrested has agreed to talk yet?' Peter asked, as they turned out on to the main road and headed towards the northern by-pass.

'No,' Stella answered. Then, after a short pause, 'I mean, no, he hasn't. I – I …,' she sighed and then took a deep breath and began again. 'DCI Porter got called away and I was left with him on my own in the interview room – well his mum and his lawyer were there too. I thought about what you said – about young black kids needing police officers they could identify with.'

'Yes?' encouraged Peter, gently.

'Well, I thought … maybe he'd be more likely to talk to me than to a middle-aged white guy like … anyway, in the end I decided to have a go.'

'Good for you!'

'I'm not so sure.' Stella sat for a few moments turning her police bowler round and round on her lap. Then it all came out in a rush. 'I told him I know what it's like to get out of your depth because of pressure from other people. I told him about Leroy – like you said – and I told him Kenny was my friend and he didn't deserve to be run over like that. And he – he –.' She gulped and wiped her hand across her eyes. 'He just swore at me and said … he said I was a traitor, joining the police, and he wasn't going to fall for me pretending to be his friend and – and …'

'Don't let it upset you,' urged Peter. 'You did your best. That's what counts.'

'His mum told him off for that,' Stella sniffed, wiping her hand across her face again. 'She told him he was being disrespectful, but he didn't take any notice of her. And then Sergeant Lepage came and took him back to the cells. His mum apologised after he'd gone, and said it wasn't like him.'

'Maybe it wasn't,' Peter suggested. 'Maybe he was just repeating what he'd heard other boys say. Anyway, let's get you back home and then you can get out of your uniform and sit back and relax. It was very brave of you to try to talk him round. You're doing great.'

'I hope so,' Stella mumbled. Then, a little louder, 'I heard he's been sent home on bail now. Do you think DCI Porter's given up on getting anything out of him?'

'No, I shouldn't think so,' Peter assured her. 'Maybe the court insisted on granting him bail or maybe Jonah's hoping his parents will talk some sense into him once they've got him alone. It's not that easy keeping a juvenile in custody. Don't worry. You know what Jonah's like. He's not going to give up on a case just because his main witness is a stubborn teenager!'

4. THE SIXTH DAY BEFORE CHRISTMAS

They sat waiting outside the courtroom for the inquest to begin. Chief Superintendent Alison Brown was there to represent the police and to ask for the inevitable adjournment while the investigation into Kenny's death was completed. Jonah, with Bernie at his side, was there in his role as Senior Investigating Officer. Pathologist Mike Carson was in attendance in case the court had any questions about his report of his post mortem examination of the body.

Ricky and Abigail were safely in the hands of their father that morning, so Peter had come along to support Gavin, who sat in a daze, staring silently into the distance. Chrissie, finally released from her teaching obligations by the school Christmas holiday, sat next to him with a plastic container on her lap and her knitting bag on the floor beneath her seat.

'Would anyone like one of my cherry almond puffs?' she asked, taking the lid off the container and holding it out towards Peter. 'I made them last night with the marzipan I had over from the Christmas cakes.'

'Thanks.' Peter took one of the pastries, which appeared to be a variation on an Eccles cake.

'Go on,' urged Chrissie, 'pass them round.'

Peter got up and offered the container to Bernie, Alison, Mike and finally Gavin. Bernie took one, which she broke into pieces and shared with Jonah. Alison hesitated, looking from the sticky delicacies to her spotless uniform and then toward

Chrissie, before putting out her hand and selecting the smallest of the puffs. Mike took one eagerly and bit into it at once, causing flakes of pastry to drop on to both his lap and the floor surrounding his seat. Gavin stared at the box for several seconds and then shook his head.

'Go on, Gav,' his wife urged. 'You know you like them!'

'Yeah' Gavin mumbled, reluctantly taking one. 'But I don't feel like one just now.'

'These are very good!' Alison declared, breaking the awkward silence that ensued. 'You must give me the recipe, Mrs Hughes.'

'It's one of my own,' Chrissie replied proudly, 'something I made up to use up left-overs from the Christmas baking. I always make a couple of Christmas cakes for the homeless shelter party and there's always some marzipan and cherries and stuff over.'

'Kenny always used to take one to school for his packed lunch on the last day before Christmas,' Gavin said tonelessly, as if talking to himself. 'I'm sorry, Chrissie, I'm really not hungry.'

He got up and put his pastry back in the box, which Peter had set down on the seat next to Chrissie. Then he put his hands in his trouser pockets and started pacing slowly round the room.

Everyone ate in silence, except for Chrissie who replaced the lid firmly on the box and then bent down to get out her knitting from the bag on the floor. It was a relief when an usher came out to announce that the inquest was about to begin.

The court was packed with journalists and members of the public who had read the press reports and were hoping to hear more details of the fatal incident. An usher showed the family and police representatives to seats on the front row and pointed out a space where Jonah could position his wheelchair. Then he turned to leave and almost bumped into a young woman who had followed them in. She was small and dark, with glossy black hair and deep brown eyes. Her clothes were immaculate: a well-cut black skirt suit with a gold brooch on one lapel, and a purple high-necked blouse. She mumbled an apology before slipping into the seat next to Peter, who looked at her in surprise.

'I'm Kenny's fiancée,' she murmured, seeing his questioning expression. 'Or at least, I was.'

'Bella!' Chrissie called from further down the row. 'It's good to see you. Have one of these!'

She passed the box of cherry almond puffs to Gavin, who pushed it back and whispered a warning that the coroner was about to begin. Chrissie, looking abashed, put the box back in her bag and straightened herself up, looking straight ahead at the bench. Glancing down, Peter saw that Gavin had taken her hand in his. An usher called for silence and the inquest began.

The proceedings were soon over. Mike and Alison spoke briefly confirming the contents of their respective written submissions. Then the coroner adjourned the inquest, pending completion of the police investigation, and released the body for burial or cremation – another decision for Gavin and Chrissie to make. Then it was over and they filed silently out the way they had come.

'Miss Kennedy!' Jonah called softly, as they queued for the door. 'I'm DCI Jonah Porter. I'm in charge of investigating Kenneth Hughes' death. I wonder if I could have a word?'

'How did you know my name?' The young woman sounded hostile.

'I overheard Mrs Hughes speaking to you,' Jonah confessed, smiling endearingly up at her. 'I've been wanting to apologise to you for allowing you to hear about your fiancé's death through the media. We ought to have been more careful about checking before we released his name.'

'That's alright,' Bella mumbled back, her face thawing a little.

'It must have been a dreadful shock to you,' Jonah continued. 'Coming out of the blue like that.' He paused and then went on, 'unless …?'

'Unless what?' asked Bella suspiciously.

'I was only thinking … was it completely out of the blue? I mean … police officers do sometimes make enemies. I should know! That's what put me in this contraption. Presumably he didn't mention anything like that to you?'

'No. Everyone liked Kenny.'

'That's what people keep telling me,' Jonah nodded. 'I was just hoping … maybe he'd have told *you* things he wouldn't let on about to anyone else.'

'I don't think so. Anyway, we split up. I hadn't seen him for six weeks when he ….' Bella's face suddenly crumpled and she put up her hand to prevent the tears smudging her mascara. 'I'm sorry. I don't want to talk about it anymore.'

She squeezed past a fat man who was blocking the aisle, leaving Jonah waiting for the crowd to disperse and make space for his wheelchair to reach the exit.

'I suppose we can start organising the funeral now,' came Gavin's voice from behind him.

'I don't mind helping,' Peter volunteered. 'It can be quite difficult, especially when it's so unexpected.'

'Do you think it's too late to have it before Christmas?' Gavin wondered. 'I – I … is it awful to say I want to get it over with?'

'Not in the least!' Peter assured him. 'I'd feel exactly the same.'

'If Russell and Annette want to come, they'll need a bit of notice,' Chrissie chipped in.

'Do you think they will?' Gavin asked anxiously. 'Russell's my brother,' he explained to Peter. 'He went to Australia thirty-odd years ago. I shouldn't think he'll want to come. After all, he's never met Kenny.'

'But he still might want to come,' Peter argued gently. 'Chrissie's right. You'd better ask him before making any definite plans. I doubt if it's going to be possible to have it before the New Year in any case. Everyone will be on holiday from the middle of next week – if not before.'

'And there's Clive and Irene in Inverurie,' Chrissie added. 'They're bound to want to be there, and I don't know about Mum and Michele.'

'Your mother won't be able to make it, surely,' Gavin protested mildly. 'Last time we were down there, she could hardly get out of bed.'

'Tell you what,' Peter offered. 'Why don't I come back with you now and help you make a list of people who need to be invited and things that need to be done. Then it'll be easier to see what the constraints are.'

'Yes!' Gavin responded eagerly. Then, 'if it's not too much trouble. I don't want to be a nuisance and I'm sure you've got other things to do.'

'Nonsense! I'll be all alone and lonesome in the house for the rest of the day, with Bernie and Jonah at work and the kids with their dad.'

'Thank you,' Chrissie said warmly, taking Peter by the hand. 'And you must stay to lunch. I've got one of my special stews with spicy dumplings in the slow cooker, because I thought we might be late back. There'll be plenty for all of us.'

Once outside the building, they separated. Peter went with Gavin and Chrissie to catch the bus to their home in Rose Hill while Bernie and Jonah headed for their car, which Bernie had left in a nearby disabled bay. Before they could reach it, however, they were accosted by Andy Lepage.

'Sir!' he called out. 'I thought you'd want to know: Harry Whittle has been found dead. It looks like he killed himself.'

'When? How?' demanded Jonah, bringing his chair to an abrupt halt and looking keenly up into Andy's face.

'This morning. His mum cleans offices early in the morning, before the people get in. She came home and found him hanging from the bannisters.'

'And he definitely did it himself?' Jonah asked at once.

'That's what she told the PC who came when she rang 999,' Andy shrugged. 'They've bleeped Mike Carson, but he hasn't got there yet.'

'Not surprising,' Jonah observed. 'He was behind us in the

scrum to get out of the coroner's court, but I expect he'll be on his way by now.'

'Do you want us to go over there now, or wait until he's had a look?'

'I'll go right away. Have you got the address?'

Andy silently handed a scrap of paper to Bernie. 'Rose Hill,' she murmured. 'It can't be far from Gavin's house.'

'Right! Let's get off there then,' commanded Jonah, releasing the brake and gliding on towards the car. 'This could change the whole investigation.'

* * *

PC Ben Timpson lifted the blue-and-white police tape to let them on to the premises when they arrived at the house. It was one of the middle ones in a terrace of four. The small front garden had been covered over with uneven paving, which had clumps of grass and dandelions growing up along the cracks. To the right of the front door, which was standing open despite the chill in the December air, there was a shared passageway giving access to the back gardens of both houses.

'The victim's mother is next door with Constable Otterbourne,' he told them in a low voice, pointing towards the tunnel between the houses. 'She seemed a bit hysterical when we arrived, but Louise managed to calm her down a bit. The neighbour is giving them both tea.'

Bernie hurried forward and set up the portable ramp to enable Jonah to gain entry to the house. Then she stood back and allowed him to go inside first. Andy Lepage waited until she was through the door and then followed them in.

They were immediately confronted by the sight of two feet, clad in grubby white trainers, revolving slowly above their heads. Looking up, they saw Mike Carson on the stairs gently rotating the body that was suspended from somewhere out of sight. Hearing them enter, he called down cheerily, 'What took you so long?'

'Is it suicide?' Jonah asked, getting straight to the point.

'Not in my opinion,' the pathologist replied with unusual candour. Normally he liked to hedge his bets at least until after extensive tests and scrutiny of the evidence. 'There are definite signs of a struggle and the injuries to his neck don't match the rope that he's hanging from. It's early days yet, but I'd say it looks more as if he was held face down and strangled with some sort of garrotte.'

'So, more than one person involved?' enquired Jonah.

'Probably, but not necessarily. If the attacker was powerful enough, he might have been able to hold him down with his knee while applying the ligature to his neck.'

'But you definitely think he was strung up after he was already dead?' Jonah pressed him.

'That's certainly what it looks like.' Mike put his head back to call to someone upstairs, 'OK! You can take him down now.'

The body juddered and swung round. Then a man in a protective suit appeared on the stairs and grasped it round the torso, guiding it down as his colleague paid out the rope from above. Soon Harry Whittle was lying on his back on the red quarry tiles of the narrow hall. His face was swollen and puffy and there were ugly purplish-black marks on his neck beneath a noose of plastic rope of the sort used for washing lines. Mike hurried down and stood over the body, staring at it intently. Then he bent down, loosened the rope and slid it off over the victim's head.

Kneeling next to the body, he gently turned it over and pointed down at a mark on the back of the neck. 'See this? That looks to me like the bruising you get from a knotted cord when you put a stick through it and turn it to tighten the noose. Eventually it crushes the larynx and causes asphyxiation. It's not as clear here as it would be in a lighter-skinned individual, but still quite easily identifiable.'

'And that's what's happened here?' asked Jonah.

'Well, I can't say for certain until after the PM, but … yes, I'll be surprised if that doesn't turn out to be the cause of death.'

There was the sound of raised voices outside. At a look from Jonah, Andy went to investigate and found Mr Whittle senior engaged in an angry altercation with Ben Timpson.

'It's my own house, I tell you!' Trevor Whittle roared. 'My wife's in there – and my son's body! You can't keep me out!'

'Yes, sir,' Ben replied, calmly but firmly, positioning himself across the front door, 'but it is also a crime scene and-'

'Mr Whittle!' Andy called, stepping out on to the ramp, which Bernie had left in place for Jonah's eventual exit. 'I'm very sorry, but I'm afraid we can't let you through here just yet.'

'Take him round the back way!' Jonah called from behind him, 'and ask him to wait next door with Mrs Whittle. I'll be round there in a minute to have a word with them both.'

He looked back at the pathologist, who had turned Harry over on to his back again and was peering into his eyes. 'OK Mike. I'll leave you to it. Get your report over to me ASAP, will you?'

'Sure,' Mike replied absently, turning his attention to the victim's hands, lifting them carefully and examining the fingernails. 'Right after I've finished the other four outstanding reports that are sitting on my desk waiting to be written up.'

'We should never have allowed this to happen,' Jonah muttered angrily to himself as he and Bernie made their way round to the back of the next-door house. 'We promised him he'd be safe. No wonder he was scared to talk. Why didn't we put someone watching the house?'

Shirley Prentice, the Whittle's next-door neighbour, was a plump motherly woman in her sixties with curly grey hair and kind brown eyes. She led them past a basket of clothes, lying on the floor in front of the washing machine, and a mop and bucket, abandoned part way through cleaning the floor, to a dining area, which looked out through sliding glass doors over the small back garden. Sitting at the round table were Trevor and Yvonne Whittle. Yvonne was slumped in her chair staring down into the cup of tea that she held cradled in both hands. Trevor, with his arm protectively around her shoulders, glared across the table at Andy, who was sitting with his hands in his lap and an apologetic expression on his face.

'Mr and Mrs Whittle,' Jonah began, looking first at Yvonne and then at Trevor, 'I want to tell you how very sorry we all are ab-'

'Fat lot you care!' Trevor interrupted rudely. 'All you lot were interested in was getting him convicted – one less black kid roaming the streets, worrying nice white people who think he's going to knife them!'

'I understand your anger-,' Jonah began again, but Trevor was not interested.

'You don't understand anything!' he declared, bringing his fist down on the table with a bang and making the teacups rattle in their saucers. 'My dad came over here from Trinidad when he was ten years old. He worked all his life for the council and then four years ago he applied for a passport to go back to see his sister before she died. He was told he had to *prove* he had a right to live here, because his birth certificate said he was born abroad. He died last year, still scared out of his wits that he might be sent back to a place he hadn't seen since he was a little boy.'

'That's awful!' Andy exclaimed. Then he fell silent at a look from Jonah, who had decided that it would be better to allow the angry man to air his grievances without interruption.

'The thing he wanted most was for his kids to get an education and make something of themselves,' Trevor continued. 'I've got eight O' Levels and three A' Levels[3]. I went to night school to get those, because my dad couldn't afford for me to stay on into the sixth form[4]. And what do you think I do for a living? I drive a cab! Because it's not *what* you know, it's *who* you know, and whether the boss thinks you'll fit

---

[3] Between 1951 and 1987, schoolchildren in England, Wales and Northern Ireland took General Certificate of Education Ordinary Level examinations at age 16 and Advanced Level examinations at age 18.

[4] For historical reasons, the final two years of schooling (after the statutory school leaving age) in England are called the sixth form.

in. Nobody ever rated me or my son, and now he's ... he's ....'
his voice faltered and he hastily lowered his eyes as he
struggled to get the words out. 'He's killed himself,' he gasped
at last. Then, louder and more aggressively, 'and I'm holding
you responsible!'

'You are quite right,' Jonah said quietly, judging that Trevor
had now blown himself out. 'And I am deeply sorry that we
let you and your son down.'

'Sorry!' Trevor muttered scornfully under his breath, but
he allowed Jonah to continue.

'We should have done more to assure his safety. We
shouldn't have sent him home without a police guard.'

'A sort of house arrest, d'you mean?' demanded Trevor,
who seemed to have got his second wind and to be on the
offensive again. 'What good would that have done? You drove
him to take his own life. You've been persecuting him for
years, with your stop and search and-'

'I'm afraid that's not how he died,' Jonah broke in gently
but firmly. 'I'm very sorry to have to tell you, but we believe
that your son was murdered.'

'Most probably by one of the gang who were paying him
to look after the cannabis plants,' Andy added, 'to stop him
telling us who they are.'

'Murdered?' Yvonne gasped, raising her head at last and
looking round wildly. 'You mean someone came in our house
and killed our son?'

'Yes, I'm afraid so,' Jonah replied. 'We'll know for sure
after the pathologist has done a proper post mortem
examination, but all the signs are that's what happened.'

He turned to the neighbour, who was busy pouring tea into
cups for Andy and Bernie. 'Mrs Prentice, did you notice
anyone hanging around outside at all during the morning –
before Mrs Whittle got in from work?'

'No – but then I was busy stripping the beds. I didn't have
time to be staring out of the window.'

'Or any noises coming from the Whittles' house?' Jonah
enquired hopefully.

'Now I come to think of it, maybe there was a few bangs,' Shirley said thoughtfully. 'But I never thought anything of it.'

'Can you describe what they sounded like?' Jonah asked, treating her to one of his endearing lopsided smiles.

'Like someone was dragging something heavy upstairs.'

'What sort of something?'

'I don't know – I didn't really think about it. Like I said, I never thought anything of it. There's plenty of reasons why someone might want to get something up the stairs, isn't there?'

'Yes, of course,' Jonah agreed. 'And can you remember what time that was?'

'Half past eight – nine o'clock maybe. Quite early. I did think it was a funny time to be doing it, because I'd seen Trevor going out and I knew Yvonne doesn't get back 'til ten or even quarter past sometimes. I thought it must be Harry, maybe bringing in something he didn't want his parents to know about.'

'Good,' Jonah said encouragingly. 'That's very helpful. Now Mr Whittle, can you tell me what time you went out this morning?'

'I had a pick-up scheduled for seven fifteen,' Trevor replied promptly. 'I went out for that before seven and I've not been back until I got your call a few minutes ago. You can check it all out with the switchboard. I took my passengers to the station and then I got a call to an address down the Botley Road. I took them to the hospital, which took a long time because of the traffic, and then-'

'Thank you Mr Whittle,' Jonah cut in. 'As you say, we can check all that with your employer. The important thing is that Harry was alone in the house from seven o'clock until his mother got home and found him at about ten. That time is confirmed by the emergency call that she made, which was logged at seven minutes past.'

He turned to Andy. 'Go and round up a team of officers to do a house-to-house in the road. I want to know if anyone saw anyone approaching the Whittles' house between seven and ten this morning.'

Andy got up, leaving the tea that Mrs Prentice had poured for him untouched, and headed for the door. He reached out for the handle, then paused and turned back. 'Mr Whittle?' he said nervously. 'I just wanted to say, we're going to put just as much effort into finding out who killed your son as we have been trying to find the people who killed PC Hughes, and … and some of us do know what it's like … you know …'

He turned back abruptly and went out, closing the door sharply behind him.

Jonah manoeuvred his chair round the table to a position where he could look the Whittles directly in the eye.

'Mr and Mrs Whittle,' he said in a low, but urgent voice, 'as Sergeant Lepage just said, we will do everything we can to bring whoever killed your son to justice, but we're going to need your help to do that. I know it's a very difficult time for you, but if you could answer some questions now it could make all the difference.'

'Yes, of course, anything you want,' Yvonne said, looking tearfully across the table at him. 'What do you want to know?'

'It seems likely that whoever was responsible belonged to the gang that was employing him to look after those cannabis plants,' Jonah explained. 'Did he tell you anything about who they were or how they came to offer him the job?'

'No.' Yvonne shook her head. 'I don't think so. Did he say anything to you about it, Trev?'

'No,' he growled. 'You know what teenage lads are like. He didn't want us to know anything about what he was doing. He just said it was looking after plants and they were paying him cash in hand. I tried to tell him it sounded dodgy, but he wouldn't listen.'

'Was it just at that one house, or did he go to other places too?'

'We never knew where it was,' Yvonne answered dejectedly. 'He just used to go off on his bike every morning. He never said where – did he Trev?' She nudged her husband, who grunted his agreement.

'And did anyone ever come to see him here – at your house, I mean?'

'No,' Yvonne shook her head again, 'or at least only some of his mates from school sometimes. Isn't that right, Trev?'

Trevor grunted again.

'So you really have no idea who these people who employed him were or where he came across them?' Jonah pressed them gently.

'No! We've told you that, haven't we,' Trevor snarled. 'We can't help you. Can't you see that? And can't you see you're upsetting my wife? Just go away and leave her in peace, can't you?'

'OK,' Jonah nodded. 'I'm sorry. We'll go now, but if you do think of anything – however insignificant or irrelevant you think it is – let me know.'

He backed his chair away from the table and turned it to face the door. Bernie handed cards to Yvonne and Shirley. 'There's a phone number and an email address on there,' she told them. 'The lines are manned twenty-four seven.'

* * *

'What a mess!' Jonah muttered as Bernie strapped him into the back of the car after this unsatisfactory interview. 'What on earth got into me to allow the boy home? And why didn't someone think to put a watch on the house? If we'd had someone there, we might have got the whole gang in custody by now! We should've expected them to come after him as soon as he was released. I must be going senile to have missed that.'

Bernie got out and went round to the driver's seat without speaking. She knew that Jonah was principally angry with himself for his own misjudgements, and decided to leave him alone to vent his frustration through this litany of deprecation. She manoeuvred the car out of its parking spot and set off back to the police station.

Eventually Jonah ran out of reasons for blame and fell

silent. After a few minutes, Bernie cautiously ventured an idea of her own.

'Do you think it's possible that the car that hit Kenny was aimed at Harry?' she asked tentatively. 'I mean, if they were so keen to prevent him talking to the police …?'

'Yes! You're right,' Jonah exclaimed eagerly. 'The way Stella described it, she was putting the handcuffs on Harry when the car came at them and Kenny pushed them out of the way. It obviously could've been aimed at Harry, not Kenny. And they had much more reason to want him out of the way than to kill a random police officer. After all, if he had told us all he knew, we might have been able to prosecute the lot of them. We ought to get Stella to go back to the house and do a re-enactment, so we can see exactly where everyone was, but I think …'

'I suppose it could have been Stella who was the target,' Bernie mused dismally.

'Not likely.' Jonah was too entranced by his new hypothesis to entertain any alternatives. 'Or only because she was a police officer. It couldn't have been personal – she hasn't had time to make those sorts of enemies.'

'It could've been racially-motivated,' Bernie suggested, playing devil's advocate. 'She and Harry are both black.'

'Too much of a coincidence,' Jonah declared dismissively. 'If these guys were that racist they wouldn't have employed Harry to look after their pot plants. No, I think you hit the nail on the head when you said Harry was the target. They tried to kill him before he was arrested and then they had another go when we released him again, which begs the question: what was it that Harry knew that was so important that it was worth killing for?'

'You mean, apart from the identities of his employers?' Bernie asked sceptically. 'Isn't that plenty?'

* * *

Peter heard the car drawing up when they arrived home that

evening, and threw the front door open leaving Bernie standing at the top of the concrete ramp with her hand poised to put her key in the lock.

'Any progress?' he asked eagerly the moment they entered the house. 'Is there any chance of finding the driver before Christmas?'

'Less now than there was, I'm afraid,' Jonah replied gloomily. 'Have you heard about Harry Whittle?'

'No. Who is he? And what about him?'

'He's the lad Kenny and Stella arrested,' Jonah explained. 'We charged him with drug offences and obstructing the police, but he still wouldn't co-operate, so we let him go home. I foolishly thought his parents might manage to talk some sense into him if they had some time alone with him.'

'And?' Peter prompted when Jonah paused to allow Bernie to remove the thermal gloves and warm jacket that she had dressed him in for the drive home.

'He was alone in the house for a couple of hours this morning and person or persons unknown got in and strangled him.'

'Whew!' Peter whistled through his teeth. 'That's a bit of a bombshell. And I suppose the assumption is that this *person or persons unknown* is a member of the drugs gang that was running the cannabis-growing enterprise?'

'Who will be all the more difficult to find now that the only person we had who knew who they are is dead,' Jonah agreed grimly.

'On the other hand,' Peter said, trying to see some chink of light in the gloomy situation, 'it's always possible that someone will have seen them getting into the house. And two crime scenes gives you twice as much chance of finding forensic evidence.'

'If only forensics can get a move on and do the analysis,' Jonah grumbled. 'I've had nothing back from them on that car we found yet.'

'Yes you have,' Bernie contradicted. 'They said one of the tyre marks from the grass verge matched.'

'But not the other one,' countered Jonah, 'which suggests that there had been at least two cars that went up on that grass the day Kenny was killed, or shortly before, so we still need analysis of the paint scrapings to establish that we've found the right one. And even *then,* it won't do us much good unless they can find DNA or fingerprints or something to tell us who was driving it. I wish they'd get a move on!'

'It's not their fault,' Bernie pointed out. 'They've had staff cuts too. They've got a backlog. Anna was telling me she's been waiting over two weeks for DNA analysis of blood traces that a burglar left when he broke a window. Anyway, let's not stand here talking. It's time we got you out of that chair and gave you your physio.'

'Tell you what,' Peter suggested, 'the tea's in the oven keeping warm, so I'm free to do that. Go and sit down, Bernie. I'm sure you need a rest after running around after his nibs all day.'

'I'm fine,' Bernie protested, unwilling to admit to any form of weakness. She had also rightly deduced that Peter was planning to pump Jonah for news of the case and she did not want to miss out on the discussion. 'Let's do it together.'

Jonah led the way, through doors that opened automatically in response to wireless signals that he sent from his chair, into his ground floor bedroom. Following a well-worn routine, Bernie and Peter transferred him on to the bed and gently removed his clothes, taking care not to damage his skin, which was vulnerable to inflammation as a result of the long periods that he spent in his wheelchair. Bernie detached the urine bag from his leg and went to empty it in the adjacent bathroom.

'So, what do you know about this second murder?' asked Peter casually as he poured moisturiser on to his hands and began gently massaging his friend's legs to improve the circulation.

'Not a lot. Ben Timpson was first on the scene after the boy's mother called 999. She found him there when she got in from her cleaning job. It looks as if the killer must've been watching the house, because they only had a relatively short space of time between when his dad left and when she got back.'

'According to Ben, she was in a bit of a state when he got there,' Bernie contributed, coming back in carrying a fleecy-lined tracksuit, which she put down on the end of the bed. 'He took her round to a neighbour.'

'The neighbour says she heard noises between half past eight and nine, 'Jonah resumed, 'which we assume was the killer dragging the body up the stairs and stringing it up from the bannister rail. The back door was unlocked – I gather they leave it like that when there's someone in the house – and the back gate was swinging open. It looks as if it was forced. It's only flimsy boards and they cracked round where the bolt was screwed on.'

'Didn't the neighbour hear them doing that?' queried Peter, walking round the bed to attack Jonah's other leg.

'Apparently not. She was upstairs in her front bedroom and says she didn't hear anything apart from the bumping on the stairs, which she attributed to Harry lumping something heavy up them.'

'And he definitely didn't do it himself?' asked Peter. 'I mean – if he was as scared as you say he was, maybe he decided it was better to end it all.'

'No,' Bernie shook her head. 'Mike was quite definite – very definite for him at this stage! – that he'd been strangled first and *then* hung up from the bannisters.'

'Harry's parents blame us for letting them get to him,' Jonah declared. 'And they're quite right. We ought to have protected him – or else kept him in custody. We didn't even give them any advice about keeping doors and windows locked, and not leaving him alone in the house.'

'You can't think of everything,' Peter murmured as he bent forward to examine a red patch of skin on Jonah's buttocks.

'But those are elementary things that anyone ought to have thought of,' Jonah protested. 'That's why-'

'Oh shut up, Jonah!' Bernie exclaimed in exasperation.

'We've been through all this already. Just because you're so full of yourself that you can't admit that the great DCI Porter could ever make a mistake! Put a sock in it can't you?'

'OK.' Peter straightened up and wiped his hands on a piece of paper towel. 'I think you're done. Let's get you dressed and give you some exercise.'

While Peter and Bernie worked his arms and legs into the tracksuit, Jonah continued to relate all that they knew about the circumstances surrounding Harry Whittle's death.

'The house-to-house threw up a few things,' he told Peter as he gently pulled the sleeve up his right arm. 'The woman from the house opposite reckons there was a black car parked outside that morning with a woman sitting in the driver's seat, as if she was waiting for someone. She couldn't give Andrews much of a description, though – just long-ish hair and dark glasses.'

'It was gone by the time Ben Timpson arrived,' Bernie added, 'and nobody from any of the other houses claimed it, so it's a pretty good bet the woman brought the killer to the house and waited outside ready to drive them away as soon as the deed was done.'

She brought over a hoist and, with Peter's help, manoeuvred Jonah into the sling by first rolling him on to his side, then positioning the sling behind him and rolling him back on to it. Then, while Peter attended to securing Jonah in the sling and attaching the sling to the hoist, she brought over the functional electrical stimulation machine, which would exercise the paralysed muscles in Jonah's legs. Together they moved him into position, disconnected the hoist and attached electrodes to his legs and trunk beneath the loose-fitting tracksuit.

'The neighbour couldn't say what make of car it was,' Jonah continued as he watched his legs moving in front of him in a cycling motion. 'She just said it was quite big and flashy and looked quite new, but in that neighbourhood "new" could mean anything up to five years old. There are no traffic cameras in the immediate vicinity, but I've got people going through footage from the ones on the main road and the ring road in the hope of picking it up on those, but it's like the proverbial needle in a haystack.'

'As you'd expect, there are fingerprints all over the bannister rail,' Bernie put in, 'and it'll take a while to exclude the ones that belong to the Whittles.'

'Waste of time,' Jonah grunted. 'The murderer is bound to have worn gloves. These aren't amateur villains. It's organised crime and they won't make simple mistakes like that.'

For a long time, no one spoke. Then Bernie remembered something that had been puzzling her earlier.

'Did it strike either of you as odd the way Bella Kennedy described herself as Kenny's fiancée?'

'You mean, after Gavin told us they split up a couple of months ago?' asked Jonah.

'I just assumed she thought it was the easiest way of justifying her interest in the inquest,' Peter said dismissively. 'I wouldn't read anything sinister into it.'

'I don't just mean, why didn't she use the past tense?' Bernie argued. 'I was surprised that she used the word *fiancée* at all. Gavin never gave us any hint that they'd ever had plans to get married. And that's not the way most young people go about things these days. They live together first. You'd think she'd have described herself as his girlfriend or his partner.'

'Fiancée sounds better,' Peter insisted.

'To us oldies, maybe, but-'

'Are you suggesting she was having difficulty accepting that their relationship *was* all over?' cut in Jonah. 'Or that *she* thought it was more serious than Kenny did?'

'I hadn't got as far as thinking anything,' Bernie replied hastily, realising that she had started a train of thought in Jonah's mind that might run in unpredictable directions. 'It just struck me as a funny thing to say, that's all.'

'Or maybe Gavin got it wrong,' Jonah mused. 'Could Kenny have meant something different when he told them not to expect her round at their place at Christmas?'

'Such as?' asked Peter sceptically.

'If their relationship *was* serious, maybe they were planning Christmas on their own,' Jonah suggested, 'and he was trying to let his parents down gently. If they always have a big family dinner, he might have been afraid they'd be disappointed that he would choose to be with Bella instead. Maybe he was planning on breaking it to them gradually, starting with putting them off making elaborate preparations for entertaining Bella.'

'Or maybe you've just got a very vivid imagination,' retorted Peter. 'All this from just a chance word!'

'Let's give the case a rest, shall we?' suggested Bernie. 'We're just going round in circles and getting nowhere. What about you, Peter? Tell us about your day. How are Gavin and Chrissie doing?'

'Chrissie is still intent on keeping busy,' Peter replied, glad of the change of subject. 'I get the impression it's largely designed to prevent her having time to think about Kenny, but maybe she's always like that. The latest is that she's heard that one of the current residents of the homeless shelter has coeliac disease and she's off to get ingredients to make a gluten-free Christmas pudding and gluten-free stuffing for the turkey. That's on top of knitting more warm winter woollies for them all.'

'Did you make any progress with planning the funeral?' Bernie asked.

'I think so. We've got an appointment with a funeral director tomorrow. Give Chrissie her due; she has a much better grasp on the practicalities of it all than Gavin. I think he just wants it all to be over with the least possible fuss, and for everyone to leave him alone; she understands that lots of people will be upset if they don't get a chance to be involved.'

'Our Chrissie certainly does seem to be something of a force of nature,' Bernie agreed with a smile. 'I'm starting to understand why Gavin is so laid back. I should think that's the only way to survive in their house – just lie back and let Chrissie run her course!'

5. THE FIFTH DAY BEFORE CHRISTMAS

Peter woke sweating and shaking. He had been dreaming. Not the usual nightmare in which he was stuck behind a glass screen (like the one he had sometimes used for watching Mike Carson performing a post mortem examination) looking down on their small kitchen where Angie was being stabbed repeatedly by a gang of youths. And not the other one, which came less frequently, where Angie was being sucked down into a black, peaty bog – the Great Grimpen Mire from the Hound of the Baskervilles, perhaps? And he was holding her hand and trying unsuccessfully to pull her out.

This time, she was in the road at the back of that house in Kidlington, walking along the rows of flowers propped up against the tall brick wall. Every so often, she bent down to read one of the cards attached to them, just as Stella had done the other day. Peter was not sure where *he* was. From where he was standing – or sitting or hovering in the air – he could see the whole row of floral tributes, so presumably he must be at some vantage point. On the other side of the road, perhaps? There was a police officer standing guard. No, not exactly a police officer. It was the teddy bear in police uniform, but now grown to life-size.

There was the sound of a vehicle approaching. A powerful red car appeared round the bend in the road. It swerved as it reached Peter – yes, he must be standing in the road opposite the back of the house – and headed directly for Angie. Peter tried to shout a warning, but no sound came. The teddy bear police officer ran towards her and attempted to push her out of the way, into a cavernous hole in the wall, which Peter had not noticed before. But it was too late. Both Angie and the bear were caught between the car and the wall and …

It was at that point that Peter awoke.

Bernie stirred beside him, disturbed by his sudden movement. She turned over and put her arm around him.

'Bad dream?'

'Yeah.'

Bernie hugged him close. Then, after a few seconds, she turned away and reached for the alarm clock. She peered down at the illuminated display.

'Ten to six. Nearly time to get up.'

'Not just yet. There's no rush. It's not a working day, remember.'

'Try telling that to Jonah!' Bernie retorted with a little laugh. 'After that miscalculation with the Whittle boy, he'll be metaphorically pacing up and down like a caged tiger all day, resenting every moment that he's not doing something to redeem himself for having allowed him to be killed.'

'It's a horrible way to die,' Peter murmured.

'Strangulation, you mean?'

'No – although that must be too. I was thinking of being crushed against a wall by a vehicle.'

'Aaah! Is that what your dream was about?'

'Mmm.'

'It must be pretty awful to watch too,' Bernie observed.

'Yes,' Peter agreed, shuddering as he remembered his dream. 'I meant to ask: how *is* Stella – really?'

'Coping remarkably well, as far as I can tell. They've assigned her to desk duties alongside Malcolm Appleton. She seemed cheerful enough yesterday afternoon, but I'm sure she must be pretty shaken up underneath.'

'It must've shaken up that lad she arrested too,' Peter remarked. 'Didn't you say he was only sixteen?'

'That's right,' Bernie nodded. 'I never thought of that. No

wonder he was scared stiff all the time, if he'd seen his minder crushing Kenny like that and thought he'd be next if he blabbed to the police! *He* should've been offered counselling too – but don't tell Jonah I said so. It'll only add to his guilt complex.'

The alarm went off. Bernie reached out and silenced it, then immediately got out of bed.

'Brrr! It's cold this morning,' she declared, picking up her clothes and hastening to the bathroom to wash and get dressed. 'I think we need to set the central heating timer to come on a few minutes earlier this weather. It hasn't had time to warm the house up and we mustn't let Jonah get cold – it could bring on another of those chest infections.'

* * *

'Rupert Andrews must really hate you,' Bernie observed to Jonah a few hours later as he concluded his fourth telephone call of the morning to the inspector. 'You're off-duty today. Why can't you just trust him to get on with the investigation without pestering him for updates every five minutes? He *is* a DI, after all. He knows what he's doing.'

Jonah had been restless all morning. Leaving his colleagues to pursue any investigation in his absence did not suit his energetic nature, and he felt a deep personal interest in this particular case, which made his forced inactivity all the more frustrating. In addition, as Bernie had correctly identified, he was feeling guilty about not protecting Harry Whittle adequately and was determined to make amends by tracking down his killer without delay.

'Well, he doesn't seem to be making much progress today,' he grumbled. 'He's done the rounds of yet more of our known drug dealers, but he hasn't found any connections between them and the house in Kidlington. And he's got people going through miles of video footage from traffic cameras, but they haven't identified the black car that was waiting outside the Whittles' house yesterday. It's all just plodding routine – and so far leading nowhere!'

'And I suppose *you*'d have found some key piece of evidence that everyone else has missed and made a massive breakthrough and solved the case by now?' teased Bernie. 'You know full well that it's this slow, painstaking, boring stuff that gets results nine times out of ten. And you ought to be aware that *you're* too impatient to be much good at it. So just be thankful you're out of it until Monday, by which time-'

'By which time,' Jonah interrupted, 'maybe we'll have those lab reports back on the paint scrapes from the wall and the mud on the tyres of the abandoned car, and a match for the thumb print they found on the rear-view mirror. Forensics are getting slower and slower with every case they handle. And Mike hasn't even done the PM on Harry Whittle yet! He says it's in a queue behind a suspected drug overdose and a road traffic accident.'

'Well, there you are then!' declared Bernie. 'You might just as well stop worrying about the case and enjoy your weekend. Why don't we wrap up warm and go out for a walk?'

'I have found out something interesting about Kenny, though,' Jonah informed her, ignoring this attempt to divert him on to safer paths. 'You know he's a leading light in the boy scouts, don't you?'

'I know Peter found a scout uniform in his wardrobe,' Bernie admitted. 'You shouldn't call them *boy* scouts any more,' she added with a smile. 'They're unisex these days.'

'Never mind that,' Jonah replied impatiently. 'The point is: I Googled him, just to see if there was anything he'd been up to that had got in the news and might have prompted someone to have it in for him – and I found this!'

He rotated the screen attached to his chair so that it was facing Bernie. She leaned forward to look at a report on the Oxford Mail website.

'Teenage scout drowns in tragic accident,' she read out. She looked up at Jonah. 'One of Kenny's troop, I assume?'

'That's right. They were camping somewhere down by the river and they had a raft-building competition between the different patrols. This lad, Alfie Simmons, somehow got caught between two of the rafts and was forced under and drowned. The verdict was misadventure and the coroner made some recommendations for improving their safety procedures and risk assessments.'

'Are you suggesting that friends or family of this Alfie Simmons might have blamed Kenny for the accident and wanted to do him in?' Bernie asked sceptically.

'I don't know. It certainly would give them a motive …'

'But why then? And why there?' demanded Bernie. 'How did they know he was going to be there? And why on earth choose a moment when the whole neighbourhood is swarming with police officers?'

'I know. You're right,' Jonah admitted. 'I think it would have to have been a chance meeting. Someone spotted Kenny standing there and saw red. I haven't managed to track down where the Simmons family live yet. If by any chance it's Kidlington, one of them could have just happened to be walking past and seen him.'

'Hmmph!' Bernie snorted. 'Riding a flying pig, I suppose! Look, it says here the scout troop is based at St Mark's Church in Rose Hill – just as you'd expect given where the Hugheses live. The members of the troop will all live down there to the south of the city – not up in Kidlington. His police uniform is far more likely than his scout uniform to have attracted the killer's attention!'

'The boy could have grandparents living in Kidlington,' Jonah insisted obstinately. 'It's worth looking into.'

'OK. If it makes you happy.' Bernie sighed. 'Carry on digging. It won't get you anywhere, I'm sure. If you don't want me for anything, I'll get on with cleaning Lucy's room and making up her bed. She'll be back before tea time.'

* * *

Peter arrived back shortly before noon, accompanied by Gavin and Chrissie. The mismatch between Chrissie's active mind, hopping abruptly from one consideration to another, and Gavin's apparent lack of engagement in the whole process must have made that morning's meeting very challenging for the funeral director – a quietly-spoken woman with compassionate brown eyes and an apparently bottomless supply of patience – who calmly and gently took them through the various options available. When eventually she left, assuring them that there was no rush and they should take as much time as they needed to make their choices, Peter, seeing the drained looks on both of their faces, had invited Gavin and Chrissie to lunch.

'I brought you this,' Chrissie said to Bernie, the moment she walked in the door. 'I baked it this morning before the funeral director came. I thought you wouldn't have time for ordinary baking with all the bother of Christmas coming, people coming to stay and all that.'

'Thank you very much,' Bernie smiled back, looking down at the cling-film wrapped fruit loaf, which Chrissie was holding out towards her and reflecting that Chrissie must have been much more busy than she this Christmas, especially since Peter did almost all the cooking in their household. 'Lucy will love this. We'll save it for when she gets home this afternoon. She messaged me a few minutes ago to say she's on the train.'

'It's an old recipe I got from my grandmother,' Chrissie went on. 'You soak the dried fruit in tea overnight, which is why it's so lovely and moist. Kenny always says-.' She broke off in confusion and dropped her eyes as if she had a sudden interest in the pattern of tiles on the floor.

'Go on in and sit down,' Peter urged from behind them. 'The lunch won't take more than a few minutes. It's just a matter of getting everything out of the fridge and cutting the bread. The bathroom's on the right just at the top of the stairs, if you want to wash your hands before we eat.'

About twenty minutes later, they had all taken their places round the big oak table in the centre of the kitchen. Peter handed round slices of bread and butter and urged Gavin and Chrissie to help themselves to ham, cheese and his own special winter salad, while Bernie fed Jonah, in between taking bites from a ham sandwich that she had made for herself.

'What do you think, Bernie?' Chrissie asked earnestly. 'About burial or cremation? We can't decide. Kenny never discussed what he wanted – well, you wouldn't expect him to, would you? With him being so young. We cremated my dad. My mum said she didn't want the responsibility of looking after a grave, but ... What do you think Kenny would have wanted?'

'I think he'd have wanted whatever you want,' Bernie said carefully. 'At the end of the day, funerals and graves are for the people who're left behind, not for the deceased. If you and Gavin would like to have a grave to visit, then go for a burial. If not, cremation makes a lot of sense, because it doesn't take up land that could be used for other things. Or these days,' she added after a moment's thought, 'there are green burial sites, where they use biodegradable coffins and don't mark the grave, so it all stays as natural as possible and they plant trees to soak up carbon dioxide from the atmosphere.'

'That's what makes it difficult,' Gavin sighed. 'There are so many choices – and so many people to consider.'

'We're wondering where to have the funeral,' Chrissie went on. 'Kenny wasn't religious, but he did used to go to church parade with the scouts. Did you know he was an assistant scout leader? They wanted him to be leader, but it wasn't compatible with the job. He couldn't be sure he'd never be called on duty on scout days. I suppose *they* might like to do something at the funeral – carry one of their flags or something.'

'Why not have the service at St Mark's?' suggested Jonah. 'That's where his scouts were based, isn't it?'

'Yes. How did you know?' asked Chrissie in surprise.

'I've been reading about the accident the summer before last,' Jonah told her. 'The boy who drowned?'

'Oh!' Chrissie's eyes widened and she seemed momentarily at a loss for words, but she quickly recovered. 'Yes. That was dreadful. Kenny was very cut up about it. He felt responsible, although the coroner was very clear that no one was to blame, but he was in charge of the activity so ….'

'What about the boy's parents?' Jonah asked innocently.

'Oh they were very understanding,' Chrissie assured him. 'They could see how bad Kenny was feeling and they made a point of asking him to read a lesson in the funeral service to show they didn't hold him responsible. His sister's still in the troop. She went camping with them this summer just gone. They live just round the corner from us – in Chichester Road. Her mum came round with a card as soon as they heard about Kenny.'

'The scouts all stood in two lines outside the church and saluted as the coffin came past,' Gavin recalled. 'Do you think they'd like to do that at Kenny's funeral?'

'Perhaps you should speak to the scout leader,' suggested Peter. 'They'll probably have a better idea what would be best for the youngsters than anyone else. It'll have been a shock for them all, and it might help them to grieve if they have a definite role to play.'

'Yes,' Chrissie agreed. 'That's a good idea. I'll get on to the scout leader tomorrow – and shall I ask the vicar from St Mark's to come round and discuss having the funeral there?' she added, turning to Gavin.

'Yes, I suppose so,' Gavin mumbled after a long pause, his mind evidently elsewhere. 'Yes. That's a good idea. Maybe then we'll be able to fix the date,' he added more hopefully.

'We'll have to decide between burial and cremation before we can fix a date,' Chrissie reminded him, sounding a little impatient.

'Lorraine will probably want us to go for burial,' Gavin murmured morosely. 'Like Mum and Dad.'

'Lorraine is Gav's sister,' Chrissie explained, looking round at the others with a wry smile on her face. 'She always has an opinion on everything. She's coming to stay for the weekend.'

'She lives in Hull,' Gavin added dolefully. 'They're driving down after work. We'll be lucky if they make it before midnight.'

'It *is* a long way,' Bernie agreed.

'But you need your family around at a time like this,' Peter added conventionally, immediately feeling annoyed with himself for falling into platitudes.

'Alfie Simmons's funeral was at St Mark's,' Chrissie murmured thoughtfully. 'How about a service there with the scouts and then a private one, just for family, at the crematorium?'

'Yes. That sounds good,' Gavin agreed, then more uncertainly, 'if you think we ought to go for cremation?'

'Or a burial, if you'd rather,' Chrissie sighed, sounding rather exasperated at her husband's indecision. 'I just meant, we'd better have some sort of public ceremony that the scouts and the police can come to, and then we can have something just for the family afterwards.'

'Yes, I'm sure you're right,' Gavin agreed at once. 'I didn't mean …'

'Perhaps we could ask Emerald Simmons to do a reading,' Chrissie mused. Her active mind had moved on, prompted by Jonah's question about the drowning of Alfie Simmons. 'She reads very well, and her mum said when she came round that-'

'Chichester Road?' queried Jonah suddenly. 'Was that where you said they lived?'

'Yes,' answered Chrissie. 'Why?'

'That's the same road as the Whittles live in. And you say it's not far from your home too?'

'Just round the corner,' Gavin confirmed. 'You must have passed the end of it to get to us on Tuesday.'

'Did we? I didn't notice. That's the trouble with always being in the back of the car.'

'And always with your nose in that screen of yours!' retorted Bernie.

'You're not trying to make something of it are you?' asked Peter scathingly. 'It must just be a coincidence, nothing more.'

'I don't like coincidences,' Jonah declared. 'I can't see any connection, but it does strike me as odd that three young men, all living within spitting distance of one another, should all have met violent deaths in the last eighteen months.'

Peter got up and started putting away the remains of the food. 'Would anyone like a mince pie?' he asked brightly, looking round at Gavin and Chrissie and pointedly avoiding Jonah's eye. 'I'm sure they don't measure up to Chrissie's standards, but I do always insist on making my own rather than buying the shop ones.'

'Just one,' Gavin replied with unexpected decisiveness, 'and then we'll have to be getting back. We've got to move things around to make room for Lorraine and Dennis. The spare room's only tiny – hardly more than a box room really – and we've got all sorts of stuff piled up in it at the moment. I suppose they could sleep in Kenny's room but ...' He shrugged helplessly and looked towards his wife for support.

'Yes,' she agreed. Peter could not decide whether the frown with which she said this signified dissatisfaction or merely that she was thinking. 'I suppose they would be more comfortable in Kenny's room, but ....' She definitely appeared to be thinking hard now. 'Well, it's only for two nights, so they'll be fine on the sofa-bed in the dining room, if we just move some of the other furniture upstairs out of their way.'

'Let's all go into the other room,' suggested Bernie. 'Leave the clearing away for now, Peter. We can do it later. You go on through with the mince pies and I'll make us all a brew.'

'Good idea,' agreed Jonah, immediately moving his chair away from the table and heading for the door. 'I'd like to catch the end of the lunchtime television news, to see what they're saying about Harry Whittle's death.'

When Peter turned on the television they were greeted with a close-up of Trevor Whittle, who was being interviewed by a reporter.

'The police promised him protection and then they sent him home with nothing!' Trevor was saying angrily. 'He was a key witness to a murder and they didn't bother to do anything to keep him safe.'

'He was also part of a drugs gang and had been charged

with drugs offences, though, hadn't he?' suggested the interviewer.

'He wasn't part of any gang!' Trevor retorted. 'He was just too easily taken in. He didn't know it was cannabis plants he was growing. How could he? We saw to it he never messed with drugs or anything like that. When we brought him home from the police station he was absolutely scared stiff! They must've seen that. So why didn't they do something to keep those animals out of our home?'

The scene faded and changed to a view of the television studio.

'That was an interview recorded a few hours ago,' the news reader announced. 'Thames Valley Police weren't able to provide anyone to come on the programme, but they did issue the following statement.'

Words appeared on the screen and scrolled upwards as she read out: 'We were deeply saddened to hear about the death of Harry Whittle yesterday morning. Police resources are limited and we have to make tough decisions in determining where to deploy them. As a potential witness who had refused to co-operate with us in identifying the man who killed PC Kenneth Hughes, we judged that he was not at sufficient risk to justify police protection in his home. Clearly, with hindsight, we got this wrong, and we are deeply sorry for this. We are continuing to make every effort to find the killers of both Harry Whittle and Kenneth Hughes.'

The picture returned to the newsreader, who faced the camera and continued, 'and now, in other news, President Trump's latest Tweet on climate change has sparked a wave of protest from-'

'Here you are everyone!' Bernie announced, coming in with the tea tray. 'The drink that cheers but does not inebriate, as my mam always used to say!'

Peter switched off the television set and helped his wife to hand cups of tea to their guests.

'I wonder what the boy's father would have been saying if he'd been remanded in custody instead of being allowed home,' he murmured. 'It strikes me it's one of those cases where we're damned if we do and damned if we don't.'

'We could have put an officer in the house,' Jonah growled in response. 'Or, at very least, given them some advice about keeping the place secure. The killers simply walked in through the back door, for goodness sake! The boy's parents have a right to be angry with us. We shouldn't have let it happen.'

* * *

'How was the journey?' asked Peter as he stood back to allow Bernie and Lucy into the house on their return from the railway station.

'OK,' Lucy shrugged. 'Both trains were very crowded, but it is Christmas, after all. I'm glad I booked a seat. There were people standing from Stafford to Wolverhampton.'

'At least with you living in a shared house, you could travel light,' her mother observed. 'Not like when I was at college and had to empty my room at the end of every term. Now take your bag upstairs while I make a brew.'

'Where's Jonah?' Lucy asked, hanging up her coat and staring round the hall in search of their friend.

'In his room,' Peter answered. 'We had a bit of a leakage problem, and I was in the middle of changing his trousers when you got back. I'll go and finish that while you take your bag up and we'll be ready by the time you're back down again.'

'I'll help,' Lucy volunteered at once. 'My bag can wait. I want to talk to Jonah.'

'Remember what I said, love,' Bernie said warningly. 'Don't be too hard on him.'

Lucy strode purposefully through Jonah's sitting room and into his bedroom. He was lying on the bed in his underpants. A pair of clean trousers was neatly folded on a nearby chair and the soiled garments that these were to replace lay in a crumpled heap on a plastic sheet on the floor, together with a plastic bowl containing soapy water, and a bath towel.

'Hi Jonah!' she greeted him. 'It's good to be back.'

'It's good to see you too,' he smiled back. 'Although I was hoping I'd be in a more dignified position to welcome you home!'

She went over and kissed him on the cheek. Then she turned round and picked up the trousers.

'OK,' she said to Peter, who had followed her in. 'I'll put these on, if you can just help to lift once I've got his legs in.'

She expertly manoeuvred Jonah's legs into the trousers and gently pulled them up. As she approached his hips, Peter lifted his body off the bed just enough for her to pull them up to his waist.

'There! That's better,' Lucy announced, fastening the button and pulling up the zip. 'Now let's get you back into your chair, and then I want to talk to you about Stella.'

'Stella's been remarkably resilient,' Jonah assured her, while Peter brought his wheelchair – now in a reclined position so that it resembled a hospital trolley – alongside the bed. 'She's determined not to take any time off, and she even had a go at questioning the lad she and Kenny arrested.'

'Yes, she told me about that,' Lucy replied, helping Peter to roll Jonah gently off the bed and on to the reclined chair. 'And then I heard on the news that you'd sent him home and he'd been killed by the gang to stop him talking.'

'That's just surmise,' Jonah told her at once. 'All we actually know is that someone got into his house and strangled him and then tried to make it look as if he'd hanged himself. We weren't intending to let even that much out to the press, but his father wouldn't keep his mouth shut. It would've been better if we could have let the murderers think we'd bought the suicide story.'

Peter positioned Jonah's left hand on the controls and fastened a strap round his wrist to hold it in place. Immediately, Jonah pressed a button to bring the chair up into a sitting position. He looked at Lucy across the bed.

'I feel bad about not having taken action to keep him safe. I knew he was scared of what they might do to him if he grassed on them, but he'd refused to tell us anything, so I didn't think, which was stupid of me.'

He started the chair moving forward towards the door, but Lucy intercepted him and stood barring his way.

'So what are you doing to prevent them doing the same to Stella?' she demanded.

At these words, Peter, in the act of bending down to gather up the contents of the waterproof sheet, straightened up again and spun round to look at them. He saw Jonah staring at her, apparently lost for words, most unusually for him.

'Well?' asked Lucy.

'What makes you think Stella's in any sort of danger?' Jonah asked at last, although Peter could tell that he had immediately joined the dots and realised what Lucy was getting at.

'She's a witness too, isn't she?' Lucy replied implacably. 'She saw them kill Kenny Hughes.'

'But she doesn't know who it was driving the car,' Jonah argued. 'Harry Whittle could have given us names. It's not the same at all.'

'They may not know that,' Lucy insisted. 'She told me she didn't get a clear look at the driver's face, but they can't be sure she didn't give you a detailed description.'

'Too late to stop her doing that by now,' Jonah countered.

Peter resumed clearing away the soiled clothes and dirty water. He could see that Jonah was floundering and wondered if he ought to say something in his defence. On the other hand, a small part of him felt rather pleased and proud of his step-daughter's efficient demolition of his arguments.

'But they don't know that, do they?' repeated Lucy. 'And, in any case,' she added after a moment's thought, 'her evidence might still be needed in court in order to convict them. So they still have a reason for wanting to get rid of her. I think you ought to have her under police protection!'

'We're keeping her off the streets,' Jonah informed her, speaking a little more confidently now. 'She's manning the desk with Malcolm Appleton for the next few weeks – and she's on daytime shifts only.'

'Yes, she said,' Lucy admitted, 'but she told me it was to keep her away from any incidents that might affect her psychologically, after seeing Kenny killed.'

'It is,' Jonah agreed, 'and to make sure there are people around for her to turn to if she wants to talk. It can be very lonely out there walking the beat, knowing you could have to be making life and death decisions on your own. But it also means it would be impossible for anyone to try to kill her, doesn't it?'

'What about when she's at home?' challenged Lucy.

'If it'll make you feel better, I'll talk to her about keeping the doors and windows locked,' Jonah conceded, 'but I do think you're exaggerating the risk. She's got Celeste there all the time, and at night Danny will be there too.'

'She doesn't want her gran worrying,' Peter added, coming back from the adjacent bathroom where he had been sluicing off Jonah's soiled clothes. 'She's afraid she'll put pressure on her to leave the force.'

'So why not set her mind at rest by giving Stella some proper protection?' demand Lucy.

'How?' asked Jonah. 'What is it you want us to do?'

'I don't know exactly,' Lucy admitted. 'A police escort to and from work and an officer on guard at the house, maybe?'

'I'm not sure that'd help,' Peter argued cautiously. 'That might just draw attention to her. We've no reason to believe the gang know where Stella lives at the moment.'

'Or even *who* she is,' added Jonah, flashing a grateful look at Peter. 'All we've released to the media is the fact that there was another officer with Kenny when he was attacked. We didn't give out her name.'

'The car driver must've seen her,' argued Lucy.

'It's not likely they saw Stella any better than she saw them,' countered Jonah.

'I still think you ought to be doing *something* to keep Stella safe,' Lucy repeated doggedly.

'OK Lucy,' Peter put in firmly, folding up the plastic sheet and putting it away in a drawer. 'You've made your point. Now let's go on through to the lounge. Your mam will be wondering what we're up to. Personally,' He went on, shepherding his step-daughter out of Jonah's rooms and into the hall, 'I'm much more concerned about Gavin and his wife. This has been a tremendous blow to them.'

'Let's invite them to tea tomorrow,' Lucy suggested immediately.

'I'm not sure about that,' Peter hesitated. 'It might just be rubbing it in – a family reunion when their family has just had its heart ripped out. I hadn't realised until this week that Kenny was their only child.'

'We can certainly invite them,' Bernie said, overhearing the end of the conversation as Peter and Lucy followed Jonah into the living room. 'I'll try to make it clear they needn't come if they don't want to, but I've already asked Andy Lepage, and they may like to hear the latest from him on the investigation.'

'Actually,' Peter cut in, 'I've just remembered: they won't be able to come because Gavin's sister's going to be there. Don't you remember, Bernie? He said they were driving down from Hull this evening.'

'Yes,' agreed Bernie. 'You're right. So they won't want us pestering them to come here for tea.'

'Well, we must at least invite Stella,' Lucy insisted. 'Or is she on duty this weekend?'

'She is,' Jonah informed her, 'but her shift ends in time for her to come over. Andy's working the early shift tomorrow as well, so we could ask him to bring her with him.'

'That's a great idea!' declared Lucy. 'I'll ring her right away. Will you organise things with Andy, Mam?'

6. THE FOURTH DAY BEFORE CHRISTMAS

'Do you think I'm getting past it?' asked Jonah when Bernie came in to get him up the next morning.

'What's brought that on?' demanded Bernie as she bent down to reach the controls on Jonah's special bed. She turned off the automatic turning mechanism (a function that tilted Jonah into different positions during the night to prevent him developing pressure ulcers) and then turned another handle to raise him into a more upright position by lifting a back rest concealed beneath the mattress and pillow. 'I thought the Great Detective was incapable of such self-doubt!'

'I've been thinking about what Lucy said,' her friend answered. 'I really ought to-'

'Has she been giving you a hard time?' interrupted Bernie. 'She was going on about what were you doing to protect Stella, while we were in the car on the way from the station. I told her to back off.'

'But she's right,' insisted Jonah. 'I ought to have anticipated that they'd try to kill the Whittle boy and I ought to have taken steps to make sure they didn't go after Stella. I ought to do something about that now, but I'm not sure what we *can* do.'

'We're already doing something,' Bernie reminded him. 'We're having her to high tea this afternoon. Andy's bringing her over straight from work and one of us can drop her off home afterwards. Her brother, Danny, will be there by then and he's big enough to be a match for anyone!'

Jonah fell silent, reflecting on this statement. Stella's half-brother, Daniel, was indeed a formidable figure. From a small and slight boy, he had suddenly shot up in his teens, developing broad shoulders and powerful muscles. At twenty-three, he towered above both his grandmother and his older half-brother, Leroy. He was just the kind of black youth whom timid white residents had an unfortunate habit of reporting to the police as potential muggers, and as a consequence had suffered more than his fair share of searches at the hands of officers who felt obliged to act on such "tip-offs".

The electric kettle, which stood on top of a chest of drawers on the other side of the room, clicked off and Bernie went over to make tea. She poured it into a bone china mug and brought it over to Jonah.

'Come on!' she urged. 'Stop brooding and get this down you.'

She climbed on to the bed and settled down next to Jonah, so that she could hold the mug to his lips. This was one of the very few luxuries that he allowed himself. Normally, favouring practicality over style, he took his drinks through a drinking straw from a plastic beaker with a lid. But once a day – and only on days when it was Bernie's turn to get him up – he had tea from real bone china, as he remembered his mother serving it when he was a child.

Bernie put her left arm around his shoulders and gave them a gentle squeeze. Jonah did not often allow his confident persona to slip and this made his evident distress at his own failings all the more poignant.

Jonah sipped his tea in silence.

'I'll get Peter to have a word with Danny when he takes Stella home this evening,' Bernie promised, after a long pause. 'He's a bright lad. He'll manage to find a way to stick close to Stella without making their gran suspect she's in danger.'

'Mmm,' agreed Jonah. 'Now why didn't I think of that? I think I *must* be getting past it!'

'More likely driving yourself too hard and not giving yourself time to relax and think things through,' retorted

Bernie. She put the empty mug down on a bedside cabinet and wiped a small dribble of tea from Jonah's chin before bending down her head and kissing him on the cheek. 'Now, if you've quite finished feeling sorry for yourself, I'm going to get on with emptying your urine bag while that hot tea spurs your bowels into action.'

A warm drink in bed in the morning was not merely an indulgence. It was a necessary part of Jonah's bowel management routine. Damage to the spinal cord affects control of the bowel and bladder as well as causing the more obvious limb paralysis. Emptying Jonah's bowel at the start of the day was necessary in order to avoid (as far as possible) unplanned bowel movements while he was out and about.

Bernie detached the bag from where it was hanging on a hook beneath the bed to ensure that it was low enough to allow Jonah's bladder to empty during the night, and took it through to his bathroom.

'Hi Jonah!' Lucy appeared through the other door and went straight over to Jonah and put her arms round him. 'I'm sorry if I was horrid to you last night,' she murmured contritely. 'I was just worried about Stella. Peter put me right about a few things after you'd gone to bed.'

'I expect it was good for me,' Jonah smiled back. 'Peter keeps telling me I'm too big for my boots. And your mam's come up with a cunning plan to keep Stella safe without her gran getting in a flap about it, which we wouldn't have thought of if you hadn't said your piece.'

'Oh?'

'We're going to enlist Danny as her bodyguard,' Jonah told her. 'It'll be a tough gangster who'd dare to mess with him.'

'He's not very fond of the police though,' Lucy said doubtfully. 'Are you sure he'll co-operate?'

'He will when Peter asks him,' Jonah replied confidently. 'He gets on fine with him.'

'Everyone gets on with Peter,' Lucy agreed, 'and I suppose Danny will probably like the idea of being Stella's minder. You'd better make sure *she* doesn't know about it though. She doesn't like being treated like a little sister who needs looking after.'

'OK,' Bernie announced in a business-like manner, coming back in and striding across to the bed. 'Now you two have patched up your differences, let's get you into the hoist and take you through to the bathroom.'

* * *

'It's been all go today,' Andy told them, spreading butter on a thick slice of Peter's home-made bread, 'and Craig Manson has been at the bottom of most of it.'

'Oh yes?' Jonah looked enquiringly across the table at his young colleague. 'He's the guy in the combat gear who interrupted my interview with Harry Whittle the other day – is that right?'

'Yes. He seems to have mobilised the entire homeless community to track down the gang that were running that cannabis factory in Kidlington. He came in this morning with a couple of other guys and a story of entrapment and covert surveillance.'

'They all came in asking to speak to you, Jonah,' Stella added. 'Manson wasn't pleased when we told him you weren't there.'

'That's right,' grinned Andy. 'I don't think he was at all impressed at being fobbed off with me, but he condescended to make the best of it in the end.'

'What other guys?' asked Jonah sharply, ignoring these asides. 'Anyone we know?'

'There's a Mike Lambert,' Andy replied, waving his bread in Peter's direction. 'DCI Davenport reckons you'll remember him, Peter. Something about a suspected assault and robbery in the University Parks?'

'I don't remember …,' Peter began, thinking rapidly back through all the cases of his long career in the police service. Then it all clicked into place. 'Oh yes! Of course! Gavin arrested him after this woman swore blind he'd tripped her up and taken her purse. It turned out in the end that he was completely innocent – except for being in possession of a small amount of cannabis for his own use.'[5]

'That's right,' Andy agreed. 'And his cannabis habit turned out to be very useful. He was able to give Manson the low-down on a new gang of drug dealers who've shown up selling cannabis on the streets recently.'

He took a large bite out of his slice of bread and butter and sat chewing it while everyone else waited for him to continue with his story.

'Any names?' demanded Jonah impatiently.

'No,' Andy shook his head and swallowed quickly. 'And he didn't know who was in charge of the enterprise – only the end-dealers, the retailers, if you like. However,' he continued with emphasis, 'because Lambert is a user himself, he was able to help Manson track them down.'

He took another large bite of bread and washed it down with water, clearly enjoying being the centre of attention. Peter reflected that Andy had come a long way since he started out as a tongue-tied trainee detective in Peter's own team. The young DC Lepage would never have been capable of speaking so confidently or dared to tease his commanding officer by stringing out the narration for maximum effect.

'They staged a trap,' Andy went on at last. 'Manson followed Lambert to wherever it is that the dealing takes place. (They wouldn't tell us where that was, exactly.) Lambert buys some cannabis from this new guy – we're calling him Dealer A – and then Manson follows him home.'

'They've got his address?' shouted Jonah excitedly. 'What is it? Have you checked the electoral roll?'

'We'll come to that later.' Andy grinned across the table at him, evidently very satisfied with the sensation that he had caused. 'First let me tell you what they did after that.'

---

[5] You can read about this incident in the short story *Witness Evidence*, within the collection *My Life of Crime* © 2016 ISBN: 9781911083207

He took another bite of bread and butter and chewed it slowly as if thinking about how best to continue his story. Peter watched Jonah's face, smiling to himself at his friend's evident frustration over the time it was taking for Andy to *Reveal All*. With commendable patience, Jonah repressed the urge to tell him to "get on with it!" and accepted the bite of sausage roll that Lucy was offering up to his mouth.

'Manson organised a team of rough sleepers to keep the house under surveillance,' Andy continued at last, reaching out to help himself to a slice of pork pie from a plate in the centre of the table. 'Dave Gillis – d'you remember him? – was on duty this morning.'

'Dave Gillis?' repeated Jonah in a puzzled voice. 'The name doesn't ring any bells with me. Who is he?'

'Peter'll remember,' Andy grinned back, turning his gaze from his current to his former boss.

'I can't say I do,' Peter answered, shaking his head. 'Can you give me a clue? When am I supposed to have come across him?'

'Think back a dozen years or so,' Andy replied, still smiling. 'The body in the canal boat?[6] Dave Gillis was the down-and-out who was wandering on the towpath and saw the murderer getting out of the boat.'

'Of course!' Peter exclaimed. 'Gavin tracked him down for us. He used to sleep under the canal bridge at Aristotle Lane. Surely he isn't still sleeping rough? He must be in his seventies by now!'

'It seems he is,' Andy told him. 'Still too obstinate to accept a place in a hostel and still deeply suspicious of the police. If it hadn't been for Craig telling him he owed it to Gavin to help, I doubt if he'd ever have been persuaded to come into the station voluntarily.'

'It's all coming back to me now,' Peter went on. 'You and Rupert Andrews interviewed him together. I remember

---

[6] You can read about this in *Murder of a Martian*, the 2nd Bernie Fazakerley Mystery © 2016 ISBN: 978-1911083108

listening to the tape. It was one of the things that convinced me you were going to make it as a detective. You had a much better idea than Andrews did how to get someone like Gillis to talk.'

'Thank you.' Andy felt his cheeks burning and was grateful that his blushes were disguised beneath his brown skin. He hurried on with his story. 'Anyway, to cut a long story short ...'

'Thank goodness for that!' breathed Jonah.

'He saw a posh black car drive up and park outside Dealer A's house,' Andy continued. 'He didn't get the registration, but his description matches the one the neighbours gave of the car that was parked outside the Whittles' house the morning Harry was killed. A man – who we called Dealer B – got out and went up to the front door and Dealer A let him in. Gillis reckons he saw another man and a woman in the car as well.'

'The same woman that was driving the car when it stopped in Chichester Road?' asked Jonah.

'We can't be sure,' Andy replied with a shrug. 'At the moment, we're still calling them Dealer C and Dealer D. We do, however, now have a proper name for Dealer B.'

'And it is?' asked Jonah tetchily.

'Stuart Hatton. Gillis identified him from photos on the police database. 'He's well-known in the drug squad as a "heavy" who makes a living working for various criminal gangs as their enforcer.'

'At last we're getting somewhere!' Jonah exclaimed with satisfaction.

'And that's not all,' Andy went on, with the air of a conjurer preparing to extract a particularly large rabbit from his hat. 'Dave's description of the man and woman in the car isn't too far off the passport photos of the fake Mr and Mrs McLeod. I showed them to him and he said he couldn't be sure, but he thought they did look similar.'

'And Dealer A?' demanded Jonah. 'Have you got his real name yet?'

'Not just his name, but we've had him in for questioning,' Andy told him. 'His name's Pilling – Ross Pilling – and he's admitted to supplying a class B drug. He claims he doesn't know the name of his supplier. According to Pilling, everyone just calls him "The Boss". He says he doesn't know who the man and woman in the car are or where the cannabis that he distributes comes from or … basically anything at all about anything!'

'Is he still in custody?' Jonah wanted to know.

'No. He'd like to be, but we thought there was a better chance of finding the rest of the gang if we sent him home. Don't worry!' he added, seeing Jonah's look of alarm. 'We've got officers watching the house day and night, and he's too terrified of "the Boss" to venture out. Apparently he owes them money and Hatton's visit was to apply the thumbscrews to get him to pay up.'

'Could this Hatton have been the man who was driving the car that hit Kenny?' suggested Lucy, plucking up courage to speak now that Andy appeared to have finished his narrative of the day's events.

'No.' Stella shook her head vigorously. 'I didn't get a clear view of the driver, but I'm quite sure it wasn't him. In fact, the more I think about it, the more I wonder if it couldn't have been a woman. I'm almost sure I saw a pony tail. Hatton's photo has a shaved head.'

'Could it have been the woman in the car outside Pilling's house?' asked Jonah, 'or the one outside the Whittle's house, if they were different? Hang on a minute! Let me find the fake photos of Mr and Mrs McLeod.'

He moved his chair back from the table a little way and started fiddling with the controls of his computer screen.

'We ought to take that screen away from you at mealtimes,' Peter muttered. 'Surely this can wait until everyone's finished.'

'It won't take long,' Jonah assured him without looking up. 'Ah! Here we are!' He swivelled the screen and Stella leaned across Lucy to see the passport photograph of "Mrs McLeod".

'I don't think it's her,' she said, after studying it for some time. 'But, I really didn't see them at all clearly. I'm sure the driver was white and they had long hair in a ponytail, but that's about it. This woman's hair looks quite different, but maybe if she tied it back …?' She sighed. 'I'm sorry. I just don't know.'

'Has everyone finished?' asked Peter in the lull that followed. 'There's apple pie for afters, if people are ready for it.'

'That sounds delicious!' Stella declared enthusiastically. 'You're lucky to have apple trees in your garden.'

'You're welcome to take some apples home with you, if you like,' Bernie offered. 'We've got a great pile of them out in the old wash house and we're never going to get through them all before they go off. You too, Andy,' she added. 'Take some for your mum.'

Lucy helped her mother to clear away the plates and dishes while Peter brought out an apple pie from the oven and a large jug of cream from the fridge. For the next few minutes everyone was busy with cutting the pie and passing round the cream jug. However, Jonah could not keep his mind away from the ongoing investigation for long.

'Have you got any news from Forensics on that car yet?' he asked Andy. 'And what about the PM on Harry Whittle?'

'As Andrews told you yesterday afternoon when you rang, they're still working on the car and Mike isn't going to be able to do the PM until next week,' Andy mumbled through a mouthful of pie. 'However, one of his assistants has collected some fragments of skin from under Harry's fingernails, which they're hopeful will enable them to get DNA from his killer.'

'And they've got some footwear marks from the Whittles' house that don't match any of their shoes,' Stella added. 'I know because they came round taking prints from all the uniformed officers who attended the scene – just in case they belonged to one of them.'

'OK,' Jonah murmured. 'So, if we can once track down these gangsters, there's a good chance we'll be able to place them at the scene of Harry Whittle's murder. What about the house in Kidlington? Any footprints, fingerprints or DNA from that?'

'I rang them again yesterday,' Andy told him. 'The message

I got – apart from "go away and stop bothering us!"' he added with a grin, 'was that they've got so much stuff that they're having trouble separating the wheat from the chaff, so to speak.'

'Anyway,' Bernie observed, 'it looks as if you ought to thank Craig Manson and his homeless friends for getting you the best lead you've had in this whole case. Gavin's work with the rough sleepers certainly seems to have paid off. What's that quotation about casting your bread on the waters?'

'I don't want to be a wet blanket,' Peter put in cautiously, 'but I think I ought to remind you all that, as far as I can see, we don't have any concrete evidence that these drug dealers that Craig and his friends have found for us are the same as the ones who were running the cannabis farm in Kidlington. All we've got to connect them with the case is the fact that they've been seen in a flashy black car similar to one that was parked in Chichester Road round about when Harry Whittle was killed. There could be two black cars. And the Chichester Road car could have nothing at all to do with Harry's death. We know there are more than this one gang selling cannabis around Oxford. And it's even possible that Harry had other enemies apart from the gang who killed Kenny. Or …'

'Go on,' Jonah urged impatiently. 'Or what?'

'Or …,' Pete continued to hesitate over presenting his final hypothesis. 'Or Kenny's death could even have been an accident,' he said at last. 'I had a look at the road on the way back from Chrissie's nativity play the other day. There's a sharp bend and lots of cars parked, not very tidily. I did wonder if someone might simply have been driving too fast, swerved to avoid a car parked on the side opposite the house and hit Kenny by accident.'

'Mel's van was parked opposite the back of the house,' Stella said, her voice sounding strangely loud in the silence that followed Peter's speech. 'She was just getting PD Q out of it when Harry came out of the garage and Kenny grabbed him. I suppose a car coming round the corner might have got a shock to see them there and swerved across the road.'

'And been too frightened to stop after hitting Kenny,' agreed Bernie.

'But the car we found abandoned not a mile from the scene was stolen,' argued Andy. 'It'd be an amazing coincidence if a thief just happened to be driving a stolen vehicle down that funny little back street just at the critical moment when Kenny was making an arrest, and then just happened to misjudge the corner and run into him!'

'If that *is* the car that hit Kenny,' remarked Peter.

'The tyre marks match,' Jonah pointed out.

'Which only necessarily means that a car with the same brand of tyres happened to park on that grass within a few days of the incident,' Peter countered. 'If you'd found mud from the verge on the car's tyres, I'd be more convinced.'

'Which is precisely why we need Forensics to get their finger out and finish examining the car and doing their tests!' concluded Jonah in a tone of deep frustration.

'So ... are you saying we may never find out who killed Kenny?' asked Stella in a small voice.

'Of course not!' Andy assured her with more confidence than any of them felt at that moment. 'It's just going to take a while, that's all. And, Peter's only warning us not to count our chickens. The chances are Pilling's suppliers *are* the ones we're after and it's just a matter of time before they make contact with him again and our surveillance team will be able to arrest them.'

'You said you knew who one of them is. Couldn't you arrest him now?' Stella asked.

'Stuart Hatton, you mean?' Andy turned his gaze from Stella to Jonah. 'Well, we could look for him at his last known address, but we decided against it in case that just sent the more important members of the gang deeper underground. We want to know who the man and woman who were with him are. My guess is that one of them is "The Boss" watching him to see he did as he was told.'

'Andy's right,' Jonah agreed. 'One thing we do know about this gang is that its members aren't easily persuaded to grass on their mates. This may turn into a long waiting game.'

'Which could be a bit of a problem,' Andy admitted, looking straight at Jonah now. 'The Chief Super's worried about all the overtime we're going to be clocking up with 24-hour surveillance on Pilling's house – especially if it carries on over Christmas. She's given us until Monday afternoon and then she says we'll have to review the situation.'

'Maybe we could ask Manson and his friends to watch the house instead?' Bernie suggested facetiously. 'They seem to have done a good job of it so far!'

'I'll have a chat with Alison on Monday morning,' Jonah promised. 'I know we're stretched, with so many officers having left these past few years, but this is something we can't afford to give up on. Quite apart from finding Kenny's killer, it's got to be worth a bit of overtime to take the latest new drugs gang off our streets.'

'But you don't work on Mondays,' Peter objected.

'I'm working this week. Didn't Bernie tell you? I'm not going to be in on Wednesday or Thursday this week, because of Christmas, so I thought it made sense to work Monday instead – especially now we're busy with this double murder to solve. I'll still only be working two days, instead of three.'

'Some men would resent the way you arbitrarily cancel my wife's leave,' Peter observed, pretending to be annoyed. 'It's a good thing I'm so easy-going.'

'We knew you wouldn't mind, under the circumstances,' Bernie responded, grinning across the table at him. 'You're as keen as anyone to catch Kenny's killer. And I made him promise that we won't be working at all between Christmas and New Year, whatever happens!'

7. THE THIRD DAY BEFORE CHRISTMAS

'… a son whom she will call Immanuel, a name which means "God-is-with-us",' Peter read out from the large Bible on the lectern at the front of St Cyprian's Church. He looked up and declaimed with as much ardour as he could muster, 'This is the word of the Lord!'

He paused briefly while the congregation mumbled back 'Thanks be to God,' before walking self-consciously back to his place between Bernie and Lucy, studiously avoiding catching Jonah's eye as he squeezed past his wheelchair, which occupied a space at the end of the pew. A young woman in a white robe took his place at the lectern and announced the response to the day's psalm. Then the congregation rose to their feet as she proclaimed, 'The Lord's is the earth and its fullness …'

Father Damien read from Matthew's Gospel the familiar story of the angel coming to St Joseph in a dream and telling him to take Mary as his wife and become a father to her unborn son. Then he closed the Bible and looked round at his congregation.

'And so,' he began, 'the future of the world depends on a poor Jewish couple living in an insignificant town in a remote corner of the Roman Empire. God has entrusted to them the most important job in the world: parenthood. And we know, as they can only surmise, that it is not going to end well for their new son.'

Peter found his mind wandering as Damien's sermon explored the roles of Mary and Joseph in the birth and upbringing of Jesus and compared it with the responsibilities of present-day parents. He had promised to go round to see Gavin that afternoon, to bring him up to date with the investigation. Not that there was much progress to report, but perhaps he would be touched to hear how his homeless friends had rallied round to help.

Yes. Everyone wanted to help, but what could anyone do? Really. Any words were just platitudes, which must be meaningless to a parent who has lost an only child – or any child come to that. But Kenny was no longer a child. He was a grown man. He had chosen a job that carried inherent danger. And when the danger came, he had thrust himself forward rather than running away. That was something that Gavin could be proud of. And yet, Peter knew that *he* would rather have his own children alive and well than celebrated as dead heroes.

'And what have these parents got to look forward to?' Father Damien was saying. 'Some years living as refugees in Egypt, an all-too-brief time together as a normal hard-working family in Nazareth and then … the ignominy of their son being executed as a criminal by the authorities.'

And what about Harry Whittle's parents? There were plenty of people out there who would consider their son's death to be, if not exactly deserved, at least largely self-inflicted. Most upright citizens would shed few tears over a youth who had got himself involved in the illegal drugs trade and been killed by his fellow miscreants. And yet, there had been a time when Peter's own son, Eddie, had looked to be going off the rails: bunking off school and hanging around on street corners. It would only have taken a chance meeting with the wrong person and *he* might have …

'We venerate our Lord's mother every time we say the Hail Mary,' Father Damien was continuing, 'but how often do we think of Joseph's role in the story of our salvation? He is there at the beginning, a shadowy figure, merely a supporting actor in the great drama of the incarnation, by tradition an older man with children of his own already. But he also has an important part to play.'

He looked up at this point and Peter felt his eyes resting on him and then on Lucy, sitting at his side. Was this just chance? Or was the priest drawing a parallel between his situation and that of St Joseph? Bringing up a child that was not your own wasn't so special. Why on Earth *would* Peter view Lucy any differently from Hannah and Eddie?

'And, unlike Mary,' he heard Father Damien saying, 'Joseph could not be sure that this was a divine child. There must have been times when he suspected that he was merely working to bring up another man's son. Oh yes! We heard just now about the angel talking to him in a dream, but there must have been times when he wondered if it was only a dream, if his wife had not been completely honest in her claims to virginity.'

Well, at least Peter knew exactly who Lucy's father was. Richard Paige had been Peter's commanding officer when he was a raw detective constable, long before he married Bernie. In a way, Richard had been a father-figure to Peter, the boy from the children's home. Not that Peter ever felt that he had missed out by being brought up in an institution. Except that he had worried whether he might mess up with his own children, having no role model to follow. Richard had been another police officer killed on duty – an unfortunate accident while pursuing a suspect. He died not knowing that he was to become a father. Kenny? Kenny had not even lived long enough to find a partner, never mind fathering children.

'And so,' Father Damien concluded, 'as we remember Mary and Joseph preparing for the birth of their son, who will bring them so much joy and also such great pain, we think also of all parents today. At this time of feasting, let us remember those parents who are struggling to put a meal on the table, sometimes going without themselves so that their children can eat. At this time of giving and receiving presents, let us remember those parents whose resources are stretched to the limit to provide even the basic necessities of life. At this time of family gatherings, let us remember those who have no family and those whose families are far away. And let us especially remember those families for which this will be the first Christmas without a loved one. Let us pray for God's blessing on all families in this Christmas season.'

He left the words hanging in the air for a few moments before turning to face the altar and beginning to recite the creed. Peter fumbled with his service sheet, anxious not to get the words wrong and envying those cradle Catholics sitting in the rows behind him who seemed to know everything by heart.

It did not take long for the congregation to file out after the service. The early Mass was never as well-attended as the main service at the more popular time of eleven o'clock. It catered largely for older people, who disliked the livelier songs and sometimes noisy children of the later service, and those whose work or other commitments required them to get their religious observance out of the way before daily duties began.

© Catherine Young

Today, they were prevented from rushing off straight away by Father Damien who buttonholed Jonah, wanting to know how the investigation into Kenny's death was progressing.

While this conversation was going on, Peter wandered over to

121

his favourite part of the church and stood looking up at the statue of the Virgin and Child positioned by a pillar that divided the main church from the Lady Chapel. The Christ child, with his pale brown skin and curly black hair, reminded him of his son Eddie as a baby squirming in Angie's arms and even then fighting to be free.

He read the inscription beneath the virgin's feet: "And thy own soul a sword shall pierce." That must be how Gavin was feeling right now – and Chrissie too, although she was making herself too busy to admit to it. It would surely be different for her on Christmas Day, when everyone else was pulling crackers and eating turkey, and they were alone together, just the two of them and an empty chair where Kenny should have been. Should he invite them round to show that they cared? Or would the homely chaos of their family Christmas simply be rubbing salt in the wounds?

'Time we were off!' declared Bernie, coming over and touching him on the arm. 'It's the carol service this morning, so the church will be full.'

It was their habit to attend morning worship at their Methodist church after fulfilling the Sunday Mass obligation as Catholics, partial Catholics or … well, Peter was never quite sure what Jonah's position was these days. If asked, he would no doubt rehearse all the arguments that his Baptist father had raised him with about the idolatrous practices of Rome, and yet … Peter had a feeling that his attitude towards smells, bells, saints and statues was mellowing gradually.

Bernie was right, there was a hum of conversation in the church as they entered and more than half of the chairs were already occupied. Lucy scanned the room with her eyes, searching for Stella. There she was! Near the back on the left-hand side, sitting with her grandmother. They were both dressed in Sunday-best dresses and Celeste had on a wide-brimmed red and green hat with a sprig of holly tastefully arranged on it. Stella's brother Danny was there too, looking rather uncomfortable in a shiny grey suit, which appeared to be a little too small for his muscular frame.

Lucy hurried forward and sat down next to Stella. Bernie watched as they began whispering together; then she turned to Peter. 'There's space on the row in front of the Gilberts,' she told him. 'I'll just move the end chair to make room for Jonah.'

The service proceeded smoothly with all the usual carols and readings and a short address by the minister. Then, as the congregation stood for the penultimate carol, "It Came upon the Midnight Clear", Bernie became aware of a quiet snuffling sound behind her. Lucy murmured something that was drowned out by the music as the singing began. Resisting an impulse to turn round, Bernie tried to concentrate on the words of the hymn. The sound came again just as they reached the middle of verse three: "beneath the angel strain have rolled two thousand years of wrong."

Then there was a shuffling of feet and Bernie glanced over her shoulder to see Lucy and Stella heading back towards the door. For a moment, she considered following them, and then decided that the young people would probably be better off without any of the older generation clucking around them. Turning to look over her other shoulder, she saw that Celeste was also watching them. Then she caught Bernie's eye and smiled briefly before addressing herself to the music again. She clearly agreed with Bernie's assessment of the situation.

The cold air hit them as they came out on to the street. Lucy put up the hood of her duffle coat and thrust her hands into her pockets.

'Are you OK?' she asked Stella anxiously.

'Yes,' Stella nodded, sniffing and wiping her eyes with a tissue. 'I don't know why it got to me like that. I just couldn't help thinking of Kenny and how things like that just keep on happening and … I mean, I knew all that already, but it suddenly just seemed so awful as if everything we do is just a waste of time.'

'But think how it would be if we all stopped,' argued Lucy, putting her arm around Stella's shoulders. 'If there weren't any police officers patrolling the streets, like Gavin and Kenny, or solving crimes, like Jonah and Andy, then people like the driver who ran Kenny over would just keep getting away with it, wouldn't they?'

'I know.' Stella sniffed again. 'But right now, it all seems just so hopeless, as if ....' She hesitated as if unsure whether to go on.

'As if what?' prompted Lucy.

'I don't know. I just ... He was protecting me!' Stella burst out suddenly. 'The car was coming for me and Kenny pushed me out of the way. *I* should've been the one crushed against the wall!'

'That's nonsense,' Lucy told her firmly. '*Nobody* ought to have been crushed against a wall. If the car *was* coming for you, the chances are it was that Harry Whittle who was the target, not you. And I bet if you'd seen a car coming towards Kenny, you'd have done the same thing he did! It was just bad luck that he didn't manage to get you both out of the way.'

'I know,' Stella groaned. 'The counsellor said it's "survivor guilt" and I have to work through it, but ... I can't help thinking, why me? And I'm not sure how I'm going to face Gavin when he comes back on duty, knowing ... knowing that ...'

She made a hiccupping noise and blew her nose on the tissue.

'I'm sure Gavin won't be thinking of it that way,' Lucy said confidently. 'I don't really know him, but Mam and Peter seem to think that he always sees the good in everyone. I mean, think about the way all the homeless people trust him, when usually they're dead suspicious of the police. He won't blame you for what happened and Jonah will soon find out who really *was* responsible. You heard what he said yesterday. They've already identified one of the gang and they've got people watching out for the rest of them to give themselves away by having another go at that dealer the homeless guys found. It'll all be done and dusted before Christmas, just you wait and see!'

'That won't alter the fact that I didn't even get a scratch and Kenny's dead,' Stella argued dismally.

'Well I'm sure Kenny wouldn't want you to make yourself miserable about it,' Lucy declared. 'And I'm sure he wouldn't agree that you being a police officer is a waste of time. I'd say you owe it to him to carry on and finish your training and then get out there making a difference, like you always wanted!'

'I suppose so.'

Lucy was a difficult person to argue with when she was sure of her ground – which was most of the time. Stella could not help thinking that everything was more complicated than her friend was acknowledging and that people's feelings did not always follow such clear logic.

From inside the church they could hear the final carol reaching its climax: "O come let us adore him, Christ the Lord!"

'Come on,' Lucy said, 'We'd better go back in. There are mince pies in the hall now – unless you'd rather just go home? I'll walk with you if you like.'

'No,' Stella shook her head. 'I'm fine now. Thanks for coming out with me.'

* * *

'Can't I come with you?' asked Lucy that afternoon as Peter prepared to go round to Gavin's house to update him on the investigation. 'Stella's worried that it'll be difficult for her to work with Gavin again after this, and I thought-'

'No,' Peter cut in firmly. 'I know you mean well, but I'm not at all sure about going round myself, with Gavin's sister and her husband being there. But I promised I would, so I better had. Besides,' he added, conscious that his words might have sounded rather brusque, 'you've got the Christmas tree to decorate. We left it for when you got home, because you do it so much better than either of us.'

'Crawler!' Lucy teased. 'OK. But promise me you'll try and find a way of dropping something into the conversation about

Stella so I'll be able to tell her she doesn't need to worry.'

'I'll do my best,' Peter conceded, 'but only if the subject comes up. There'll be plenty of time later on. I can't see Gavin being back on duty at least until after the funeral's out of the way.'

He decided to cycle the 4 miles to Gavin's home. It would give him time to think through what he was going to say and avoid any difficulty over finding somewhere to park when he arrived. And if Gavin's sister were to question his presence there, he could portray it as simply calling in while passing, on a ride in the December sunshine or as part of a fitness drive.

He was right to be anxious about parking. The road outside Gavin's modest semi-detached house was crammed with vehicles. Peter recognised a TV van amongst them and shuddered as he realised that his friend's home was being watched by a dozen or more pairs of eyes. Two reporters with cameras slung around their necks were standing on the pavement chatting while glancing over the hedge every so often to check on any movement within the house. A television camera operator was poised at the end of the drive, with her lens directed over the top of Chrissie's car, presumably in the hope that someone would emerge from the house. A group of young men in puffa jackets stamped their feet and walked up and down to keep warm. The front room curtains were closed and Peter could see that a cardboard box had been propped up inside the small window on the other side of the front door, which provided light to the hall, to obscure that too.

Peter dismounted and leaned his bike against a hedge on the opposite side of the road. Immediately, he was approached by an earnest young woman brandishing a notepad. Ignoring her, he took out his mobile phone and rang the police station.

'Hi Jordan. Could you send a few officers round to lift the siege on PC Hughes's house?'

He waited until PC Ben Timpson had arrived and started moving on the journalists before approaching the front door. At his ring, it opened a crack and a woman's face appeared. It had blue eyes beneath a fringe of fair hair, but that was where any family resemblance to Gavin stopped. Her nose was long and pointed, her lips thin and pale, and her expression was one of deep suspicion.

'We're not at home to visitors,' she barked at Peter, closing the door in his face.

He stood on the step pondering. Then he turned and watched as the reporters got into their cars and drove off. Eventually they were all gone and PC Timpson came up the drive to speak to him.

'I don't think they'll cause any more trouble,' he told Peter. 'I've made it clear that they'll get no more news from us if they continue to harass PC Hughes and his family.'

'Good,' Peter smiled back. 'And now, perhaps you could knock on the door and let them know that they've got their lives back again.'

Timpson did as he was asked. For some time nothing happened. Then Peter noticed a movement of the curtain over the window of the front room. Shortly after that the door opened again. This time it was Gavin who looked out. He smiled apologetically at Peter and Ben.

'I'm sorry. Lorraine didn't mean to be rude. It's just, we've had that many journalists knocking on the door wanting to know how we feel about what happened and what we think of the police investigation and …'

'How high they ought to hang the guys who did it?' Peter suggested with a wry smile. 'Believe me, I know their routine.'

'I've sent them off with a flea in their ear,' Ben told him. 'I don't think they'll be back for a while, but if this case goes on much beyond Christmas, you'd maybe better think of finding somewhere else to stay until they get bored.'

'Come in, both of you,' Gavin urged them. 'I was just saying to Chrissie that it was time for another cup of tea.'

'I'd better not, thanks all the same,' Ben excused himself. 'I've just had a call to a disturbance in Temple Cowley. No rest for the wicked, eh?' he grinned.

He turned and walked back down the drive, while Peter

followed Gavin inside the house.

'This is my sister, Lorraine,' Gavin introduced the woman with the pointed nose and thin lips. 'Lorraine, this is DI Peter Johns.'

'Ex-DI,' Peter corrected him. 'I've been retired for eight years now. I was just out for a cycle ride – trying to keep fit and keeping out from under my wife's feet for a bit – and I was passing, so I thought I'd pop in and see how Gavin and Chrissie are doing.'

'And Peter lives with the DCI who's in charge of investigating what happened to Kenny,' Gavin added quickly. 'He promised to bring us up to date on how it's going.'

'Don't all stand around in the hall gossiping!' Chrissie emerged from the kitchen carrying a plate of mince pies. 'Go on in and sit down. These are fresh out of the oven. I've made them for the party on Christmas Day, but there are plenty. Go on! Try one.'

Peter took one of the pies and then made his way into the front room. Before he could sit down, Lorraine strode past him and took the middle one of the three armchairs, picking up a clipboard and a sheaf of papers from the coffee table as she did so. Leaving the other two chairs for Gavin and Chrissie, Peter selected an upright chair just inside the door.

'You'd better fetch another chair from the kitchen,' Lorraine told Gavin. 'Dennis will be back down in a minute.'

As if on cue, the door opened and a small man with black plastic glasses obscuring his pale eyes came in, carrying a large cardboard box. 'I've cleared the drawers,' he announced. 'Where shall I put this?'

'Oh just dump it in the kitchen!' Lorraine called out commandingly. 'We'll go through it later and decide if there's anything worth keeping or if it all needs to go to the charity shop.'

The man backed out of the door followed by Gavin on his mission to collect another seat. Peter heard footsteps in the hall receding and then growing louder again.

'My brother-in-law, Dennis,' Gavin explained, ushering

him back in and closing the door. 'He and Lorraine have been helping us to plan the funeral.'

'Oh!' Peter said in some surprise. 'I thought that was more or less settled.'

'Except that we have to take into account the need to choose a time that will fit in with Clive and Irene getting here from Inverurie,' Lorraine put in before Gavin could answer, 'and, of course, there's the catering to organise.'

'Lorraine's very good at organising things,' Gavin said loyally, but not, Peter suspected, completely sincerely. 'They've been clearing out Kenny's room in case we need to put anyone up.'

Peter bit into his pie to avoid having to say anything. In his opinion, Lorraine's, no doubt well-meaning, intervention was making life considerably more stressful for Gavin and his wife. He was also dubious of the wisdom of clearing out Kenny's possessions so soon, even if his room was needed to accommodate guests.

'Now before we forget,' Lorraine said, picking up a glossy leaflet from a mobile catering firm and pointing at an illustration halfway down one page, 'are we all agreed that this buffet is good value for money and covers the dietary requirements of everyone who is likely to be there?'

Gavin and Chrissie nodded, and Chrissie added, 'I can always make some of my cheese straws and vegan sausage rolls if we need anything more. I'm not sure, but I have a feeling that Flora is vegetarian.'

'Good! That's settled then,' Lorraine declared, noting down these details on her clipboard. 'Now, has the scout master got back to you yet about what they're doing?'

'I don't think we need to go into that now,' Gavin ventured apprehensively. 'If you don't mind, I'd rather hear what Peter has to say about the investigation.'

He looked entreatingly across at Peter, who cleared his throat and hastened to gather his thoughts.

'I'm afraid I can't report that *an arrest is imminent*,' he said, trying to keep things light. 'As Gavin will know, an investigation like this one takes time and there's a lot of scientific work to be done, which can't be rushed. The abandoned car, for example, has to be gone over with a fine tooth comb for evidence that it *is* the one that was involved in the incident. They've found some fingermarks inside it, which may help to prove who was driving, but so far-'

'If they've got fingerprints, surely that ought to mean they know who it was,' interrupted Lorraine.

'Only if they can match them to someone on the police database,' Peter explained patiently. 'We aren't allowed to keep records of everyone's prints, so if the driver doesn't already have a criminal record it's unlikely they'll be any use until we have some suspects to compare them with.'

'And *do* you have any suspects?' Lorraine demanded, ignoring Gavin's open mouth as he attempted to formulate his own response.

'Well, there are a couple of people that we think may belong to the gang,' Peter said cautiously, 'but so far nothing to link them directly to the house in Kidlington or to the car that hit Kenny. It was your friend Craig Manson who found them,' he added, turning to Gavin. 'He organised a posse of homeless people with knowledge of the drugs scene to track them down.'

'Craig's a good fellow,' Gavin nodded. 'It's a disgrace the way he's been treated since he came out of the army. He shouldn't be sleeping on the streets, but he won't try hostels any longer, after being chucked out for disturbing other people's sleep.'

'Oh?' Peter queried encouragingly, sensing his friend's relief at being back on familiar territory and addressing a subject in which he was more expert than his domineering older sister.

'He suffers from post-traumatic stress disorder,' Gavin explained. 'He gets night terrors and shouts out in his sleep, which upsets people – especially if they're vulnerable themselves. He needs to have his own place and proper mental health treatment, but being a single man, he's not a priority for social housing and private landlords don't like taking on someone who's been sleeping rough.'

'Quite understandable,' Lorraine said emphatically. 'They've got their investment to protect, after all, and a lot of rough sleepers have drug or alcohol addictions.'

'Craig doesn't,' Gavin argued doggedly. 'And he's bright. There's no reason he couldn't hold down a job, if he could find the right one.'

'I'm surprised that's been a problem,' agreed Peter. 'I'd have thought lots of people would be pleased to have an ex-military man in their security team – or what about the police? I'd say he's proved his worth just now, tracking down this gang of drug-dealers. And he's obviously got leadership qualities too. I wouldn't have thought the likes of Dave Gillis and Mike Lambert would've been easy people to persuade to turn out and help.'

'But would you want to be relying on someone with a history of panic attacks watching your back in a critical operation?' asked Gavin.

'I thought we were supposed to be becoming more understanding of mental health issues in the police service,' Peter countered. 'But I see what you mean,' he added after a moment's thought. 'Maybe not on the front line then – a civilian role, perhaps?'

'It seems to me it's a pretty poor show if the police are having to rely on those sorts of people to do their work for them,' Lorraine observed censoriously. 'Why didn't *they* go out and find these suspects instead of waiting for members of the public to point them out to them?'

'The critical thing is that some of them had inside knowledge of the illegal drugs trade,' Peter explained. 'They could talk to the sorts of people who don't trust the police. We now know the names of two of the gang who are most likely responsible for the cannabis factory. The assumption is that it was one of this same gang who killed Kenny and also Harry Whittle.'

'Yes, I was meaning to ask about Harry,' Gavin began, but

Lorraine cut across him.

'Who's he?' she demanded. Then, without waiting for Peter's reply, she rounded on Gavin. 'Why didn't you tell us somebody else had been killed?'

'Harry Whittle is the teenager that Kenny was arresting when the car drove into him,' Peter explained. 'We assume that he was working for the gang, but he refused to answer any questions – too frightened, I think.'

'He lived just round the corner from here – in Chichester Road,' Gavin added quickly, trying to get in before Lorraine took over the conversation again. 'I think I've met his dad. He drives a taxi.'

'That's right,' Peter agreed. 'The police allowed Harry home after questioning and someone got into the house and killed him while his parents were both out at work. It's a tragedy for them, but it's also a blow for the police investigation, because he was the one person who could've identified the driver of the car.'

'So why was he released?' demanded Lorraine. 'I would have thought he'd be kept in custody until he did answer all the police questions!'

'It's not as simple as that,' Peter explained, mustering all his patience. 'He was a minor, which means that a police cell isn't really suitable for him. And every suspect has a right to silence. The miscalculation was not giving him protection after he'd gone home.'

Lorraine looked unconvinced but did not comment further. For a minute or two nobody spoke. Then Gavin suddenly got to his feet.

'I need some fresh air,' he announced. 'I'm going for a walk. Will you come with me, Peter?'

'That's a good idea,' Chrissie agreed heartily. 'It'll be good for you to catch up with an old workmate, and if we're going to be talking food, we'll get on better just me and Lorraine. Take a couple of these with you,' she added, holding out a white paper bag towards Peter. 'It's chocolate fudge. I always make up some bags at Christmas for the kids at the Women's

Refuge, but there's plenty to spare.'

'Lorraine means well,' Gavin confided to Peter a few minutes later as they strolled along the road in the fading afternoon sunshine, sucking squares of homemade chocolate fudge, 'but I always feel a bit like I've been flattened out by a steam roller after she's been here for a few days. She was the only girl in the family, you see, and she thinks the rest of us need keeping in order. I'm the youngest and she doesn't rate me at all.'

'Hannah can be a bit like that with Eddie,' Peter agreed with a laugh. 'I think all big sisters tend to think their brothers can't be trusted to behave sensibly.'

'She's offered to stay on for a while to get the funeral sorted,' Gavin continued mournfully. 'Dennis has to get back to his work, but she's off until after Christmas. She's a teacher too, which means she and Chrissie have a lot in common, but even she agrees that it'll be more peaceful if we can convince Lorraine that her place is at home. Mind you,' he added dutifully, 'she's quite right about the catering. We hadn't thought about where people would go after the service – especially if they've come a long way.'

'Isn't that something the scouts might like to do,' suggested Peter. 'They could probably earn badges for that sort of thing.'

'I dunno.' Gavin sounded doubtful. 'I wouldn't like to ask. It would be alright if they volunteered but … I reckon Chrissie will probably make enough stuff for everyone whatever Lorraine or I do!' he smiled. 'She enjoys that sort of thing. She's still planning to do the Homeless lunch on Christmas Day. I told you about that, didn't I? I suppose I'd better go too, and thank Craig and the others. I never thought they'd do what they did.'

'They're grateful to you for being on their side when most officers just move them on or arrest them for begging,' Peter told him. 'It's their way of saying thank you.'

'I just wish I could do something for Craig in return,' Gavin sighed. 'Some of the others … Mike Lambert, for example, just drifted into drink and drugs and doesn't seem to have the drive to get himself out again. And Dave Gillis – he claims he *prefers* sleeping out to a bed in the homeless shelter. But Craig! Did I tell you how it was he ended up on the streets?'

'Well, I know he was discharged from the army and then couldn't hold down a job because of his PTSD,' Peter answered.

'Yes, but there's more to it than that. His dad was in the army too. He served in Northern Ireland and was killed by the provisional IRA when Craig was only four. According to Craig, his mother fell apart after that and he was handed round between his grandparents, an aunt and various army families, while she went in and out of mental hospitals. That's one reason he's not keen on having treatment himself. I think visiting her in some of those places was probably the start of his own mental health problems. Anyway, he joined up as soon as he was old enough, looking for the security of a regimental "family", which is why he feels so bitter towards the army when he didn't get any support after his medical discharge. I don't know the ins and outs of it, but the way he sees it, they used him until he broke and then didn't want anything more to do with him. Faults on both sides, I expect but …' Gavin sighed. This was a long speech for him and the exertion seemed to drain him of energy for further conversation.

'Chichester Road,' Peter murmured a few minutes later as they turned a corner. 'Any particular reason for this itinerary?'

'I thought we might pay a call on Harry Whittle's parents,' Gavin admitted sheepishly.

'Are you sure …?' Peter began. Then he reflected that, of all the officers in Thames Valley Police, Gavin was perhaps the only one who might receive something better than an extremely frosty reception at the Whittles' house. 'I suppose *they'd* probably like to know how things are going too,' he amended, 'but we'd better be careful not to tell them anything we don't want made public. I'm not sure they feel very co-operative towards the police at the moment.'

When they arrived at the house the drive was empty, suggesting that Trevor Whittle was out in his taxi. A boy of eleven or twelve was standing with his back to them preparing to shoot into a basketball net attached to the blank wall next to the tunnel between the two adjacent houses. He turned round as they approached and stared at them belligerently.

'Is your mum in?' asked Gavin, smiling towards him in a friendly fashion.

'Who's asking?' the boy mumbled back, looking rapidly from Gavin to Peter and back without allowing either of them to make eye contact.

'I'm Gavin – PC Gavin Hughes. What's your name?'

'Leo Whittle. What do you want to know for? I haven't done anything!' the boy was suddenly on the defensive.

'I live just round the corner. I heard about what happened to Harry and I wanted to see if there was anything I could do.'

'No thanks.' The boy stared hard at Gavin for a moment and then turned away and appeared to be planning to continue his shooting practice.

'Well, we'll just have a word with your mum.' Gavin advanced up the drive, but Leo darted across in front of him.

'She's in bed,' he said urgently. 'She's not well. She can't see visitors. Just go away and leave us alone, can't you?'

'I'm sorry to hear that,' Gavin answered calmly. 'What about your dad then? I'd like to talk to them. We've got some news about the hunt for the people who killed your brother.'

'Dad's out. He's working.'

'Do you mind if we wait for him to get back?' Gavin asked with gentle persistence. 'Or maybe if you told your mum we're here …?'

'I told you, she's not well.'

'Has she seen a doctor?'

'No. She doesn't need one. She just needs to rest, that's all.'

'OK.' Gavin sat down on the door step and motioned to Peter to join him. 'We'll just wait here for your dad then.'

'He might not be back for hours!'

'We've got plenty of time – or at least, I have. What about you Peter?'

'As long as it takes,' Peter nodded, settling down beside his friend. He was not sure what Gavin's game was, but he sensed that it was important for them to get to speak to Harry's parents.

'Have one of these,' Gavin invited Leo, holding out his bag of fudge. 'It's good. My wife made it.'

Leo stared back looking first hostile then puzzled. Finally he stepped forward and put his hand in the bag. Peter and Gavin also took pieces of fudge and for several minutes they all sucked in silence. Two women walked past. Peter felt their eyes on him as they paused momentarily to stare at the group on the doorstep and then hurried on pretending not to have noticed anything.

'If you won't go away, I suppose you'd better come inside,' Leo growled. He had evidently also seen the women and wanted to avoid attracting any more attention. 'Come round the back.'

He led the way through the tunnel into the small back garden and then in through the kitchen door.

Peter was immediately struck by the stench of alcohol. On the floor, just inside the door lay a cardboard box crammed with empty bottles. On the worktop next to the sink, which was piled high with dirty crockery, stood a glass and a half-empty bottle of vodka. He glanced towards Gavin, who seemed unperturbed by the scene. Had he somehow guessed the nature of Mrs Whittle's "illness"? Was that why he had been so uncharacteristically insistent on being admitted to the family home?

'Come through to the other room,' Leo urged them, hurrying across to open the door and usher them out of the disorderly kitchen.

As he passed the gas cooker, Peter noticed a pan of something brown and glutinous, which had boiled over and congealed on the surface of the hob. The walls were greasy and the floor sticky. A flip-top bin in the corner nearest the door was overflowing with polystyrene containers and crisp wrappers. Was this a normal state of affairs or was it a sign of the affect that Harry's death had had on his family and his mother in particular?

Leo led them into a small front room with a large television set on one wall and a large sofa opposite it. The bay window was filled with an artificial Christmas tree decorated with coloured lights, tinsel and an assortment of ornaments. The cards standing on surfaces around the room were all on a Christmas theme – no sign yet of friends and neighbours sending condolences for Harry's death.

They all sat down and Gavin handed round the fudge again.

'We're very sorry about what happened to your brother,' he said, 'and we're working hard to find who did it.'

Leo nodded, but said nothing. His eyes darted suspiciously from Gavin to Peter.

'I know the officer in charge of the investigation,' Peter told him. 'He thinks they've found two of the gang, but they don't want to arrest them yet, because that may frighten off the others and they want to catch the lot of them.'

Leo nodded again, but he seemed to be distracted by sounds overhead. Someone was walking around in the room above. Floorboards creaked and a door squeaked. Then a voice called down from the top of the stairs.

'Trevor! Is that you?'

Leo leapt to his feet and raced out into the hall.

'No Mum!' they heard him call. 'It's two policemen. They want to talk to Dad.'

'Tell them to go away!'

'I just did, but they said they'd wait until he got back.'

Footsteps started descending the stairs. Then there was a slithering and bumping and louder steps going up. Alarmed, Peter went into the hall to see what was going on. He looked up the stairs and saw Leo halfway up, in the act of helping his mother to her feet. She had evidently lost her footing on the stairs and slid part way down.

'Let me help you, Mrs Whittle,' Peter said with the voice of authority that he had learned during his time in the police service. He took hold of her arm and gently escorted her downstairs and into the sitting room. 'You look as if you could do with a nice cup of tea – or maybe some coffee. Why don't you go and sit down and I'll put the kettle on?'

He deposited her next to Gavin on the sofa and then, without waiting for an answer, headed back into the hall. He walked briskly to the kitchen and started making tea. He selected four mugs from a glass-fronted wall cupboard and found teabags in a jar next to the kettle. While waiting for the water to boil, he tightened the lid on the vodka bottle and put it away in the cupboard under the sink. Then he removed the pan from the hob and scraped the contents into the bin.

'What are you doing?' demanded Leo, who had followed him into the kitchen.

'Just making tea for your mum, and then I thought I'd help her by clearing up a bit.' Peter poured water on to the tea bags and stirred each mug with a teaspoon. 'How does she like it?'

'Dunno.' Leo seemed bemused both by the question and by the sight of a strange man squeezing out teabags in his kitchen.

There was a bag of sugar lying next to the jar of teabags. Judging that this was an indication that at least one member of the family took sugar in their tea, Peter added some to two of the mugs. Then he opened the fridge and got out a bottle of milk. He poured some into each mug and stirred them again.

'OK then,' he said, handing the two sugared mugs to Leo. 'Take these for your mum and PC Hughes and then come back in here. Let's see if we can't get all these dishes washed up before your dad gets back.'

Leo stood staring for a few moments, then nodded and headed out of the door. Peter turned back to the sink and began lifting the dirty crockery out and running hot water. By the time Leo returned, he was busily scrubbing at the hob, trying to remove the burnt-on remains of whatever had been in the pan.

'Why're you doing that?' Leo stood in the doorway staring as Peter applied a squirt of washing-up liquid and scoured the surface vigorously.

'Like you said: your mum's not well; so I thought we'd help her a bit by doing some of the jobs round the house that she's not feeling up to,' Peter replied without looking up. He scooped up the dislodged gunk and went over to the sink to rinse the scouring pad. Then he turned to face Leo and pointed down at the box of bottles on the floor.

'Would you be able to carry those outside? If you leave them by the front door, we'll take them and drop them off at the bottle bank for you.'

Leo continued to stare for a moment or two. Then he stepped into the kitchen, picked up the box and headed out into the hall with it. Peter gave the hob a final wipe and then turned his attention to the dirty crockery. As he filled the sink with hot water he heard the front door open and then close again. Shortly after that he sensed Leo's presence behind him.

'Find yourself a tea towel and dry up for me,' Peter instructed. 'You'll know better than I do where to put everything away.'

Without speaking, Leo went over to a drawer and pulled out a check-pattern cloth, which he used to dry the glasses that Peter had washed and set down on the draining board. For several minutes they worked in silence.

'Are you going to report us to Social Services?' Leo demanded eventually.

'What makes you think that?' Peter asked casually, taking care to avoid sounding judgemental.

'Seeing mum … and … all this ….' Leo looked round the kitchen. 'Harry says-.' He broke off and became suddenly very busy wiping the wet dinner plate that he had in his hands.

'Yes?' Peter prompted gently.

'It doesn't matter.' Leo put down the plate and reached for another.

'Did Harry ever talk to you about his job?' Peter asked after a few moments.

'Not really. Why do you want to know?'

'We think – I mean the police think – that the people who employed him to look after their pot plants were probably the same as the people who killed him,' Peter explained. 'So if you knew who they were ...'

'Why would they do that?' Leo put down the plate and stared at Peter.

'We think that Harry didn't realise what they were doing was against the law, and after the police raided the house where he was working, they were afraid he'd tell on them. So they killed him to make sure he didn't.'

'And if I tell you anything about them, what's to stop them killing me too?'

'It'd be too late by then, wouldn't it?' Peter pointed out. 'And in any case, how would they know it was you? *Did H*arry tell you any names?'

'He sometimes talked about a guy called Terry,' Leo muttered. 'I think he was Harry's boss, but I don't know.'

'Terry,' Peter repeated. 'Thanks. I'll pass that on to the officer who's in charge of finding who killed Harry. Now, that's the washing up done, so let's drink our tea and then the floor could do with cleaning and maybe you could take the rubbish out to the wheelie bin.'

'You never said if you're going to report us to Social Services,' Leo complained, as they stood leaning against the worktop drinking the tea.

'What makes you think I'm going to do that?'

'Harry said we had to be careful 'cos Social Services would take us into care if they found out about Mum ... you know ...'

'I can see she has a drink problem,' Peter nodded, 'but I can also see that there's food in the fridge and you've got decent clothes and shoes on. There's no sign that you've been physically abused in any way. You've got two parents, both in work. If Social Services forcibly removed every kid whose parents ever went on a bender, the children's homes would be crammed full and bulging at the seams!' He grinned and gave Leo a friendly nudge with his elbow. 'If your mum and dad are fed up with looking after you, they're going to have to try a lot harder than this to get you taken away!'

'Are you sure?'

'Look, Leo.' Peter rinsed out his mug and put it down on the draining board. 'I was brought up in a children's home. Most of the kids there were there after their parents gave them up voluntarily because they couldn't cope for one reason or another. The very few that had been removed from their homes had experienced much, much worse than …,' he looked round the room, 'than a bit of neglected housework. Your mum has had a very traumatic experience just now,' he went on earnestly. 'She came home and found your brother's body. Nobody's going to blame her for turning to drink to try to forget what she saw for a while.'

'Are you sure?'

'Yes,' Peter said firmly. 'But that's not to say it wouldn't be a good idea for her to come off the booze. There are people who can help. Has anyone from Victim Support been round yet?'

'A lady came round on Friday. I think that was where she was from.'

'Well, she ought to be able to put your mum in touch with the right people to help her. See if you can persuade her to ask about it next time she comes round. Now, have you finished?' Peter took Leo's empty mug and washed it under the tap. 'Go and ask your mum and PC Hughes if they'd like another cup, while I go over this floor with a mop.'

'How did you know what Mrs Whittle's "illness" was?' Peter asked Gavin as they made their way home, taking it in turns to carry the heavy box of bottles.

'Dunno,' Gavin shrugged. 'Just something about the way the boy behaved. It felt like he was covering up for something. I've seen it lots of times. Kids don't want people to know their parents' weaknesses – or sometimes … sometimes they're afraid to let on.'

'What's your assessment of Mrs Whittle?' Peter asked cautiously. 'Leo's scared we might tell Social Services and get him taken into care. Is she a danger to him at all, do you think?'

'No.' Gavin's answer was unequivocal. 'She's all messed up by this business with Harry, but … She told me she'd been off the booze for months until this trouble with Harry came up, and I believe her. You can't blame her: first her son goes missing; then he's been arrested for supplying drugs; and then she finds him hanging there and it looks like he's topped himself – except that it turns out he was murdered. It's enough to drive anyone to drink!'

'Yes. That's about how I saw it too,' Peter agreed. 'I just thought – better to be safe than sorry. Do you think we ought to put in a safeguarding report?'

'I've told her I'll come round again tomorrow and talk her through the inquest and stuff,' Gavin replied. 'I'll keep an eye on them. No need to bother Social Services.'

'Good.' Peter walked on in silence for a few minutes. Then, just as they were turning in at Gavin's drive, he asked, 'and did she tell you anything about Harry or Harry's job – or a man called Terry that Harry knows?'

'No.' Gavin put down the cardboard box and felt in his pocket for his keys. 'I'm sure she doesn't know anything about it. Harry kept all the details to himself.'

'He did mention this Terry to Leo,' Peter told him. 'If you're speaking to him, see if you can't get any more details from him. It's a new name that doesn't match either of the two we've got our sights on so far, so you never know, it could be this mysterious "boss" that is proving so elusive to find!'

8. THE SECOND DAY BEFORE CHRISTMAS

When Bernie and Jonah arrived at work on Monday morning, they immediately knew that something was going on. The moment they entered the building their ears were assailed by angry voices coming from the Reception area. Bernie pressed the large square button on the wall to open the double doors and allow Jonah's chair through. Opening the door also allowed them to make out the words as Craig Manson stormed at Malcolm Appleton, who was once more manning the desk. He leaned across and grasped the sergeant by his collar and shouted in his face.

'You've no right to keep him here! I've already told you: he only-'

'Can I help you, Mr Manson?' Jonah asked smoothly, gliding silently across the vinyl tiles and coming up behind him.

Letting go of Malcolm's lapel, Craig swung round and stared down at him.

'Are you responsible for this?' he demanded. 'Did you order them to arrest Brendan?'

'I haven't had anyone arrested – yet,' Jonah replied, smiling up at him, 'but I'm open to suggestions. Assaulting a police officer really isn't a good idea, you know.' He turned to Malcolm. 'Can you tell me what this is all about?'

'It's all perfectly simple,' Craig cut in before Malcolm could speak. 'Some of your lot arrested Brendan last night for no reason, and now they won't let him out.'

'Brendan?' Jonah looked towards Malcolm and raised his eyebrows.

'Brendan Connolly. He's an offender out on licence,' Malcolm explained. 'One of the conditions of his parole is that he lives in the probation hostel down Iffley Road and he gets back there by ten every night. Inspector Andrews had officers out watching a house in Cowley, and they saw him lurking in among the bushes in the front garden. They nicked him for suspicious behaviour and then discovered he was out after hours.'

'He was watching for that dealer I told your sergeant about,' Craig broke in urgently. 'He was there on my orders. Doug here was supposed to relieve him at eight.' He gesticulated towards a bearded man in a dirty duffle coat, who was sitting hunched up on one of the plastic seats at the side of the room. 'But he was too pissed to crawl round there, so Brendan stayed on.'

Jonah looked at each of them, assessing the situation. Then he turned back to Malcolm.

'OK. I'll deal with this,' he told him. 'You two! Come with me.'

When they reached the open plan office housing the team of officers and civilian staff who were working on the double murder case, Rupert Andrews accosted them at once.

'We've got four males in custody,' he informed them. 'Stuart Hatton came back to Pilling's house late last night and these other two men were with him. They're brothers: Shane and Terence Butler.'

'Terry?' asked Bernie at once, remembering what Peter had told her about his conversation with Leo Whittle.

'Yes,' Andrews nodded. 'His brother did call him Terry. Why? Have you come across him before?'

'Harry Whittle's brother told Peter that Harry was working for someone called Terry,' Bernie explained.

'Harry Whittle's brother?' exclaimed Andrews in surprise.

'I didn't even know he had one. Have we interviewed him? Where was he when Harry was killed?'

'He must've been on his way to school, I should think,' Jonah answered tersely. '*We* didn't know about him either until Peter and Gavin came across him by chance. I suppose the parents didn't want to get him involved. But you said *four* men. Who's the other one? Or ... let me guess. It wouldn't be a Brendan Connolly, by any chance?'

'Yes! How did you know? They found him hanging round outside the house. He's an offender out on licence. The parole board only let him out last month and it looks as if he's already broken his probation conditions. Like I said, he was hanging around the house. It all looked very suspicious, so they brought him in for questioning with the others. Of course, the chances are he's no more than an addict on the lookout for some weed, but ... well, better safe than sorry, and then when we found he'd got a record ....' The inspector shrugged and gave Jonah a meaningful look.

'But that's all nonsense!' Craig burst out. 'He was just watching, like I said. We were just trying to find the bastards who killed Gavin's boy.'

Andrews, who had been too busy reporting on the successes of the night to pay attention to the men who had accompanied Jonah into the room, stared at him in surprise. He opened his mouth to demand an explanation of this outburst, but Jonah got in first.

'OK.' He said briskly. 'I've got the picture. Now tell me: have any of them been interviewed yet?'

'No Sir. By the time we'd got them all checked in to the cells it was past midnight, and ... and we thought you'd probably prefer to do it yourself, Sir.'

'Yes.' Jonah looked at Bernie. 'I think I'd better see Connolly first. He'll be scared stiff he's going to be sent back to jail for breaking the terms of his probation. It won't do any harm to leave the others to stew for a bit. But first,' he added, turning back to Andrews, 'I need to have a little chat with Mr Manson and his friend. I shouldn't think it'll take more than a few minutes, so you might as well get Connolly settled in an interview room. Give him a cup of tea and tell him I won't be long.'

'Yes Sir. I'll arrange with the custody officer to have him brought up from the cells.' Andrews turned to go. Then he remembered something and swivelled round on his heel to face Jonah again. 'Oh! There was one other thing. We've had the car they were in taken away for forensic examination. It's a black Alfa Romeo, and when we checked out the registration it didn't match anything on the DVLA[7] database.'

'OK.' Jonah nodded. 'I can't see they're likely to find much, but it had better be done. Presumably there's no news on the red car – the one we think hit Kenny?'

'Not yet, Sir. I'll chase them up again after I've spoken to the custody officer,' Andrews promised.

'And organise search warrants for all of their houses!' Jonah called out after him.

Andrews left the room and Jonah turned to address Craig.

'Don't worry. I'll get this sorted, but I need you to answer a few questions first. Come over here and sit down, both of you.'

He led the way into an enclosed section of the room, separated from the main working area by glass walls. Bernie moved chairs to enable him to position himself behind an oval table and gestured to the others to sit down opposite him. Craig deposited his rucksack on a spare chair and sat down. The man whom he had called Doug hesitated before following suit. Once they were both seated, Bernie took her own place next to Jonah and waited for him to begin the conversation.

'First, let me tell you that I think I know Brendan Connolly[8]. Wasn't he sleeping rough before he went to jail?'

'That's right,' Craig agreed. 'PC Hughes gave evidence at

---

[7] The Driver and Vehicle Licensing Authority holds records of all cars registered in the UK.

[8] Brendan first comes across Jonah's radar in *Organ Failure* © 2018 ISBN: 978-1-911083-38-2.

his trial – like a character witness. It was ridiculous putting him away for something he did back when he was only a kid!'

'And his evidence cleared up a forty year old mystery,' nodded Jonah. 'Which is why he got such a light sentence and was paroled after only serving half. But if he wants to *stay* out of jail, he *must* stick to the conditions, which means being back in the hostel on time *whatever.* As you'll have realised by now, there was no need for your Baker Street Irregulars to have been watching the house, because we had officers out there doing just that.'

'Pity you didn't think of that before the Whittle boy was killed,' Craig muttered sulkily.

'Yes, it is,' Jonah agreed, 'which is all the more reason why we weren't going to make the same mistake twice. Now, I'm going to speak to Brendan, and he'd better tell me the same story you've just done. And if he does, I'll do my best to smooth things over with the probation service. OK?'

Craig nodded.

'But, before that,' Jonah continued, 'is there anything else you and your friends have found out that I ought to know about?'

Craig shook his head.

'Doug?' Jonah asked.

Doug, who was sitting slumped in his chair apparently contemplating the surface of the table, looked up and shook his head too.

'OK.' Jonah manoeuvred his chair out from behind the table and headed for the door. 'Let's get you both back down to Reception. You can stay there until I've finished with Brendan. And if you talk *very* nicely to Constable Gilbert, she might even be persuaded to get you both some tea and mince pies while you're waiting.'

'OK now, Brendan,' Jonah greeted Connolly, without waiting for Bernie to close the door behind them. 'Welcome back to Interview Room two. If I remember correctly, this was where we first met, back in March 2018.'

Brendan looked back with moist, sunken eyes. He looked less weather-beaten than Jonah remembered from their previous encounter and his sparse grey hair was more neatly trimmed. A casual observer would have put his age at around seventy, but Jonah knew from his records that he had not yet reached his fifty-fourth birthday.

'Your friend Craig has been giving me an earful,' Jonah went on, when he received no reply. 'He thinks we ought to forget about you breaking the conditions of your parole and let you stay out on licence. He told me a fine story about what you were up to last night. I'm inclined to believe him, but I need to hear your version. So now, tell me: what were you doing hanging around that house in Cowley?'

Brendan stared back without speaking.

'Come on!' urged Jonah impatiently. 'I'm giving you a chance to vindicate yourself. Answer the question.'

'You know about Kenny Hughes?' Brendan asked at last.

'Yes,' Jonah confirmed, sighing in exasperation. 'Yes. I'm the SIO investigating his murder. Now go on – what were you up to last night, lurking in the bushes in a quiet residential area?'

'I was watching the house. Craig said the bloke who did it was a dealer, and he had it in for the bloke who lived there. Craig reckoned he'd be coming back. I think the bloke owed him money or something. I don't know. I just did what Craig said and watched the house to see if he came round.'

'And did he?' asked Jonah.

'Well *someone* did. I don't know if it was him. This flash black car drove up and this big bloke got out.'

'Can you describe him?' Jonah asked eagerly.

'It was dark. All I could see was he was big and he'd got something in his hand – a rope maybe – and, and I saw the light from the street lamp shining on the top of his head.'

'Good,' Jonah said encouragingly. 'Now go on.'

'Then these two other blokes got out as well. One of 'em had long hair in one of them daft pony-tails. They all went up the path, like they was going to knock on the door.'

'And then?' prompted Jonah.

'All hell broke loose, dinnit? There was cops everywhere. The next I knew, I was being put in a squad car and brought here.'

'I see. And what time did these events take place?'

'I dunno, do I?' Brendan's voice rose and he looked Jonah in the eye for the first time. 'I don't have a watch, do I? Craig told me Doug would be along at eight to take over, and he hadn't come so I thought it must be before that. I didn't know the lying bastard was standing me up, did I?'

'OK.' Jonah pondered for a few moments. 'I believe you. Tell you what: we'll take you back to the custody sergeant and she'll give you your things back. Craig and Doug are waiting for you in Reception. Don't whatever you do make a scene with Doug,' he added warningly. 'I'll contact your probation officer and see if we can't forget about you not getting back to the hostel last night. I'll tell them we needed you as a witness – which is perfectly true. I'm also going to tell Father Damien that you're back in town. He'll be pleased to know you're out of prison, and you never know, he may be able to help you get a job or something. I gather you Catholics all stick together.'

A few minutes later Jonah was back in the open-plan office debating with Rupert and Andy the best approach to take in questioning their three suspects.

'We think Terry Butler was Harry Whittle's boss,' Jonah said thoughtfully, 'but is he Mr Big or could that be his brother Shane?'

'Or might they both be just cogs in the machine and there's someone else pulling their strings?' suggested Andy.

'If there is, we can't do anything about it,' Jonah observed grimly. 'These three are all we've go to work with. 'The question is: what's the best way to get them to talk?'

'Hatton's like a sort of mercenary. He just sells his services to the highest bidder. He might be willing to shop the others in exchange for a lighter sentence,' Rupert suggested.

'Mmm,' murmured Jonah. 'On the other hand, if the chain

of command doesn't stop at the Butler brothers, he's unlikely to be able to point us to the real boss, because the chances are he has no idea who he's actually working for.'

He pursed his lips in thought. The others waited in silence for his verdict.

'OK,' he said at last, speaking briskly now that his mind was made up. 'We'll interview them all simultaneously. That way, there's no danger of just looking for confirmation from one of them for what another has just told us. Andrews!'

'Yes Sir?'

'You tackle Stuart Hatton. Take DC Ray with you. Sometimes having a woman in the room knocks these big fellows off guard.'

'Right-oh Sir!'

'I'll take Shane. He's a bit of an unknown quantity. And I'll let Stella Gilbert sit in on it. It's time she saw a bit of the action. It'll make her feel she's doing something.' He looked towards Andy. 'Will you be OK interviewing Terry? You'll have to have Josh Pitchfork; there's nobody else free.'

'I'm fine with that,' Andy assured him. 'He's the one we think was running the cannabis factory – is that right? Do we know anything more about him?'

'Not much,' Andrews answered at once. 'We ran checks on both of the brothers. Neither of them has got a record. Terry – the older one – is married. Her name's Holly. No kids that we could trace She's been informed that he's in custody – as per protocol.'

'But she's not here, asking after him?' asked Bernie in surprise.

'She came round last night,' Andrews replied. 'Asked to see him – which we refused – and said she was arranging a solicitor. He arrived while you were talking to Connolly.'

'What about his brother?' Jonah asked at once. 'Has he got legal representation too?'

'Yes,' Andrews nodded. 'Mrs Butler seems to have organised a full team of legal eagles! It makes you think they must've been expecting to need them sooner or later, doesn't it?'

'That's good,' Jonah smiled. 'I was afraid you were going to say that they were all demanding to have the same lawyer with them, which would've put paid to our plans to do all the interviews at once.'

'They've missed a trick there, haven't they?' suggested Bernie. 'I'd have thought any delay was in their favour, because you might run out of time before you'd finished questioning them all.'

'Oh there are always ways of getting round that,' Jonah said dismissively. 'Now, speaking of delays, let's get on with it and see what those three have to say for themselves.'

* * *

'Now Mr Butler – or may I call you Shane?' Jonah began, looking across the table at the younger Butler brother. Shane had long black hair tied at the back of his neck with a piece of black ribbon. He had a matching ribbon around the collar of his pale blue shirt, which was a fancy number with frills down the front. The stubble on his face was evidence that he had not had the opportunity to shave that morning. He looked contemptuously back at Jonah with deep-set brown eyes.

'Mr Butler?' Jonah repeated.

'Yeah,' Shane mumbled, 'Shane's fine.'

'Good. Now would you like to tell me what you were doing in Ridley Avenue at ten-thirty last night?'

'Minding my own business,' growled back Shane.

'And exactly what is your business?' asked Jonah.

'We was visiting our good friend Ross,' Shane expanded. 'It's Christmas. That's what people do, innit? Call round on their friends.'

'Oh! I see,' Jonah said agreeably. 'You were just calling round with a card, and maybe a Christmas present. Is that it?'

'Yeah.'

'So what was it you were giving him? You weren't carrying any nicely wrapped presents when the officers arrested you.'

'No, well …,' Shane appeared to be thinking. 'We left them in the car, in case he wasn't in.'

'So he wasn't expecting you?' enquired Jonah.

'It was gonna be a surprise, wasn't it?' Shane's lips curled in a sneer.

'I see. So, when our people take your car apart looking for evidence of what you were really up to, they'll find some nice gift-wrapped parcels in the boot, will they?'

'Unless your officers nicked 'em!' retorted Shane. 'Which I wouldn't put past 'em.'

'I see,' Jonah said calmly. 'And the bicycle chain that your friend Stuart had in his hand when he was arrested, was that a present for Ross too? He does a lot of cycling, does he?'

'Nah! You'll have to ask Stuart about that. Nothing to do with me!'

* * *

In the adjacent interview room, DI Andrews was doing exactly that. In response, Hatton leaned back in his seat and cracked his knuckles.

'I always like to take some protection with me when I go out at night,' he said, folding his muscular arms across his massive chest. 'There's some dangerous people out there, and a few people who've got a grudge against me – know what I mean?'

'Are you quite sure you weren't planning to use it to threaten Mr Pilling with?' Alice Ray asked, smiling sweetly across the table at him and toying with her long blond hair, which she had released from its usual neat bun at the back of her neck.

'Threaten Ross?' Stuart gave a guffaw of contemptuous laughter. 'Why would I want to do that?'

'Because he owed your boss money,' Andrews replied coldly. 'He admitted that much to us when we had him in here last week.'

'We could charge you with carrying an offensive weapon in public,' Alice told him.

'A bike chain?' Stuart laughed scornfully.

'When you're carrying it loose in your hand on the way to visit a man who's reported to the police that he's scared you might be going to come and get him – yes,' Andrews confirmed coldly.

* * *

'That's a fine beard you have there,' Andy commented, gazing across the table at Terence Butler, who stared impassively back at him. 'How long've you had it?'

'What's that got to do with anything?' Terry opened his eyes wider as if in amazement at the question and glanced towards his lawyer.

'Just answer the question.' Andy's voice was firm and unemotional.

'Off and on for years,' Terry shrugged. 'The wife doesn't seem to be able to make up her mind if she likes it or loathes it!' he added with a grin. 'But I don't see why it matters to you.'

'I'd like to try a little experiment.' Andy opened a folder that lay on the table in front of him and took out a sheet of paper. It was a copy of the photograph from the bogus Mr McLeod's passport, blown up to life-size and enhanced to show the features more clearly. He leaned across the table and held the picture up next to Terry's face. Then he took another piece of paper and held it in front, obscuring his mouth and chin. 'What do you think?' he asked, looking towards DC Pitchfork. 'Are they the same do you reckon?'

'Could be,' Joshua replied cautiously. 'There's a definite similarity around the eyes. The hair's a bit different though.'

Andy peered at the photograph and then at Terry's face. 'Have you got a comb on you, Josh?'

'No. Sorry Sir. Shall I see if any of the-'

'Take this,' the solicitor said impatiently, holding out a black plastic comb, which he had taken out from the breast pocket of his suit. 'Let's get this charade over with.'

Andy took the comb and carefully altered the parting in Terry's hair to the opposite side. Then, after further study of the passport photograph, he combed the hair at the side of his face back behind his ears. Then he held up the photograph next to Terry's face once more.

'Well?'

'Yes,' Joshua nodded. 'I'd say they're the same.'

Andy put the photograph down on the table and pushed it towards Terry and his lawyer.

'This is the photograph on a false passport, which was used to take out a tenancy on a house in Kidlington in the name of a Mr and Mrs McLeod of Dundee.'

'That's very interesting,' the solicitor responded, 'but I fail to see what it has to do with my client.'

'Your client just happens to be the spitting image of the so-called Mr McLeod,' Andy told him coldly. Then he turned to Terry. 'Mr Butler? Can you explain this uncanny resemblance?'

'I'd say it's all in your mind,' Terry smiled back. He pushed the photograph back towards Andy. 'This could be almost anyone! Dark hair, brown eyes, maybe a similar shape nose! There's nothing else! Look at the eyebrows for instance! They're nothing like mine.'

Andy looked down at the photograph and then up at Terry's face. He was quite right: the man in the photograph had thick black eyebrows that met across his nose. Terry's were narrower and separated by a centimetre or more of bare pale skin.

'You could easily have shaved them,' he said at last, 'or plucked them out.'

'Or it could just be that this is someone else completely,' Terry said emphatically. He sat back in his chair and smiled complacently. 'Come on! Admit it! You've got nothing on me. Let's just call it a day and all go home, eh?'

'Are you denying that you impersonated Mr John Alexander McLeod in order to take out a tenancy on this property?' Andy placed a photograph of the house in

Kidlington on the table in front of Terry.

'Yes. I am.' Terry said smoothly. 'I don't know anything about this house, any more than I know anything about where Ross Pilling gets his drugs from – assuming that you're not making up all that stuff about him being a dealer. Like I told you, we just went round to pay him a friendly visit, the way mates do.'

'We've got people over at your house right now,' Andy told him menacingly, 'with sniffer dogs. If you've had drugs stored there, they'll find the evidence. It'd be better for you if you come clean now. Your friend Ross told us he was scared of your other friend, Stuart, because he was working for his supplier and he owed money. I think you were round there last night to get him to pay up.'

'You can think what you like,' Terry smiled back, 'but it won't make it true.'

There was a knock on the door and a young uniformed officer entered. 'I'm sorry to disturb you,' he said nervously, 'but Sergeant Appleton said you'd want to see these.'

He held out two evidence bags. Andy took them and turned them round in his hand looking at them intently. Each bag contained a passport, open at the photograph page. Then he studied the labels attached to the outside of the bags. Finally he looked towards Terry and smiled.

'Mr Butler,' he said in a satisfied tone. 'These two passports were found in your house. They are in the names of a Mr and Mrs McLeod. Would you care to explain how they came to be in your possession?'

* * *

'Right!' Jonah called out when the team reconvened after the interviews were complete. 'We've made some good progress, but the Butler brothers are still holding out and denying everything. It looks as if the passports, and hopefully other forensic evidence, are likely to be enough to establish that they were running the cannabis farm, but we've got nothing so far to link them with Kenny's death.'

'They're bringing Terry's wife in for questioning,' Andrews added. 'It looks like she was probably the fake Mrs McLeod. Maybe she'll be willing to talk in exchange for a lighter sentence on the grounds that she was acting under duress from her husband and brother-in-law.'

'Except that she may not have been,' Jonah observed bluntly. 'Stella said she thought the driver of the car that hit Kenny might have been a woman. We'll have to play it by ear when we see what she's like. For all we know, she could be the brains behind the whole operation, and the men are all just taking her orders! Meanwhile, let's see what else we can do to tie up some of these loose ends.'

'I rang the letting agent earlier,' Andy volunteered. 'He says he'll be in the office all day and we can come round any time to show him the passports.'

'OK,' Jonah nodded. 'Better wait on doing that until we've got photos of Mrs Butler to show him. If he can confirm that Terry and Holly *are* the couple he showed round the Kidlington house then it's going to be impossible for them to continue with this pretence of outraged innocence that they're putting on. Once we've got them on the back foot, they may start making mistakes.'

He paused for a moment in thought before addressing Andrews.

'Tell me again: what was Stuart's alibi for the afternoon Kenny died?'

'He claims he was working out at the gym. I've got it in mind to follow up on that later. He gave the names of a couple of the staff there that he says he spoke to.'

'And when Harry Whittle was killed?'

'He says he was playing squash with Shane Butler from eight until ten that morning.'

'That's what Shane says too,' agreed Jonah. 'We'd better follow up on that with the leisure centre. And Shane claims that he was at the races at Plumpton the day Kenny was killed. He produced a receipt from an on-course bookie confirming a bet on the three-twenty race. My immediate thought was: why did he keep it, and carry it round with him in his pocket, unless it was for the purpose of establishing an alibi?'

'That doesn't mean it isn't true though,' Bernie pointed out. 'If one of the others – or someone else from the gang that we haven't come across yet – warned him that their drugs factory had been raided and a police officer had been killed, he'd want to make absolutely certain that he could prove he wasn't there when it happened, wouldn't he?'

'Yes, you're right,' Jonah agreed. 'I'll get on to Sussex Police and ask them to check it out.'

He turned to Andy. 'What about Terry? I suppose he has alibis for both days too?'

'He told me a long story about how he and his missus had gone to see an elderly aunt of hers in a dementia care home in Norwich,' Andrews reported. 'They stayed overnight and drove back the morning Harry was killed. He showed me the booking on his phone. It was an Airbnb place over a hairdressing salon. They leave the key in a key safe outside the door and the guests do everything for themselves. So there's no way of checking if they actually did stay there.'

'You'd better follow it up, though,' Jonah said. 'The owner may be able to confirm that *someone* was there – if the bed was slept in or if the kitchen was used. Or someone from the hair salon may have seen them going in. And you'd better check out the care home too – see if the staff remember them visiting.'

'I've already been on to Norwich CID,' Andrews told him. 'They're going to pay them both a call. And I've checked – it would take about three and a half hours to drive from Norwich, so they could've done everything they say they did and still got back in time to kill Harry Whittle, if they set off by, say, five-thirty in the morning.'

'And what about the other day?' asked Jonah. 'The afternoon when Kenny was killed.'

'According to Terry, he was with his wife again,' Andy reported. 'They were doing some Christmas shopping in the centre of Oxford. He says Holly will be able to show us all the receipts.'

'OK,' Jonah nodded. 'We'll see what she says when they bring her in. Shopping in Oxford isn't a very strong alibi for a murder that took place in Kidlington. If they had a friend with a fast car, they could easily get back there within a few minutes of dumping the car that hit Kenny. The times on those till receipts are going to be crucial.'

'And there was only one person driving, as far as we know,' Andy added, 'so one of them could've been shopping while the other was outside the Kidlington house watching the police raid – or they could've had someone else collecting the till receipts for them.'

'Mmm,' Jonah nodded in agreement. 'Once we know which shops they claim to have been to, we'd better get some officers out there asking the staff if they remember them.'

'Remember one couple?' Bernie exclaimed. 'At this time of year!'

'We can only try,' Jonah sighed, 'and it's not as if we *want* them to be identified. It suits us if there aren't any witnesses to prove they weren't in Kidlington running down poor Kenny Hughes.'

'Only if they were,' Bernie commented darkly.

'There'll be CCTV cameras all round the shopping streets,' Jonah continued, ignoring this remark, 'so, if they really were there, they should appear on some of them.'

'I'll get on to that,' Joshua Pitchfork volunteered.

'Good. You do that. Andy! You get over to the letting agent with those passports as soon as we've got the photos of Mr and Mrs Butler.'

'I've sent off copies of all the suspects' fingerprints for matching with prints from both houses and the abandoned car,' Andrews reported. 'I'll add Mrs Butler's to them as soon as we've got them. If they are guilty, surely they'll have left some in one of those places!'

* * *

'Thanks for coming over,' Gavin greeted Peter as he let him into the house. 'Chrissie will be down in a minute. She's just packing the things into bags. Come and sit down.'

Peter followed his friend into the front room and sat down in one of the armchairs. Gavin reached out and opened a tin that lay on the coffee table.

'Have a mince pie while you're waiting,' he said, holding it out towards Peter. 'We said we weren't doing Christmas this year, but Chrissie can't stop baking whatever. I suppose it helps to keep her mind off things.'

'And it's a good idea to have something to offer people when they come round,' Peter observed. 'I suppose you'll have had a lot of visitors?'

'Yes and no,' Gavin nodded. 'We've had lots of cards pushed through the door and people popping in on the way to somewhere else, but not many wanting to stay for long. People don't know what to say, I suppose. And everyone's busy at this time of year. I hope we're not getting in the way of things you ought to be doing,' he added anxiously.

'Not, not at all,' Peter assured him. 'Eddie's off work now until the New Year, so I haven't got the kids to worry about, and Jonah and Bernie are slaving away trying to get this case sorted, so I'm at rather a loose end at the moment. Even Lucy deserted me this afternoon in favour of catching up with some of her school friends.'

He paused, wondering how to put into words what he wanted to say next. Gavin had rung him that morning to ask him to accompany Chrissie as she went through the streets distributing the gloves, scarves and hats that she had knitted for the city's rough sleepers. While he was happy to undertake this duty, he was anxious that Gavin's reluctance to do it himself might be a sign that he was not coping well with the shock of Kenny's death. Cancelling Christmas was understandable, but it was not like him to avoid an opportunity to interact with the homeless community, many of whom seemed almost to have become part of his family.

Lost in thought, he gradually became aware that his friend

was speaking.

'We usually go round them together,' Gavin was saying, 'but somehow I can't bring myself to do it this year. I know it's stupid, but hearing about what Craig and the others did only makes it worse. I don't think I can face them – not yet. But I don't want Chrissie to be out there on her own. It's not the homeless guys I'm worried about,' he added quickly. 'It's the young executives who've had a few too many at the office party and the respectable folk who think helping the rough sleepers is only encouraging them to bother people with begging.'

'Like I said, I'm happy to do it, but …,' Peter hesitated again. Then, throwing caution to the winds, he went on bluntly, 'but I'd rather you came too. You'll know the right places to find the guys, and … and they'll be worried not to see you.'

'Do you think so?' Gavin asked. He sat ruminating on this idea, which was clearly completely new to him.

'Craig's already been expressing concern that he's not seen you around since Kenny died,' Peter told him, pressing home his advantage. 'We've told him you're busy organising the funeral and stuff, but that won't wash if Chrissie's out there handing out winter woollies.'

Before Gavin could formulate a reply to this, the door burst open and Chrissie came in carrying two large shopping bags. She was dressed all in red, apart from a white knitted hat with a pattern of reindeer around it.

'Peter!' she called out, putting them down on the floor and coming over to give him an unsolicited hug. 'It's good to see you! And it's very good of you to agree to help. I've split the things into these two bags. The hats and scarves are all one-size-fits-all, but there are two sizes of gloves. This bag has the larger size in it. We'll do the rounds of all the usual places and then, if there're any left, we'll drop them off with Mike Bannister at the homeless shelter.'

'OK,' Peter nodded, smiling to himself at Chrissie's irrepressible energy. 'I think I've got the idea.'

'And this one is for you!' Chrissie bent down and took out from one of the bags a red hat, trimmed with white fur fabric and with a large white pom-pom on the top. 'We can't have you getting frostbite on your ears, can we?'

'Thank you, but it really isn't as cold as all that,' Peter protested as Chrissie stretched the hat over his head, 'and I'd rather your hard work went on someone who hasn't got a drawer full of woolly hats that I never remember to put on. Tell you what,' he added, seeing the disapproving look on Chrissie's face and feeling as if he were back in Primary School arguing that he did not need his coat on a playtime, 'I'll wear it while we go round and then I'll drop it off at the shelter with the others.

'I think I'll come along too, after all,' Gavin mumbled, hauling himself to his feet and looking round at them both. 'I ought to thank Craig and the others for trying to find the guy who ran Kenny down.'

'Are we all ready then?' Chrissie asked in the tone of voice she used for rallying her class to action. She glanced up at the clock. 'Five to two, if we get off now we should be able to get round before it gets dark.'

'Yes,' Gavin murmured in a rather dreamy voice. Then he added tentatively, 'I suppose it must've been about this time last week that …'

'Yes,' Peter confirmed, immediately catching his drift. 'The incident was logged as occurring at thirteen fifty-three. That's when Mel Stanton radioed for backup.'

Chrissie put down the bags and looked apologetically towards Peter.

'I'm sure you'll think this is very silly,' she said with a nervous little laugh, quite unlike her usual confident demeanour, 'but, I wonder, could you show me the place that it happened? I don't know why, but somehow, when Gav said it was exactly a week ago, I suddenly thought I ought to see it. I'd like to be able to picture how it happened.'

'Of course I can take you,' Peter assured her, 'and it isn't silly at all. Do you want to go now? It'd be better to do it in the daylight. I don't suppose the lighting's very good down that back street.'

'Yes please.' Chrissie sounded more like one of her more diffident pupils than the self-assured teacher that Peter had been presented with up until now.

* * *

'OK, Stella,' Jonah said gently, 'you've seen them all now. Can you identify any of them as the person who was driving the car that hit Kenny?'

'No Sir. I'm sorry.' Stella shook her head. 'I just didn't get a good enough look at them. It definitely wasn't the big guy – Stuart, was it? – because I'm sure they didn't have a shaved head like he's got, but … like I say, I really don't know.'

'Don't worry,' Jonah told her kindly. 'We wouldn't have got a conviction without forensic evidence to back up your identification anyway. Provided we've got the right car, there's a good chance there'll be fingerprints or DNA to prove which one of them was driving – if only the labs can hurry up and get back to us with the results!'

'And presumably, once those alibis have been checked out, we may be able to narrow it down by the process of elimination,' suggested Bernie.

'Yes.' Jonah pulled a face. 'We'll have to hope one of them turns out not to be as watertight as it seems. Andrews has already reported that two of the gym staff have confirmed that Stuart was there on the afternoon of the day Kenny died. He arrived about twelve thirty and didn't leave until sometime after two pm. So that rules him out – but Stella's just told us she's sure it wasn't him in any case. We're still waiting on Sussex Police for news on Shane's little flutter at Plumpton and it'll take days to go through all the CCTV footage looking for Terry and his wife.'

He turned back to Stella. 'OK. You'd better get back to the front desk. Thanks for trying.'

Stella left the room. Bernie sat down on the desk, swinging

her legs and watching Jonah, waiting for him to decide what to do next. He frowned as he flicked impatiently through pages of case notes on his computer screen, looking for some line of enquiry that he could pursue while waiting for news from the various investigations that he had set in motion. The telephone rang. It was an inspector from the Lewes police station.

'DCI Porter? You wanted confirmation of a bet placed at Plumpton on the three-twenty last Monday?'

'Yes!' Jonah replied eagerly. 'Have you traced it?'

'Yes. The slip's genuine. The horse came in next to last. It wasn't well-favoured, so it didn't attract a lot of bets. And you're in luck – or rather your suspect is – when I mentioned his name the bookie immediately remembered a man telling him that he was betting on that horse because the jockey was called Rory McShane and the punter's name was Shane, so he thought it was a good omen. It sounds like that must've been your man.'

'Yes,' Jonah agreed. 'The incident took place earlier that afternoon. If he heard about it from one of his friends, he might have tried to make himself conspicuous in order to establish his alibi. Anyway, I'll send over photographs of all four of our suspects for your bookie to have a look at, just to be sure. Thanks for your help.'

'Well, it's beginning to look as if it's between Terry and Holly,' he observed to Bernie. 'But then, they were always the most likely.'

'Sir! You might want to have a look at this.' Jennifer Moorehouse, one of the civilian staff, called out from behind her computer screen.

Jonah immediately headed over to see what she was looking at.

'This is from a camera at one of the entrances to the Westgate Shopping Centre,' she told him. 'See there! Isn't that Mrs Butler going in at fourteen eighteen?'

Jonah watched as a woman in a green coat appeared from the right and joined a crowd of people heading into the shopping mall.

'Yes,' he agreed. 'It certainly looks like her. Good work! Make a note of that and then carry on watching to see if she comes out again. If she comes back the same way, we should get a better view of her face.'

'If Holly Butler *was* in the Westgate at half past two, there's no way she could've been in Kidlington, driving that car at one fifty-three,' Bernie said to Jonah as they returned to his desk. 'On the other hand, there was no sign of Terry, which would fit in with our idea that one of them was creating an alibi for them both.'

'But Stella said the driver of the car had long hair,' Jonah objected, 'so I was rather assuming it must be *Mrs* Butler, rather than her husband.'

* * *

Peter drove and Gavin and Chrissie sat holding hands together in the back of the car. The road was crowded with parked cars, forcing him to pull up some distance from the crime scene. They got out and walked slowly back to where the many bunches of flowers still lay piled up against the wall – some very faded now, others apparently fresh – all the worse for a period of wet and windy weather that had battered delicate blooms and saturated cards containing messages of condolence.

'My understanding is that Kenny and Stella were waiting here,' Peter told them, stopping outside the garage door, 'and the Whittle boy opened this door from the inside trying to get away from the police who were coming in at the front door. Stella was just in the act of putting the cuffs on him when the car came round that corner.' He turned and pointed along the road. 'Kenny saw it coming and pushed Stella back inside the garage, but he didn't have time to get inside himself before it hit him. Mel Stanton had her van parked on the opposite side of the road – over there somewhere. She was just getting PD Q out of the back when it happened.'

Gavin stood in the road, turning slowly round, taking in

the crime scene. Chrissie walked along the line of floral tributes, occasionally bending down to look closer. When she came to the police bear, now looking very woebegone as it lay propped up against the wall, spattered with mud, the card attached round its neck soggy and disintegrating, she picked it up.

'Aren't you a little sweetie?' she exclaimed, as water from its saturated fur fabric ran down her sleeve. 'What are you doing out here, poor thing? We'd better take you home and give you a wash and brush up, hadn't we?'

* * *

'Have we been missing something?' Jonah muttered, impatient at the long wait while his team carried out the painstaking work of corroborating the suspects' stories. 'Have we been jumping to conclusions? What if *all* these alibis check out OK?'

'I suppose then, we hand those four over to the drugs squad and carry on looking for the driver of that red car,' Bernie said, trying to sound upbeat. 'It's only a week since it happened. You can't expect to have got the case wrapped up so soon. And assuming it *is* all to do with that cannabis factory, one or other of them may give in and tell us who was driving, just to get you off their backs.'

'But what if it isn't?' demanded Jonah. 'What if we're barking up the wrong tree altogether? Come on!' he commanded a moment later. 'I'm going to talk to Bella Kennedy. We need to broaden this out. Ever since Craig found us Ross Pilling, we've had tunnel vision, chasing after the gang who were supplying him. But what if Kenny's death was more personal?'

'If it was, then Harry Whittle's murder is almost certainly unrelated,' Bernie pointed out. 'How likely is that?'

'We ought to check on Bella anyway,' Jonah continued, apparently ignoring this remark. 'She has a right to be kept informed, given her relationship with the victim.' He glanced down at the time on his computer screen. 'Come on! If we go now we may catch her on her own, before her parents get back from work.'

In the event, it was Bella who was not yet back home. Her mother, greeting them at the door wearing reindeer antlers and a Christmas jumper featuring a jolly snowman surrounded by sprigs of holly, explained that she had gone to sign on at the job centre.

'She won't be long,' she assured them. 'You'd be welcome to come in and wait if you like.'

They accepted the invitation and followed Mrs Kennedy into a spacious room decorated with fairy lights and garlands of tinsel. A large Christmas tree, surrounded by packages in gay paper wrappings, stood in the bay window.

'We're doing our best to give Bella a good Christmas,' she told them, seeing Bernie looking at the heap of presents. 'It was a terrible blow to her losing her job like that. It came completely out of the blue; and with all the uncertainty surrounding Brexit, there hasn't been much chance of finding another. At least perhaps that's out of the way now. Maybe once we're out of the EU people will start investing again and there'll be more jobs. But I mustn't bore you with all that. Sit down! Make yourselves at home. Would you like a coffee? And some mince pies?'

'That's very kind of you,' Jonah replied, 'but no thank you.'

'We've already had more mince pies than is good for us,' Bernie added, carefully moving aside a cushion featuring a large Christmas pudding in order to sit down on one of three two-seater settees, which were grouped in such a way as to make the Christmas tree the central feature of the room. She knew that Jonah would not want the embarrassment of being fed like a baby in a stranger's house.

'It's not as if she hasn't tried,' Mrs Kennedy went on. 'Poor Bella's been out looking for work every day since Cook's collapsed, but there just aren't any jobs out there. She thought she'd at least be able to pick up some seasonal work in the run up to Christmas, but no. The shops and restaurants are only interested in young people who don't have to be paid the adult minimum wage.'

'And losing her fiancé so suddenly must have been a terrible shock,' Jonah commented innocently, having decided that feigning ignorance of the split-up between Bella and Kenny might encourage her mother to open up on the subject.

'Oh! But didn't you know? That beast Kenny dumped her only a few weeks after she lost her job. I could hardly believe it! How could anyone be so callous? Talk of kicking someone when they're down!'

'I suppose perhaps -,' Bernie began, but Mrs Kennedy was not listening.

'You'd have thought he'd have given her some support, wouldn't you?' she continued, 'but no! All of a sudden he was working every weekend! And even if they did go out somewhere, he'd get a call and say he had to leave. I've seen her sobbing her eyes out because he didn't return her texts.'

'The police service can be like that sometimes,' Bernie told her coldly, stung by what appeared to her to be unfair criticism of someone who could not defend himself. 'I've been married to it for twenty-odd years, on and off. You just have to get used to it.'

'But I can see why it would be upsetting for your daughter, under the circumstances,' Jonah added, flashing a warning look in Bernie's direction. 'And she still seemed very fond of him when we bumped into her at the inquest.'

'Of course she was! It was *him* who dumped *her*! And that's something I'll never understand.'

'Perhaps he just came to the conclusion that they were incompatible,' Jonah suggested mildly. 'Or maybe he had difficulties of his own. That was one of the things we came to see Bella about – that and to bring her up to date with the progress of the investigation. We were hoping she might have thought of someone who could've had a grudge against him.'

'Maybe some other old girlfriend that he deserted for no good reason,' Mrs Kennedy suggested scornfully. 'But poor Bella won't tell you that. She still thinks the world of him and believes it must have been her fault. Imagine that! He walks out on her and then she blames herself! It's really undermined her confidence – just when she needs it most, to get another job. I know he's dead, but I believe in speaking my mind, and he should've behaved better. He *must*'ve been able to see how low she was after losing her job.'

'Some people find it difficult to deal with that sort of thing. Maybe it was Bella being depressed after losing her job that frightened Kenny off,' Jonah suggested, looking across at Bernie again to forestall any reaction from her in Kenny's defence.

'It's a pretty poor sort of man who can't stand by his girl when she's in trouble. That's all I can say!' Mrs Kennedy retorted.

There was the sound of a car backing up the drive. Mrs Kennedy pulled back the curtain (dark green with a pattern of silver stars and bright red poinsettias) and peered out. Then she hurried across the room to the door.

'That's Bella. I'll tell her you're here.'

They heard the front door opening and voices in the hall.

'There's a plain clothes policeman here wanting to speak to you.'

'What about?'

'Kenny. He *said* it was just to bring you up to date with the investigation into his death, but then he said something about wanting to ask you if you knew about anyone having a grudge against him.' Mrs Kennedy lowered her voice, but the door to the living room was ajar and Jonah heard her whisper, 'I'd be a bit circumspect with what you tell him, if I were you. No point encouraging them to try to get you involved.'

There was a rustle of coats and then Bella entered the room followed by her mother.

'Oh! It's you again,' she exclaimed when she saw Jonah. 'I wasn't expecting … Mum said … I'm sorry,' she said at last, flopping down on the sofa furthest from where Bernie and Jonah were sitting, 'that must've sounded rude. Can we start again?'

'Of course,' Jonah smiled kindly. 'I suppose I probably didn't introduce myself properly last time we met. I'm Detective Chief Inspector Jonah Porter and this is my personal assistant, Dr Bernadette Fazakerley. You can call us Jonah and Bernie. I'm the Senior Investigating Officer in charge of finding out who was driving the car that killed your fiancé. I thought it was time we gave you an update on how we're getting on.'

'I see,' Bella nodded.

'We're following a few lines of enquiry,' Jonah went on, 'and we've actually made some arrests. Presumably you know that Kenny was there because the house was being used to grow cannabis? We think we've got hold of some members of the gang that was running the business, but it's looking rather as if we're going to have to dig deeper to discover which, if any of them, was the driver of the car.'

'I see,' Bella repeated.

'Did Kenny ever talk to you about his work?' Jonah asked casually.

'Sometimes.' Bella's face assumed a puzzled frown. 'Why?'

'Well, with this cannabis factory being only just round the corner from here, I just wondered if he might have mentioned to you that there were suspicions about it.'

'No. He never said anything to me, but then I haven't seen Kenny since the middle of November.'

'Yes, of course,' Jonah nodded understandingly. 'It was a long shot, but I just can't help feeling that this might be a bit more personal than just a random attack on a police officer. That's why I was hoping he might have mentioned something to you. Did he ever give the impression of being nervous at all? Worried that someone could have been out to get him?'

'No. Not at all.'

'Ah well! As I said, I just had to ask – just to be sure we hadn't missed anything.' Jonah sounded as if he were bringing the conversation to an end. 'You may hear on the news that some people have been arrested in connection with Kenny's murder. I thought you ought to know that there's still some way to go before we'll be able to charge anyone with anything more than drugs offences. Meanwhile, just for the record, do you mind telling me where you were last Monday afternoon?'

'She was at a job interview, weren't you Bella?' Mrs Kennedy cut in immediately. 'For a receptionist at one of the hotels in North Oxford – what was the name of it? I keep forgetting.'

'Norham Lodge,' Bella answered. 'Yes. Mum's right. I was there.'

'Again, just for the record, can you remember what time the interview was?' Jonah pressed her gently.

'One – one thirty – I can't remember!' Bella became agitated and suddenly seemed close to tears. Her mother moved over and put her arm round her.

'That's alright. It doesn't really matter,' Jonah said soothingly. 'I'm sorry to have bothered you about it. It's just, as I said, dotting the i's and crossing the t's, making sure we've got everything down in case we need it. We'll go now.'

'Don't bother coming again,' Mrs Kennedy said coldly, as she held open the front door for them to leave. 'Bella doesn't need any more updates from you. We can find out all we need to know about this business from the news reports.'

'Yes, of course,' Jonah smiled up at her. 'I really am sorry that we upset your daughter. I hope she finds a job soon.'

As she bent down to pick up the portable ramp Bernie heard the front door snap shut. She turned to follow Jonah down the drive and was surprised to see that he had stopped next to a red car parked there.

'Look at that,' he said when she came up alongside him. 'See that graze on the front wing? Doesn't that look to you as if the car scraped along a wall or something?'

'Maybe,' Bernie acknowledged cautiously.

'And don't you think this car's the same colour as the traces of paint the SOCOs found at the crime scene?'

'It's red,' Bernie agreed, still reluctant to commit herself to the new narrative that Jonah was clearly building in his mind, 'but plenty of people drive red cars and get them scratched.

And we've already got a car that we think was the one.'

'But what if we're wrong about that?' Jonah persisted, releasing the brake and allowing his wheelchair to roll silently down to the bottom of the drive. 'Let's get back and find out if they've finally got the analysis done to prove that one way or the other.'

9. CHRISTMAS EVE

'We've been going back through all the footage from the cameras in Kidlington,' Joshua Pitchfork greeted Jonah when he and Bernie arrived at work the next morning, 'and we've picked up that other car you were asking about on a couple of them.'

'Tell me more,' Jonah urged him eagerly.

'It came off the roundabout near Sainsbury's at thirteen twenty-seven, heading into Kidlington,' Joshua told him. 'And it didn't get to the traffic lights at Lyne Road until fourteen-O-three.'

'So what took it so long?' Jonah demanded. 'That can't be more than a few hundred yards.'

'And what was it doing as far up Banbury Road as that?' Bernie chipped in. 'If Bella Kennedy was heading home from her interview, why didn't she turn off down Yarnton Road?'

'I reckon she did,' Joshua told them smugly, producing a map and putting it down on Jonah's lap. 'Don't forget, there was a police operation going on down there. Her natural route home would've been along Gladstone Road, but that was blocked with police vehicles from one-thirty onwards that afternoon. Maybe she waited around for a bit and then doubled back to the main road and went round Lyne Road and then down Grovelands to get through from the other side.'

'Or maybe she tried to get past the blockage by going round the back,' Jonah murmured. 'Palmerstone Crescent, where Kenny was killed, goes off Gladstone Road and then joins it again further along. Suppose she tried going along there, and then she saw Kenny and something snapped and she ran him down.'

'But why?' demanded Bernie. 'OK, she was pissed off with him for dumping her, but deliberately crushing him against a brick wall? It doesn't make sense!'

'Maybe Peter's right and it wasn't deliberate,' Jonah argued. 'Maybe she was in a hurry to get home and driving too fast. She wasn't expecting Mel's van, swerved to get past it and hit Kenny accidentally. When she sees what she's done, she panics and makes off back to Banbury Road and home the way Josh described.'

'And the other car?' Bernie asked sceptically. 'Where does that come in?'

'A coincidence. Cars get stolen all the time.'

'I thought you didn't like coincidences,' grumbled Bernie.

'That doesn't mean they don't happen.' Jonah turned to Joshua. 'Get her in here. I'm going to interview her under caution. She's got a bit of explaining to do.'

'It doesn't stack up,' Bernie told Jonah in a low voice, after the young constable had left. 'If she carried on along Palmerstone Crescent, she wouldn't have needed to go back to Banbury Road – look!' she jabbed at the map, which Joshua had left lying on Jonah's lap. 'The whole point of going down there was to get home without turning round. And we know she didn't turn in Palmerstone Crescent, because Stella and Mel would've see it.'

Jonah, busy with something on his computer screen, said nothing. Then he looked up with an expression of satisfaction on his face.

'But she was in a panic, remember. Look at this!'

Bernie came round behind him and peered over his shoulder at the screen. It displayed a map of the part of Kidlington where Kenny had been killed.

'See there?' Jonah pointed with the cursor on the screen. 'Where Palmerston Crescent comes back out on to Gladstone Road? It's a cross-roads. If you were driving recklessly, trying to get as far away as you could as quickly as you could, don't you think you might just go straight over there? And then in a few hundred yards you'd be back at the Banbury Road.'

'OK, you win!' Bernie sighed. 'But I'm still not convinced Bella did it. It doesn't make sense!'

'Now Miss Kennedy,' Jonah said a short while later, looking across the table at Bella, who was sitting nervously in the interview room next to the duty solicitor. 'As I've just explained, you are here because we suspect that it may have been your car that hit PC Kenneth Hughes last Monday afternoon, resulting in his subsequent death. If you are innocent, you have nothing to worry about. Just answer our questions and we'll be able to let you go.'

'What do you want to know?' Bella asked so quietly that Jonah had to strain to hear the words.

'Let's start with you telling me the truth about where you were between one and three on Monday the sixteenth of December.'

'I told you before – I had a job interview.'

'At the Norham Lodge Hotel, yes,' Jonah nodded. 'We checked with them. They say your interview was over by one twenty. Where did you go after that?'

'Home – I drove home. I was parked in the visitor's car park at the hotel. I just drove up Banbury Road and straight home.'

'Yes,' agreed Jonah. 'Your car was picked up on the camera by the Sainsbury's roundabout at ….' He made a play of consulting his notes on the screen. 'That's right – at one twenty-seven. What time did you get home?'

'I don't know exactly. A bit after that, I suppose.'

'Is there anyone else who might be able to vouch for that?' Jonah asked innocently. 'Was your mother at home when you got back, for instance?'

'No. She was at work.'

'What route did you take?'

'How d'you mean?'

'You presumably went up Banbury Road and across the ring road. What then?'

'I just carried on past the Sainsbury's roundabout and into Kidlington.'

'That's right,' Jonah nodded. 'And you passed there at twenty-seven minutes past one. I'm asking where you went after that?'

'Straight up the road.'

'All the way up to the traffic lights at Lyne Road?'

'Yes.'

'Was the traffic very heavy?'

'Not specially.' Bella looked puzzled.

'Only, it seems to have taken you thirty-six minutes to drive just over a mile.' Jonah smiled enquiringly towards her.

'That's because I turned off at Yarnton Road,' Bella explained, looking more confident now. 'I was going to go along Gladstone Road, but it was blocked, so I went back to Banbury Road and came round the other side.'

'You're sure of that, are you? You didn't try getting past by going along Palmerstone Crescent?'

Bella hesitated and glanced towards the solicitor, who remained impassive. Jonah pressed his advantage.

'We have a sample of paint from the wall behind where Kenny was killed and tyre marks from the grass opposite. I've arranged for your car to be taken away for forensic examination. If it did go down Palmerstone Crescent that afternoon, we'll find evidence; so, it will be better for everyone if you tell the truth now.'

'OK.' Bella pushed her long black hair back from her face. 'I got to where the police had blocked the road, like I said. I was just turning round when I saw Kenny with that black girl he's been hanging round with.'

'PC Gilbert?'

'Is that her name? All I know is, I tried to see him a couple of times after we split up and both times he was with her.'

'She's a trainee constable,' Bernie put in, hiding her resentment of this implied criticism of her young friend with difficulty. 'Kenny was her mentor.'

'They went off together, just the two of them,' Bella continued, ignoring Bernie's intervention. 'I finished turning the car and went back down Gladstone Road. I saw them walking along together, talking and laughing. And then they turned into that other road – the one that goes round the back of the houses.'

'Palmerstone Crescent?' enquired Jonah.

'Yes.'

'And you decided to follow them?'

'Yes.' Bella hesitated, then went on the defensive. 'It's a shortcut. It goes round and back to the main road.'

'So, you weren't following Kenny, you were just making your way home by the quickest route?'

'Yes. Well … yes and no.'

Jonah waited without speaking.

'I wanted to see what they were up to,' Bella admitted at last. 'I didn't get what was going on. There was a whole van load of police officers there and only Kenny and that – that – that … only the two of them went off round that other road. I wanted to see what they were getting up to together.'

Bernie took a deep intake of breath, preparatory to an indignant refutation of this suggestion of impropriety. Then she thought better of it and let the air out again in a silent sigh.

'So, you followed them along Palmerstone Crescent,' Jonah continued evenly. 'What then?'

'There was a high brick wall all along the right-hand side of the road,' Bella told him. 'A little way along, there was a white garage door in it. They stopped next to it and just stood there together, like they were waiting for something. I didn't want Kenny to see me, so I carried on past and pulled in a bit further on.'

'And then what?'

Bella looked nervously round from Jonah to Bernie, a quick glance at the solicitor and then back to Jonah again. Then she took a deep breath, as if steeling herself to get an unpleasant job over and done with.

'I got out of the car and went back and hid behind a tree to see what was going on,' she admitted at last. 'There was a police van there by then – not a big one like the one I saw Kenny get out of, a little one, the size of an ordinary car. A woman got out of it and went round to get something out of the back. Kenny was still just standing there with – with–.'

Her voice rose as she remembered the scene and she seemed to be fighting back tears, whether of sorrow or anger Jonah could not determine.

'I could've understood him finding someone else,' she went on hysterically, 'but what could he have seen in *her*?'

Bernie reached into the storage compartment at the back of Jonah's chair and took out a small pack of tissues. She put it down on the table in front of Bella, who stared at it for several seconds before pulling one out and dabbing at her eyes.

'Take your time,' Jonah said kindly, 'and, when you're ready, tell me what happened next.'

Bella took several deep breaths and wiped her eyes again.

'The garage door opened a bit – it was one of those funny ones that slides across and then bends round inside the garage – and this big black man came out,' she gulped, eventually. 'Kenny grabbed hold of him, and so did that PC whatever-she-is that he was with. Then there was this roaring noise from somewhere and this red car came round the corner and smashed into Kenny and – and-'

She dissolved into tears, putting both her hands up in front of her face. Bernie replenished the paper cup of water that stood on the table in front of her. Jonah waited patiently until the sobbing subsided and she looked up at him again.

'What did you do then?' he asked gently.

'I – I – well, I just went back to the car and drove home.'

'Did you see where the other car went – the one that hit Kenny?'

'It went the same way as me – on up Palmerstone Crescent.'

'And when it got to the crossroads?'

'I don't know. It was gone by the time I got there.'

'OK. What about the driver? Did you see them?'

'No.' Bella shook her head. 'It all happened so fast.'

'You didn't even see if it was a man or a woman?'

'No.'

'Did you really go off straight away?' Bernie asked. 'If it'd been my boyfriend – or even ex-boyfriend – I'd have wanted to know how badly hurt he was.'

'I was scared. I didn't know what was going on. Everyone was shouting and there was this big police dog barking and running after the black man and – and that girl was down on the ground with her arms round Kenny, like she owned him. I couldn't ….'

She pulled another tissue out of the pack and blew her nose. Then she wiped her eyes again and looked Bernie in the face. Her expression had changed. There was something fanatical about it.

'I just wanted to get out of it all. And I didn't want Kenny to think I'd been following him. It was bad enough … I didn't want her to have the satisfaction …'

Bernie stared back at her uncomprehendingly as Bella continued her rambling tirade.

'She'd got Kenny! I didn't want to give her the chance to crow over me too. The worst was the way he refused to be honest about it. He said it wasn't that he'd found someone else, and then I kept seeing him with that black tart. What did he see in her, I'd like to know!'

'OK, OK,' Jonah intervened. 'I get the picture. You wanted to get away, so you got in your car and drove off. Are you quite sure you can't remember anything about the other car or its driver that might help us to identify them?'

'No, nothing,' Bella said earnestly, shaking her head vigorously.

'Alright.' Jonah thought for a few moments. It was Christmas Eve. They did not have enough evidence to charge Bella with any offence. Her story could well be true and only forensic evidence from her car, which would not be available until after the Christmas shutdown, would prove otherwise.

'OK,' he sighed at last. 'You can go home now. I'll get someone to drive you back, but we will have to keep your car and I may need to speak to you again later.'

'Do you think she's right about Kenny and Stella having been in a relationship?' Jonah asked Bernie when they were back in the open-plan office a few minutes later.

'I shouldn't think so. I'm sure Stella would have told Lucy if there was anything like that going on. I reckon it was all wishful thinking on Bella's part. It must be bad enough to be dumped like that, without being told that your boyfriend would rather have nobody than you! She owed it to her self-respect to imagine that he'd been bowled over by some scheming hussy, and she obviously has a problem with ethnic minorities, so it probably suited her pride to think that he was lowering himself by taking on someone who was clearly inferior to her.'

'Mmm,' Jonah murmured in agreement. 'That's how I read it too, but still … Even if she was wrong about that, if Bella *believed* that Stella had stolen Kenny from her, might she have tried to run Stella down – in the heat of the moment, seeing them together?'

'I suppose so, but if she's telling the truth about watching from outside her car, how would she have had time to get back in and launch her attack?'

'It depends exactly where that tree she says she was hiding behind is and where she left the car and-'

'She said she drove past where they were standing and parked further on. So, she'd have had to turn the car round and come back in order to drive it at Stella,' Bernie objected. 'And even then, she'd have been going the wrong way!'

'She could be lying about where she parked,' countered Jonah. 'The car that hit Kenny must've started from further back round the corner, out of sight from where Kenny and Stella were. I think we need to go and have another look at the crime scene and try to work out where that tree that Bella claims to have hidden behind actually is.'

Jonah hated inaction and was feeling increasingly frustrated with this case, which seemed to involve more than the usual amount of waiting for the results of time-consuming evidence-gathering procedures. He started towards the door, then stopped abruptly, nearly causing Bernie, who was hurrying after him, to collide with his chair.

'Or hang on!' he exclaimed. 'We shouldn't need to waste time going there. Where's that plan of the scene that the SOCOs drew?'

He spent the next few minutes staring intently at his computer screen, flicking through pages, frowning in concentration.

'Ah! Here we are!' he said at last. 'I knew I had it somewhere. Now let's see …'

Bernie came round behind him and looked over his shoulder, resting her arms on the back of his chair, her face close to his.

'There's only one tree marked on there,' she pointed out, 'and it's further on, beyond Mel's van.'

'Yes,' Jonah nodded. 'You're right. If Bella's telling the truth about getting out and hiding behind a tree, she must've left her car further on, round that bend. If it was back the other way, she'd have had to walk right past Mel to get to it. But suppose she was lying. What if she never got out of the car at all? She could've come round that corner, following Kenny and Stella, as she said she was, seen them standing there and driven at Stella just as the garage door opened and Harry came out.'

'No,' Bernie disagreed. 'Stella said they were waiting for a little while before Mel arrived and before Harry came out. If Bella followed Kenny into Palmerstone crescent, she must've stopped the car and waited for a bit before everything kicked off. And if she parked there,' she added, pointing to a position on the map, 'Mel would've had to drive past and would've seen the car as she arrived.'

'Who says she didn't?' challenged Jonah, reluctant to give up on his latest theory. 'We haven't asked her about that. And even if she did pass it, a parked car wouldn't necessarily register with her. There were lots of cars parked in the road when we were there the other day. So long as it was far enough back not to be in the way of the operation, why would she notice it?'

'I still think we were on the right track when we arrested those drug dealers,' Bernie insisted. 'They seem much more likely murderers than Bella – even if her attitude towards ethnic minorities does leave a lot to be desired. And what about *Harry*'s murder?' she added, suddenly remembering that Kenny's was not the only suspicious death under investigation. 'That *can't* have been her!'

'Yes, you're right,' Jonah sighed. 'We'd better go through their alibis again. Where's Andy got to?'

'He's not on duty today,' Bernie reminded him. 'It is nearly Christmas and you let him have the day off so he could take his mum to visit her sister.'

'Then who's been collating the information on those alibis?' demanded Jonah irritably. 'We need to go through it all and see if any of them don't quite stack up.'

'I've got it all here, Sir,' Joshua Pitchfork broke in. He had been listening to the conversation, eagerly awaiting an opportunity to contribute. 'Where would you like me to start?'

'Terry and Holly Butler,' Jonah replied immediately. 'They were the closest to the scene and they may be covering for one another. Is here any chance we can establish that one of them had time to sneak off to Kidlington during the time they were supposed to be shopping together?'

'They claim to have left home at round about half-past one that afternoon,' Joshua told him, 'and we've got a picture of Mrs Butler driving a silver Volvo into the underground car park at the Westgate Centre at thirteen thirty-eight. No sign of Terry, though. According to them, she dropped him off on the way and they met up again later, but …'

'But he could've been somewhere else entirely,' Jonah continued for him – Kidlington, for example. Is there any evidence he was in Oxford at all?'

'Yes. At fourteen eighteen Holly Butler is caught on camera going into the centre. According to her, she was returning from a visit to Marks & Spencer on Queen Street. She produced a till receipt from there, which confirms that. A few minutes later, she orders coffee for two at a café inside the centre – again, she gave us the receipt and we've got CCTV of her sitting in the café drinking coffee with a man, who looks like Terry, but he's got his back to the camera all the time, so we can't be absolutely sure.'

'Could he have got from Kidlington to the Westgate Centre between when Kenny was killed and when they were in the café?' Jonah asked.

'It'd only take fifteen minutes in a car,' Joshua told him, 'or maybe a bit longer in the Christmas traffic, but we're assuming that he abandoned the car after hitting Kenny.'

'How about the bus?' suggested Bernie. 'It'd take a bit longer, but they're reasonably frequent during the daytime, and he might have been lucky and had one come along straight away.'

'I can check up on that,' Joshua said eagerly. 'You never know, the driver may remember him.'

'Good idea,' agreed Jonah, 'but let's just finish going through their movements after they both got to the city centre. We need to be systematic or we may miss something. Are there any other sightings of them together? Or any of Terry on his own?'

'They turn up together several times on the CCTV between fourteen forty and fifteen thirty three, when they left the car park together,' Joshua reported. 'Mrs Butler provided a sheaf of till receipts covering the period from when she arrived to when she left. Terry had a receipt for a pair of earrings, which he claims he bought as a surprise present for his wife between when she allegedly dropped him off in New Road and when they met up again at the café, but it only had a date on it not the time, and nobody in the shop remembers him particularly. Apparently they sold three or four of the same pairs that day.'

'How did he pay for them?' Jonah asked briskly.

'Cash. And the same goes for all the items that they attribute to him. Mrs Butler used a credit card for her shopping – well, apart from the coffees.'

'So she could've bought the things that they claim he bought,' Jonah murmured. 'How about this for a scenario? Holly Butler goes shopping, as she claims. Meanwhile, Terry goes to visit the Kidlington house for some reason. When he gets there, he sees the police outside, so he drives round the back to watch from there. He sees Harry making a break for it and tries to stop him talking by running him down, but this attempt misfires and he ends up killing Kenny. He drives off and dumps the car as soon as he reckons he's lost his pursuers, all the time working on how he's going to establish an alibi if he needs one. He rings Holly and arranges to meet up at the Westgate Centre – and he tells her to go round buying things with cash and keeping the receipts.'

'Then he makes his way into Oxford as quickly as he can,' Bernie continued enthusiastically, 'either by stealing another car or on the bus. They meet in the coffee shop and then spend a while wandering round the shops together, making themselves as conspicuous as possible to create the impression that they've both been there since before the incident in Kidlington.'

'Precisely!' Jonah agreed. 'It all fits perfectly. Josh! Go through their phone records and see if you can find evidence that they communicated with each other that afternoon. I'm going to find Stella and get her to have another look at Terry and see if she can't identify him as the driver of the car.'

In this he was disappointed. Stella shook her head vigorously at the suggestion.

'No,' she said decidedly. 'I'm sure the driver didn't have a beard. I told you – I think it may have been a woman. They had long black hair tied back in a ponytail.'

'How long would it take to grow a beard like Terry's?' pondered Bernie.

'Longer than the week he had between Kenny's death and when we picked him up,' Jonah replied in a dejected voice. He turned back to Stella. 'So you're saying it couldn't have been Terry or Stuart, what about Holly – *Mrs* Butler?'

'But she was in central Oxford all the time,' Bernie objected before Stella could reply.

'Not necessarily,' Jonah argued. 'Go on, Stella. Could she have been the driver?'

'Yes, I think so.' Stella stared down at the four photographs. 'I think it could have been her or this other one,' she added, pointing at the image of Shane Butler.

'Yes,' Jonah nodded. 'I was wondering about him, but as far as we can tell, he was down in Sussex at the time betting on horses at Plumpton racecourse. OK, thanks.' He turned to Bernie. 'I suppose we'd better have another look at Shane's alibi as well as considering whether there's any way Holly Butler could've got back from Kidlington in time to be on that CCTV picture at fourteen eighteen.'

Half an hour later, they were still no closer to breaking Holly Butler's alibi. Assuming that she had immediate access to another vehicle, it was just possible that she could have driven from Kidlington to central Oxford in time to be seen walking into the Westgate Centre on schedule, but she could not have made purchases in Marks & Spencer's twenty minutes earlier using her credit card, and the assistant who had served her was adamant that she would have noticed if the customer had been a man – especially one with such a prominent beard as Terry Butler's.

'Could it have been Shane driving?' suggested Bernie. 'And someone else gave him the betting slip that proved he was at Plumpton.'

'Don't forget whoever it was told the bookie that his name was Shane,' Jonah cautioned glumly. 'He could've been lying, but that means that he must have known that Shane was going to need an alibi.'

'OK. So Shane rings him, whoever he is, and tells him about the incident in Kidlington and asks him to place the bet in an ostentatious way to convince us that Shane was miles away when it happened.' Bernie countered. 'Did the bookie have a description for the man who claimed to be Shane?'

'We sent photographs of both Butler brothers and Stuart Hatton to Sussex Police,' Joshua reminded them. 'Shall I give them a buzz and see if they've shown them to the bookie yet?'

'Yes – you do that,' Jonah murmured. 'Mind you, I don't see how it could have been any of them other than Shane. We've got Terry's movements pinned down pretty well now – particularly from half past two onwards – so there's no way he could've been placing bets in Plumpton shortly after three. Stuart signed in at the Gym at twelve thirty. I suppose if he left right away he just *might* have got down there in time, but didn't one of the staff say he was still there later on?'

He sat for several minutes restlessly flicking through the case files on his screen. Then he looked up and caught Bernie's eye.

'Right!' he declared briskly. 'I think it's time we had another word with Bella Kennedy.'

He headed for the door. Bernie hastened to go ahead to open it for him and then followed him at a rapid pace along the corridor. They had just entered the lift when Jennifer Moorehouse called after them.

'Before you go, Sir!' but it was too late, the doors had closed before she could continue, 'I think you might like to have a look at this. It's the forensics report on those paint scrapings on the wall.'

* * *

Peter glanced down at his watch: eleven-thirty. Ricky and Abigail would be tucked up in bed, tired out after a strenuous day in the park with their father, designed to make them sleep despite their excited anticipation of the day ahead. Christmas was always particularly special when there were young children in the house, but Peter was not sorry to have got beyond that stage in his life. Midnight mass and then bed, uninterrupted by small people wanting to share the contents of their stockings in the early hours, suited him just fine.

The lights dimmed as Father Damien made his entrance accompanied by two altar servers dressed in white and carrying candles, which they set down on either side of the altar. The congregation got to their feet, casting dancing shadows in the flickering light from candles ranged along the windowsills and in holders on the pillars supporting the arched roof. Looking up, Peter saw the painted angels on the ceiling shining eerily as the candlelight caught the gilding on their wings and halos. The blue sky and puffy white clouds were hidden in darkness and, for the first time, he noticed small silver stars glinting among the angels.

Then he hastily brought his mind back to the words that were being spoken as Father Damien invited the people to confess their sins prior to receiving the sacrament.

'You were sent to heal the contrite,' intoned the priest. 'Lord have mercy.'

'Lord have mercy,' responded Peter and the rest of the congregation.

'You came to call sinners: Christ have mercy.'

'Christ have mercy.'

'You plead for us at the right hand of the Father: Lord have mercy.'

'Lord have mercy.'

A few moments of silence followed. Then a single spotlight came on, shining on Father Damien as he stood on the sanctuary steps holding up his hand in blessing and proclaiming absolution:

'May almighty God have mercy on us, forgive our sins, and bring us to everlasting life.'

'Amen,' everyone chorused.

The lights came back on and the congregation fumbled with their service sheets as the organ struck up the first hymn, which was Hark the Herald Angels Sing. When it was finished, they sat down again and Father Damien stepped forward and stood with his arms outstretched at the top of the sanctuary steps.

'Let us rejoice in the Lord!' he declaimed dramatically, 'for our Saviour is born to the world. True peace has descended from heaven.'

There were some prayers and then one of the servers stepped forward to read the familiar verse from the prophet Isaiah: 'The people that walked in darkness has seen a great light …'

Peter found it hard to concentrate. His mind kept drifting away from the familiar hymns and readings to Gavin: Gavin sitting bewildered in the hospital waiting room, Gavin packing Christmas away in a box before it had even begun, Gavin hunting for that last missing paper angel, and Gavin patiently coaxing Harry Whittle's brother to trust him.

And then there was Chrissie, with her bags and boxes of food that she handed round to anyone and everyone, while endlessly knitting garments for other people to wear. No doubt somewhere there was a lovingly-crafted jumper or scarf, painstakingly gift-wrapped all ready for Kenny to open on Christmas morning – except that there would be no more Christmas mornings for him. Had that reality permeated her mind yet? Or had all this busy-ness that she had occupied herself with succeeded in crowding out the painful truth?

They had both been out when Jonah called earlier that evening, hoping to give them a last progress report before he finally went off duty for the holiday period. Peter hoped that this meant that they were among friends who would make their time of waiting a little less unbearable.

As was his custom, after he had taken communion himself and given it to the servers, Father Damien came down the steps to the body of the church and stood waiting, with the ciborium in his hands, while the congregation formed a queue in the left-hand of the two aisles.

Feeling rather guilty for his inattention, Peter hastily crossed himself and genuflected towards the altar before following Jonah and Lucy out of their pew. Two years on from his decision to become a Catholic, these actions still felt clumsy and unfamiliar. He prayed silently for forgiveness as he waited his turn, glancing for reassurance towards the statue of Mary, which appeared more life-like than usual in the flickering light from candles encircling her feet.

After receiving the elements, they all processed across the front of the church and back up the other aisle. As they neared the back of the church, Peter was surprised to see a familiar figure sitting on the last row. What on earth was Gavin doing here? What could have induced him to come and sit in a Roman Catholic church in a different part of town from where he lived? Chrissie was there too, looking very smart in a black hat and coat with a silver brooch on the collar. She looked up and smiled at them as they approached. Then she nudged her husband and he slid along to the end of the pew to speak to them.

'We're only here because of Brendan,' he whispered to Peter. 'He got permission to come, but only with a police escort. I've promised to see him safely back to the hostel after the service.'

Peter nodded and then placed his hand briefly on Gavin's shoulder before following the procession of people, which wound round behind the pews and back down the left-hand aisle to their seats. Gazing round the building, he spotted Brendan Connolly on his way up the other aisle, having received communion from Father Damien shortly before.

'Don't run away after the service,' came Jonah's voice from behind him, whispering in Gavin's ear as he passed. 'I've got some news for you.'

They resumed their seats and waited expectantly as Father Damien went back up the steps and replaced the ciborium on the altar. Then he turned to face the congregation and pronounced the solemn blessing. There was silence for thirty seconds; then the organ started playing the final hymn: O Come, All Ye Faithful.

'Can you just give me a moment to take off these glad rags?' Father Damien said to Peter and the others after he had closed the door on the last of his parishioners. 'I'm all agog to hear the latest news. Just go on through to the lounge – Peter knows the way. That will be alright, will it? You can spare a few minutes?' he added anxiously, looking towards Brendan.

'Yes,' Gavin answered for him. 'We've got permission. Just so long as we get him back to the hostel before two, everything will be fine.'

'Good,' Damien smiled, 'and help yourselves to coffee. There's a jug keeping warm in the kitchen – Peter will know where to find everything.'

Peter led the way through the vestry into the adjoining presbytery.

'This way,' he said, opening a door on the left and ushering them into a large room furnished with an assortment of easy chairs and sofas. He felt rather awkward, acting as host in someone else's home – except that this room felt institutional rather than homely. It was reserved for church meetings, with Damien choosing to spend his own time – insofar as a priest ever has time that can truly be called his own – divided between the kitchen and his study.

'Sit down,' Peter urged them, gesturing vaguely round the room. 'I'll get the coffee.'

He escaped to the kitchen, leaving the others to settle into chairs and make awkward conversation while they waited for Father Damien to join them so that the real talking could begin. How strange it was that they had all landed up here tonight – or rather this morning! Who would have thought that Brendan would suddenly get the urge to come to mass at his boyhood church, which he had not attended for – what? Thirty years? Perhaps nearer to forty. And what a coincidence that Gavin had been there and had volunteered to accompany him so that he could get round his curfew!

'You're managing OK?' Damien's voice broke through Peter's thoughts. He entered the kitchen, dressed now in black trousers and a turtle neck sweater. 'Good! Put the cups on this tray here. If you carry that, I'll go ahead and open the doors for you. And we mustn't forget these,' he added, picking up a large biscuit tin. 'Raisin cookies! Deirdre's Christmas gift – just in case I was in any danger of starving myself over the festive period!'

Soon everyone was settled with a cup of coffee and a biscuit from the huge supply that Damien's ever-solicitous parishioner had given him. Gavin looked expectantly toward Jonah, who cleared his throat while Damien tapped on the table with a teaspoon for silence.

'I'm glad you're both here,' Jonah began, looking towards Gavin and Chrissie, 'and you too, Brendan. I wanted to let you know the latest news before it gets out in the media. We've charged Shane Butler with murdering Kenny, and his brother, Terry, and sister-in-law, Holly, are both being charged as accessories.'

'Those are the drug-dealers that you arrested at the same time as Brendan – is that right?' Gavin asked. 'I thought you said they all had alibis?'

'They did,' Jonah nodded, smiling grimly, 'but we managed to see through them – in the end!'

'The final breakthrough was when Sussex Police had another talk with the bookie at Plumpton who supposedly took a bet from Shane Butler that afternoon,' Bernie explained, with a satisfied grin. 'He said that the man calling himself Shane had a black beard, which meant that either he was wearing a false one or it *wasn't* Shane Butler!'

'And when we re-checked the CCTV footage of *Terry* Butler's activity in Oxford that day, his whole face was never visible,' Jonah continued. 'Either he had his back to the camera or the lower part of his face was covered with a scarf.'

'Which we should've realised was suspicious, given how mild it's been for December,' Bernie added.

'Piecing everything together,' Jonah went on, 'we reckon this is how they managed it. Terry went off to Plumpton that morning. (We've got Sussex Police working on finding more sightings of him, now we know it was him who was down there.) Mrs Butler was at home all morning and went off for her shopping expedition in the afternoon, just as she said, except that Terry wasn't with her. Meanwhile, Shane goes over to Kidlington to check up on the cannabis business. He takes a stolen car as a matter of routine, just to be sure he doesn't leave any sort of trail back to any of the family. We assume he was intending to bring some supplies back with him, and didn't want his own car to have traces of an illegal substance left in it.'

'It turns out to be a good move from his point of view,' Bernie grinned, 'because, lo and behold! What does he find when he gets there, but a police raid going on?'

'He goes round the back, where he can watch without being seen and the first thing he sees is Harry Whittle making a break for it and getting caught by Kenny and Stella,' Jonah continued, clearly enjoying himself. 'His first thought is that Harry could land them all in it if he talks to the police, so he hits the gas and does his best to silence him permanently; but Kenny's too quick for him and he pushes Harry and Stella out of the way, getting hit himself as a consequence.'

'Now Shane's in the position of having potentially killed a police officer,' Bernie took up the tale again, 'and he's desperate not to be caught. So he drives off and then dumps the car as soon as he thinks he's lost his pursuers. He rings his brother and his sister-in-law-'

'We've got evidence of those calls from his phone records,' Jonah broke in, 'and also a call from Holly Butler to Stuart Hatton, who drops everything and drives from the gym, where he's working out, to pick Shane up. He drops him off in the centre of Oxford and heads off home where he makes a point of picking a fight with one of his neighbours over who parks where in front of the houses, thus establishing that he was back there before three.'

'Which is the time that Shane was supposedly placing a bet at Plumpton and Holly was drinking coffee in the Westgate Centre, ostensibly with her husband,' Bernie added.

'And less than an hour after Stuart was reported to have been seen at the gym,' Jonah put in. 'In other words, they successfully created the illusion that they were all elsewhere for the whole of that afternoon. Our first thought was that it must have been Terry driving the car, because he was the only one who could have had time to get from the crime scene to the first sighting of him after the incident. Actually, it was Bella who gave us the tip-off that cracked the case.'

'Bella?' queried Gavin, looking puzzled. 'You mean Bella Kennedy?'

'That's right,' Jonah nodded. 'When we thought the alibis were stacking up and it couldn't have been any of the Butler gang, we brought her in for questioning again.'

'Again?' Gavin continued to stare at him in bemusement.

'I suppose we never told you,' Jonah apologised. 'Bella was there. She was driving back from a job interview in North Oxford. She saw Kenny and Stella getting out of the police van and going round to the back of the house together. She told us that she got out of her car and watched from behind a tree.'

'But why?' demanded Chrissie, who up until now had not appeared to be taking much notice of the conversation. She sat with her discarded coat lying across the back of her chair nervously picking pieces of fluff off her skirt, as if she needed something to do with her hands in the absence of her, until now ubiquitous, knitting. 'What was she expecting to see?'

'She seemed to have got the impression that Kenny was in a relationship with Stella,' Bernie explained. 'She didn't seem to be able to accept that it was just work.'

'Anyway,' Jonah continued, 'when it started looking as if the Butlers were innocent – of murder, at least – we brought her in and went through it all with her again. I was really starting to think that she might have done it out of jealousy – especially after I'd seen the marks on her car where she'd scraped the front wing.'

'But that was nothing to do with the incident, as it turns out,' Bernie added. 'Bella told us it had been there for months.'

'But we didn't know whether to believe her until we read the forensic report confirming that the paint on the wall came from the stolen car after all,' Jonah continued, 'and that wasn't until after we'd got her back and were interviewing her under caution. That put us in a bit of a fix, I have to admit. All five of our suspects seemed to have been ruled out.'

'But you said that Bella told you something that cracked the case,' Gavin reminded him. 'What was that?'

'She identified Shane as the man in the car,' Bernie explained. 'We showed her pictures of them all and she picked him out.'

'Which was a bit of a puzzler for us, because we thought we'd established that he was a hundred miles away at the time!' put in Jonah cheerily. 'That's when we had to do a bit of lateral thinking, and we worked out that, if it was *Shane* who was going round the shops with Holly, then Terry could've been standing in for his brother down in Plumpton. All the logistics that we'd worked out when we thought Terry was driving worked just as well if it was Shane. All we had to do was to find someone who could give a positive identification either of Terry in Plumpton or Shane in Oxford and we'd have them banged to rights!'

'Which is where the bookie remembering that "Shane" had a beard comes in,' Bernie added triumphantly.

'I'm sorry, could you go through it all again?' Gavin asked, shaking his head slowly and frowning in puzzlement. 'I'm confused now. Which of these two Butler brothers has the beard?'

'Terry – the older one,' Jonah told him promptly. 'He probably grew it so as to avoid being recognised as the bogus Mr McLeod who rented the house in Kidlington.'

'Now you've got *me* completely lost!' Damien declared. 'Who's this Mr McLeod? And where does he come in?'

'Terry Butler and his wife, Holly, used those names when they rented a house for the purposes of growing cannabis,' Jonah explained. 'That's where all this started. The real Mr and Mrs McLeod are living totally blameless lives in Dundee, so just forget about them. The point is, the Butlers stole their identities in order to rent the house, but then they didn't want to be associated with the tenancy in case the cannabis factory was discovered, so they changed their appearances from the photos on their false passports.'

'I see,' Damien nodded. 'So "Mr McLeod" was clean-shaven and – *Terry* Butler, was it? – grew a beard, so as to look different?'

'That's right,' Jonah confirmed. 'And Holly changed her hair and wore different makeup. But, to get back to the day Kenny was killed, we now know that it was Terry's brother, Shane, who went to the house in Kidlington and found that there was a police raid going on. He must've known that Harry Whittle was inside and might reveal their identities if he talked to the police, so–'

'I'm sorry,' Damien interrupted. 'You've lost me again. Harry Whittle?'

'He was a teenager that the Butlers recruited to cultivate their cannabis plants. We don't know how he came to be mixed up with them, but we think it's quite possible he didn't actually know what he was getting himself into – or at very least, not until it was too late to get out again. He was clearly terrified of what they might do to him if he grassed on them, and he was probably right to be, seeing as it looks as if Shane's first thought when he made a run for it was to silence him by ramming him with the car.'

'So you're sure it was Harry who was the target?' Lucy asked eagerly. 'Not Stella or Kenny?'

'That's certainly what it looks like,' Jonah replied, 'and that's the story that Terry eventually came up with when he finally accepted that we'd sussed his brother's alibi. Of course, he may just have worked out that admitting to covering up the intentional killing of a police officer would be a bad move. Shane's insisting that it was an accident, but with his brother and sister-in-law telling a different story, I can't see any jury buying that defence.'

'Stella will be relieved,' Lucy told him. 'She felt guilty that they might have been aiming for her and got Kenny instead. The worst would have been if it really had been Bella driving and it was all about her being jealous of Stella.'

'Was she …?' Chrissie began suddenly. Then, in some

confusion she amended her words. 'I mean, were she and Kenny … close? He never said anything.'

'They weren't going out together,' Lucy answered confidently, 'but I know she liked him a lot.'

'Everyone did,' Bernie confirmed. 'I know that everyone suddenly becomes the most popular person in the place as soon as they die, but everyone who worked with him seems genuine when they keep saying how much they depended on him.'

'Did you – did you just say that this Shane has *confessed* to killing Kenny?' Gavin asked slowly, turning over what he had heard in his mind and trying to make sense of it. 'He actually said that?'

'Yes,' Jonah confirmed. 'It was a long time before he came round to it, but-'

'You can say that again!' Bernie broke in. 'I was on the very verge of putting my foot down and telling you, you *had* to call it a day because it was Christmas Eve and you were *not* going to be allowed to make us late home, when he finally cracked. I suppose it was me mithering you to go home that tempted you to use that underhand trick with Bella's cigarette?'

'Bella told us she'd seen Shane drop a cigarette end out of the car,' Jonah explained, seeing the puzzled expressions on the faces of his audience. 'I merely told Shane that we'd got it and sort of hinted that the DNA on it would prove he was there. I'm sure we *have* got it,' he added, grinning round unrepentantly, 'along with far too much other stuff to have wasted resources on random DNA testing. The SOCOs were very thorough.'

'But Shane didn't know how expensive DNA tests are or how long they take,' Bernie added, 'so he was taken in.'

'But it was only when he discovered that Terry and Holly had admitted to covering for him that he realised there was no point keeping up the pretence,' Jonah went on. 'I confronted Terry with the statement from the bookie, confirming that he was the one who placed that bet. He immediately started to backtrack, and so did his missus. They both knew they were going down on drugs charges anyway and they decided they'd better co-operate with us in the hope of mitigating their sentences. The same goes for Stuart Hatton – except that he's claiming he had no idea why Shane needed him to drive him into town. According to him, he was only following orders!'

'Stuart Hatton?' asked Damien.

'Oh, he's not important!' Jonah declared dismissively. 'He's just a professional heavy that the Butlers employed to put the fear of God into anyone who didn't dance to their tune. We're holding him on a charge of being an accessory after the fact, but it's possible he may manage to slip through our fingers on that one, if he holds his nerve. I've got better hopes of pinning him down to the death of Harry Whittle – strangulation definitely seems just up his street! That'll most likely all come down to the forensic evidence – which won't be ready until the labs start working again after the holiday. It's a real nuisance that this all kicked off just before Christmas!'

'OK Scrooge,' Bernie laughed, 'save your bah humbugs for later. Just be pleased we've got them all in custody for killing Kenny. I expect you'll be able to pin them down for the other murder once everyone gets back to work next week. At least there you've got some genuine DNA evidence to go on!'

'Have you?' Gavin looked enquiringly at Jonah.

'Yes. Harry fought back. There were some fragments of skin from this attacker under his fingernails. So long as he wasn't killed by someone new that we don't know about yet, we should have that sorted too, as soon as the labs are working again after Christmas.'

10. CHRISTMAS DAY

Christmas Day felt strange this year. The routine was the same: the morning service at the Methodist church, where they met Bernie's old friends, Stan and Sylvia, and brought them back to spend the rest of the day as part of the family; opening presents around the big tree in the hall; the traditional Christmas dinner of roast turkey followed by one of Sylvia's Christmas puddings; and then, in the afternoon, the grandchildren coming round, eager to show off their new toys; but somehow it all felt different this time. Peter could not quite put his finger on it, but there was something not quite right.

For no reason that he could make out, he felt tears pricking at the back of his eyes as he watched the children rolling on the floor giggling happily in some riotous game with their father. Then later, when little Abigail fell asleep in his arms, exhausted by the excitement of the day, he had to pull down the paper crown from his cracker over his face to hide the moisture on his cheeks, as an overwhelming sadness engulfed him at the thought that Angie had not lived to see her grandchildren.

After he had composed himself again, he pushed the tissue paper back up and looked across the room at the smiling portrait of his first wife, which stood on the mantelpiece. Although he thought of her often, it was a long time since he had felt the pain of losing her so acutely. People assumed that he had "got over it" and "moved on". So he had, but he was not the same person he had been before she died.

Where was she now? Did she know that she was a

grandmother? Could she see them now? – Abigail contented in her grandfather's arms and Ricky riding his father's back, as Eddie crawled round the floor pretending to be a horse. Father Damien seemed to think so. He did not laugh when Peter confessed that he sometimes still talked to Angie. He spoke of the Communion of Saints as if the dead were still quite close and still interested in the antics of those left behind.

Even so, it was still so unfair! Angie might be able to see her grandchildren growing up, but she would never be able to reach out and touch them. They would never fall exhausted on to her lap or smother her with wet kisses or tell her that she was the best gran in the world! Surely that must make her sad, if she were really looking down on them as Damien seemed to think?

But maybe it was Jonah who had got it right? He said that praying to saints was nonsense, because when you died you knew nothing more until the Resurrection. In a way, that was a more comforting thought: Angie asleep, unaware of what was going on in the world that she was no longer part of. Perhaps it would be more like a form of torture for her to watch and be unable to intervene – unable to share their joys or comfort their sorrows? And yet, he did hope that she could see and care.

'Let me relieve you of Abby,' Eddie's voice broke through Peter's thoughts, jerking him back to reality. 'It's time we were going. After such a long day, I don't want the kids getting a late night.'

'Time we were making a move too,' Stan said, pushing himself up by the arms of the upright chair near the window, which was reserved for him because it suited his arthritis. He smiled round at everyone. 'Thank you for having us again – and thank you, Eddie, for bringing the kids. It's lovely to see them growing up.'

'Thank you for putting up with them,' Eddie grinned back. 'They can be a real handful sometimes. And thanks especially for letting them hold one of your pigeons. Ricky's really made up about it.'

'He's welcome,' Stan smiled back. He had been a pigeon fancier most of his life and loved showing off the small flock of birds, which he kept in a loft at the bottom of Bernie's extensive garden.

'Before you go,' his wife, Sylvia, added, 'we've got one more present each for the kids. She took two small gift-wrapped packages out of her handbag and held them out towards Eddie. Then she turned to look at Ricky, who was gazing up expectantly. 'They're for you both to open after you're in bed,' she said firmly. 'And if you give Daddy any trouble, he has my permission to keep them for himself instead. Do you understand?'

'Yes, Aunty Sylvie,' Ricky answered, nodding vigorously.

'Thank you very much, but you really shouldn't,' Eddie protested.

'Don't be a daft ha'p'orth!' Stan clapped him on the back. 'We don't have any grandkids of our own, so we're grateful to you for sharing your bairns with us.'

As he and Bernie helped their friends into their coats, Peter debated with himself whether to ask Stan and Sylvia to visit Gavin. He knew that they would be willing. When the news came out that a young police officer had been killed, they had come round with a card, "for his poor parents," even before they knew that Gavin was a personal friend. They had lost their son, Stephen, to suicide forty years previously and wanted Kenny's mother and father to know that they were not alone in their sorrow.

Wouldn't they be the ideal people to help Gavin and Chrissie to cope with their grief? Perhaps, but then again, maybe it was too soon. Would whatever words Stan and Sylvia used create the impression that they were over their loss? Would their demeanour offer no outward sign that their hearts were broken and their world ended? Did Gavin and Chrissie want to know – now when their loss was so new and their pain so raw – that a time would come when they would discover that life goes on, but in a different way?

Anyway, it was too late now. Bernie was helping Sylvia and

Stan into the car ready to drive them home. He would mention it to Gavin next time he saw him. It would be better if he and Chrissie decided when, and if, they wanted to meet other bereaved parents.

He stood on the step waving to Eddie, who had Abigail in the pushchair and Ricky at his side, as they walked away down the drive. He was so lucky, he reflected. He had two wonderful children – not to mention a most exceptional stepdaughter – and four adorable grandchildren, and so much to look forward to in the years to come. How could he begin to imagine what it was like for Gavin now that all that had been so cruelly snatched away from him?

He closed the door, nodding absently to Lucy who was volunteering to help Jonah with his evening physiotherapy. He suddenly felt the need to contact Gavin urgently. Whether or not he had gone with Chrissie to the Christmas lunch with the homeless community, that would all be over by now and they would be alone at home. And it was the first time that they would be spending Christmas night without Kenny there with them.

He half expected that there would be no answer when he rang Gavin's mobile number, but the response was immediate, almost as if Gavin had been waiting for a call; and he sounded different – anxious and confused. Of course, he hadn't been himself since Kenny died, but this was a different sort of anxiety somehow.

'Hi Gavin. I just thought I'd give you a ring. See how you and Chrissie are doing.' Peter wished he could think of something less banal and stupid to say, but this was the best he could manage.

'Oh, hello Peter. Thanks for ringing.'

Something in Gavin's tone of voice and the short intake of breath at the end of his words set alarm bells ringing in Peter's mind. 'Are you OK?'

'Yes. Yes, we're fine; just a bit all-in after the Homeless party.'

There was something wrong here, but Peter did not want

to intrude. He floundered around trying to think of words to keep the conversation going in the hope of learning more, or else of obtaining reassurance that his worries were unfounded.

'How did the party go?' he asked at last.

'OK.' Gavin paused momentarily, 'It was good, I suppose,' he added. 'Chrissie's Christmas puddings and mince pies went down very well, as usual.'

There was still something wrong in his voice, but Peter could not work out what it was. Perhaps he was just tired after a busy day.

'Good. Was Craig there – and the others?'

'Yes. They were all there.'

'It was good of you to come to midnight mass with Brendan. I know it meant a lot to him to be there.'

'It was the least I could do, and … and I haven't been sleeping very well recently, so having an excuse to be out late was all to the good as far as I was concerned.'

'Would it be OK for me to come round?' Peter asked, suddenly making up his mind that *he* needed to see Gavin and assure himself that there was nothing amiss – well, nothing more than the obvious, anyway – even if Gavin did not need his company. 'We've got loads of sausage rolls and samosas, which we got in for tea and then didn't eat because we'd stuffed ourselves with turkey at lunch time. It'd save you cooking – if you're both tired.'

'Oh, I couldn't possibly ask you to!' Gavin exclaimed at once. Peter noted that he did not suggest that such a visit would be unwelcome. 'You must be busy, with the family and everything.'

'They've all gone off and left me!' Peter declared. 'The grandkids have gone home to bed now, so I'm all alone and lonesome while Bernie's off to Cowley with some old friends and Lucy's seeing to Jonah's physio. You'd be doing me a service, getting me out of the house for a bit and helping us to eat up some of that food.'

'Well, if you're sure?' Gavin answered tentatively. 'I wouldn't mind a bit of company, if I'm honest. And it would probably help Chris-.' He broke off suddenly and then resumed in a slightly different voice, speaking much quicker than usual. 'I mean, I'm sure Chrissie would like to see you too.'

'Good. I'll be over in about twenty minutes then.'

'Thank you for coming,' Gavin murmured apologetically as he let Peter into the house. 'Come through to the kitchen,' he added looking down at Peter's foil-wrapped parcels. 'We'll put those in the fridge for later.' Then he leaned over the bannister rail and called up the stairs, 'Chrissie darling! Peter's here!'

Looking round the kitchen, Peter spotted the refrigerator and went over to put away the packets of food. He squeezed them in on the bottom shelf next to a half-eaten meat pie. Straightening up, he turned to see Gavin at the sink, filling the electric kettle.

'Sit down.' He indicated a high stool next to a breakfast bar, which extended from the wall near to where the kettle was plugged in. 'I'll make us some tea.'

Peter climbed on to the stool and leaned his elbows on the counter. He watched silently as Gavin replaced the kettle on its stand and then crossed the kitchen and opened a glass-fronted wall cupboard containing crockery. While his back was turned, Peter reached over and pressed down the switch on the kettle prompting the power light to come on and the kettle to hiss encouragingly.

Gavin returned with a stainless-steel teapot and three cups and saucers, which he put down on a metal tray that lay on the working surface next to the kettle.

'I don't suppose Chrissie will be long,' he said, reaching for a packet of teabags and starting to count them out into the teapot. 'She's in Kenny's room, sorting out his things.'

'I thought your sister did all that when she was here at the weekend?'

'Umm. Well that's another thing,' Gavin mumbled miserably, adding two more teabags to the pot. 'I made her stop. I behaved very badly about it. I don't know if she'll ever forgive me.'

'Of course she will,' Peter told him emphatically, grasping Gavin's hand gently in his and moving it away from the teapot, 'unless you keep giving her tea as strong as the pot you're making for us just now!' he added, smiling across the breakfast bar at his friend.

Gavin gazed down at the teapot. Then he turned it over and shook it. A dozen or more teabags fell out on to the work surface. He looked up at Peter and managed a brief grin in return.

'I don't seem to be able to concentrate on anything these days,' he muttered, shaking his head at his own ineptitude. 'This morning I squirted Chrissie's face cream on to my toothbrush instead of toothpaste!'

'Don't worry. It's all part of the process,' Peter assured him gently. 'That part won't last for ever. Just try not to let it bother you too much. And seriously: your sister will understand that whatever you did was only because of what you're going through. I'm sure she won't hold it against you.'

Gavin put three teabags into the pot and then busied himself trying to squeeze the remaining ones back into the packet.

'I haven't shouted at Lorraine like that since the time she deliberately broke the head off my action man when I was seven,' he told Peter morosely. 'I don't know what got into me. It was after we got back from our walk. Remember? You didn't come in because you needed to get off home, so I said I'd say your goodbyes to Chrissie and the others.'

Peter nodded.

'I was feeling a lot better for having got out in the fresh air for a bit,' Gavin continued, 'and I thought we'd be able to finish agreeing on the funeral arrangements before it was time for them to get off to the station, and then Chrissie and I would have the house to ourselves again.'

The kettle clicked off and Gavin picked it up and added boiling water to the teapot.

'But then, when I got in, there was Chrissie in the kitchen, weeping buckets into that box of Kenny's things that Dennis had brought down from his room. Do you remember?'

Peter nodded.

'She said she wanted them to stop. She said she didn't want anyone else messing with Kenny's things. I just grabbed the box and stormed upstairs with it and threw it down on the bed and told them to put everything back where they'd found it and then get out of the house.'

'I don't blame you,' Peter said with feeling, imagining how he would have felt if anyone had touched any of Angie's possessions uninvited. 'And I'm sure, when she thinks about it, your sister won't either,' he added firmly. 'She's probably stressed out too, with thinking about the way Kenny was killed, and I'm sure she thought she was helping.'

'I know,' Gavin groaned. 'That's what makes me shouting at her like that so awful.'

'Not at all,' Peter insisted. 'Honestly. At a time like this you really can't be held responsible for what you do. I'm just amazed at how well you're both holding things together. I still can't get over how Chrissie coped with that nativity play. She was wonderful.'

'It was because she didn't want to let down the kids,' Gavin told him, wandering over to the fridge and getting out a bottle of milk. He brought it across the room, and set it down on the working surface next to the tray. 'It was the same this morning. She was up at six getting everything ready for the Homeless party; and then, while we were there, she was pulling crackers and joking with them, almost as if … as if …'

He picked up the milk and returned it to the fridge.

'Chrissie's always been the practical one,' he resumed, leaning across the worktop so that his face was close to Peter's. 'She keeps the house running like clockwork, and she always likes to keep busy. I think all the time she had things she had to do, she could push what happened to Kenny to the back of her mind and just get on with getting them done. That's why Lorraine coming in and trying to take over was such a disaster. And that's why …'

He wiped his hand across his face and turned away to look for something in one of the wall cupboards.

'You don't take sugar, do you Peter?' he enquired, turning round again and holding up a bag of it.

'No, but I would like some milk, if that's OK.'

'Haven't I just …?' Gavin stared blankly at the empty cups and then shuffled over to the fridge again.

'As I was saying,' he resumed as he poured milk into each cup. 'Chrissie was there being the life and soul of the party and I was just sitting in the corner wishing it was all over and we could go home and maybe just sit for a bit and watch a film on the telly. But then, when we got home … I suppose it was the anti-climax, and not having any reason to keep going anymore.'

Peter picked up the milk bottle and returned it to the fridge to give Gavin time to collect his thoughts.

'When we walked in the door, the first thing we saw was that teddy bear in the police costume – you know, the one somebody left with the flowers?'

'Mmm,' Peter nodded. 'I remember.'

'Chrissie had washed it and put it on the radiator in the hall to dry. Anyway, she just picked it up and went upstairs with it. She said she needed to sort out Kenny's things. I did try to persuade her to leave it for a bit – at least until we'd had a sit down – but she said she needed to feel close to him again. I realised afterwards that Wednesday was her day for tidying Kenny's room. She used to do it while he was out at the Scouts. I suppose it probably helped her to keep to the old routine. Anyway, I made us a mug of tea and took hers up to her. I know I ought to have stayed with her and helped, but I just couldn't face it.'

'Don't beat yourself up about it,' Peter said gently. 'Everyone grieves differently. And if Chrissie always tidies Kenny's room on her own, she may not even have wanted you there.'

'The thing is: when I got up there, she wasn't tidying the room. She was just sitting there on the bed holding that teddy bear and staring into space. I put the mug down on the bedside table and came downstairs again. I've been up again a couple of times, but she's still just the same – staring ahead like she was in a trance. So that's where she is now,' he finished. 'I don't think she can have heard me call. I'd better go up and get her. She won't want to have missed you.'

He looked towards the door, but made no attempt to move from his position, leaning on the worktop. Then suddenly he looked up and caught Peter's eye across the breakfast bar.

'Why did it happen to Kenny?' he demanded in an anguished voice. 'Why was he the one who got sent round the back of the house? With his whole life before him! Why couldn't it have been me they picked instead?' He brought both fists down heavily on the work top, staring across at Peter defiantly for a moment before dropping his head and gazing down at the marble-effect work surface.

For a long time, neither of them moved or spoke. Then Gavin straightened up and gave Peter a sheepish grin. 'I'm sorry. I didn't mean to …. I'll go and get Chrissie.' He looked down at the teacups. 'Could you take those through to the front room? We won't be long.'

Peter came round to the other side of breakfast bar to pick up the tray. As he passed Gavin he gave him a pat on the shoulder. 'Please believe me. It never goes away, but it won't always be as bad as this.'

Peter put the tray down on the table below the television set and stood back to wait for Gavin to return with Chrissie. Should he sit down? There were just the three armchairs in the room now, looking as if they were grouped together, clearly designed for family evenings-in watching the television. It suddenly occurred to him that one of them must be Kenny's chair – but which one? And would it be worse to sit in it himself or to force Gavin or Chrissie to do so?

'Hello Peter! How lovely to see you!' Chrissie entered the room, still holding the police teddy bear. She opened her arms wide and gave Peter an unexpected hug, which he forced himself to accept, but did not make eye contact. Peter did not go in for this sort of thing in public, even with Bernie, and he was glad when Chrissie released him and gestured towards the chairs. 'Sit down please! Don't stand on ceremony.'

Peter hesitated. Having thought of the chair issue, he did not like to choose any of them for fear of getting it wrong. Gavin immediately collapsed into the middle chair but Chrissie seemed to be waiting for Peter to sit down first. Perhaps that meant it didn't matter which chair he picked, but …

To gain time he decided to broach the subject of Stan and Sylvia.

"There are a couple of friends of mine,' he ventured tentatively. 'Well, they're Bernie's friends really. Their son died young too – even younger than Kenny. Would you like us to introduce you to them? I'm sure they'd be happy to talk to you.'

'That's very kind of you,' Chrissie smiled back, settling down in the chair on Gavin's left. 'If you're sure they won't-'

'I think I'd rather not.' Gavin interrupted, 'or, at least … maybe later – after the funeral's over.'

'There was a card came from a couple who said they knew you,' Chrissie remembered. She got up and went across to the row of cards on the windowsill. 'This is the one I think. Yes! It says Stan and Sylvia Corbridge, and there's a phone number. Could you thank them for us, Peter, and tell them we'll be in touch later – when we're both ready.'

Peter sat down in the chair at Gavin's right and racked his brains for things to say. He must not avoid speaking about Kenny, as if their grief were an embarrassment to him, but he should not dwell on it too much either. Was there some subject of normal conversation that he could bring up? But nothing was normal for Chrissie and Gavin anymore.

'Stella and I saw that bear when we were in Kidlington the other day,' he said at last. 'Do you have any idea who left it?'

Chrissie shook her head.

'Lucy's got one a bit like it,' Peter continued. 'She's had it since she was two. He's called Richard, after her dad. He's not as smart as that one though – one of his ears is chewed and he's gone a bit bald round the back. Most of her old toys are up in the attic, or passed on to my grandchildren, but she's still got that one. She even took him with her to Liverpool when she went up there to uni.'

'Kenny gave all his toys to the scout jumble sale,' Chrissie murmured dreamily. 'I said he ought to keep some of them for when he had kids of his own, but he said he'd rather do some good with them now. It turned out he was right, didn't it?'

She looked up at Peter and this time their eyes met. He smiled gently back unable to think of a fitting response. He took a sip of tea and wondered what to say next. Chrissie turned to speak to Gavin.

'I was wondering what to put in the coffin with Kenny. You remember the funeral director said people often put in some personal effects. That's why I wanted to go through his things. I thought I might find something that he'd have liked to have with him. But in the end, I couldn't face it.'

'Maybe Lorraine was right: pack it all in boxes and then go through it bit by bit,' suggested Gavin.

'So I was wondering if there was something else that we could use,' Chrissie continued as if she had not heard this remark. 'I want to put in *something*. I don't know why. I'd just like to … well, it just seemed like a nice idea when she suggested it … sort of our last … Oh! I don't know!' She sighed rather helplessly and then looked down at the teddy bear. 'I was wondering about this. What do you think, Gav?'

'If you like,' Gavin answered wearily. Peter could see that he could not understand his wife's desire for this gesture and, as he had said previously in regard to the funeral, "just wanted to get it over with".

'Whatever you choose, you need to be sure you won't regret not still having it afterwards,' Peter cautioned gently. 'If I was the person who thought of leaving that bear with the flowers for Kenny, I might be really pleased if he was somewhere people could see him at the funeral, rather than inside the coffin.'

Chrissie looked towards him with a pensive expression as if she were turning this idea over in her mind.

'One or two of the parents have been in touch to say their children want to come,' she said after a long pause. 'With all the media coverage, they feel they know Kenny, even though he's only been to the school a couple of times. I haven't got back to them yet. I don't like to say "no", but I'm not sure if it'd be the best thing for *them* to be there. They've probably never been in a church before, let alone to a funeral! I suppose this might give them something better to focus on than … Or better!' She became more animated now that she was back in the role of a school teacher, thinking about what would be best for her class. 'I think I'd better call on them to explain that this is something for grown-ups only. I'll take the bear with me – we must think of a name for him – and tell them that, although they can't come, he'll be there for them, and I'll bring him into school afterwards to tell them about it.'

'That sounds like a good idea,' Gavin agreed, relieved at Chrissie's improved mood. 'Better wait for a few days to let them get over Christmas and then give them a ring.'

'Yes.' Chrissie sat back, thinking. 'I've got some books somewhere … I must look them out, so I can take them with me. "Badger's parting gift" is a good one for when children's grandparents die, but I'm not sure about … It does talk a lot about badger being ready to die because he was getting old and … Maybe "The Velveteen Rabbit" would be a better one.'

'My kids loved that one,' Peter commented. 'We read it over and over when they were small and then I caught Eddie looking at it again after Angie died. He was a young man by then, so he was dreadfully embarrassed.'

Chrissie smiled and nodded. Gavin reached out and took her hand in his. They all sat in silence, lost in their own thoughts.

'But I still need to think of something to go inside with Kenny!' Chrissie exclaimed all of a sudden, looking as if she were about to burst into tears in frustration at her own inability to decide. 'I want him to have something special, from me.'

'Perhaps you could knit something for him,' Peter suggested, spotting Chrissie's bag of wool and needles under her chair.

'Yes! Of course!' Chrissie leapt to her feet in an abrupt movement that caused the teddy bear to fall to the floor and roll underneath the table. She crossed the room and began rummaging in a drawer. She pulled out a pile of knitting patterns, settled back in her seat and started sifting through them on her lap. Gavin got down on the floor and retrieved the teddy bear from under the table. He sat down next to his wife with the bear perched incongruously on his lap.

'Oh look, Gav! Do you remember these? Noddy and Big Ears! I knitted these for Kenny's second birthday.' Chrissie held up two knitting patterns with pictures of the gaily-coloured characters. 'And here's the jumper I made for him when he was six – and the hat with the rabbit ears! I suppose all these patterns ought to go to someone with children. It's a pity to have them just gathering dust in that drawer.'

'I wouldn't be too hasty,' Peter cautioned gently. 'You might want to keep them for the memories. You could always *lend* them to people if you don't like to see them wasted.'

'Yes,' Chrissie murmured, continuing to sort through the patterns on her lap. 'Maybe you're right.' Then, 'How many grandchildren do you have?' she asked unexpectedly.

'Four,' Peter answered, conscious that his voice sounded apologetic, as if he were ashamed of his good fortune. 'My daughter Hannah has two little girls. They're nine and six. I don't see very much of them because they live in Leeds. She went there to train as a nurse and decided to stay. When she went away, I imagined she'd come back and work in the John Radcliffe with her mum, but ….' He allowed his voice to trail off, not liking to bring up the subject of Angie's death again, in case it sounded as if he were suggesting that his experience of bereavement justified him in believing that he understood their pain. He had hated it when other people claimed to "know exactly how you must be feeling" – as if anyone could even begin to comprehend the desolation that Angie's death

210

had brought to him. 'And then my son, Eddie, has a boy and a girl,' he finished quickly. 'They've got a flat in the Windrush Tower. I look after them quite often because Eddie and Crystal both work.'

'You saw them at the Nativity play,' Gavin reminded her. 'Ricky was the bright spark who kept calling out.'

'I hope he didn't put your pupils off,' Peter apologised. 'He was very taken with the wheelchair animals, and he doesn't seem to be able to enjoy anything without telling the world about it!'

'Typical pre-school child!' Chrissie laughed, looking almost like her normal self again for a few seconds. 'I'm glad he enjoyed it. He certainly joined in with the carols very enthusiastically.'

'He loves singing,' Peter agreed. 'His dad used to too at his age, but then he grew into a teenager and got all self-conscious. Ricky'll be starting school in September. It'll be strange not having him around asking questions all day.'

'Yes,' smiled Chrissie, 'I remember when Kenny was that age … he … he never seemed to – to stop asking why?' Her voice stumbled to a halt and she took refuge in her cup of tea. Peter did the same, although his cup had been empty for some time, unable to think of anything to say.

Gavin drained his cup and put it back down on the table. He leaned over and hugged Chrissie close to him as tears began running down both of their faces. Peter tipped his cup higher to avoid staring at them. As soon as he felt able to risk disturbing them, he got up with the intention of creeping out, but Gavin put out his arm and held him back.

'Don't go – or, at least, only if you've got things you need to do. I mean, we don't want to impose.'

Peter stood for a moment in thought.

'I know!' he said at last. 'Why don't we all go out for a walk? I know when Angie died, I felt exhausted all the time, but I still couldn't sleep unless I'd done some hard physical exercise to tire me out before bed.'

'What do you think, Chrissie?' Gavin asked. 'It sounds a

good idea to me.'

Chrissie wiped her face with a tissue and then looked up and nodded towards Peter. 'Yes, OK. Where shall we go?'

'Anywhere you like,' Peter shrugged, afraid that any suggestion he might make would prompt unwelcome memories.

'Would you mind driving us to Shotover?' Chrissie asked suddenly, appearing almost eager as she looked towards Peter. 'That was Kenny's favourite place. He used to take the scouts orienteering there. That's how I'd like to remember him.'

Peter hesitated. He did not want to deny Chrissie her wish or to imply that her idea was a foolish one, but it was dark and the country park on the edge of Oxford would be deserted and possibly dangerous at this time in the evening on a winter's day. His plan had been for a brisk "turn round the block" through well-lit streets, rather than a moonlight hiking expedition. He was grateful when Gavin intervened.

'Maybe save that for tomorrow?' he suggested, 'when we'll be able to see the view properly. And I think we'd better let Peter go now,' he added, getting to his feet and gathering the teacups together on the tray. 'We've kept him away from his family for long enough!'

'Yes, of course!' Chrissie stood up too, her eyes shiny with moisture, but seeming almost cheerful. 'Thank you so much for coming, Peter. And thank you for your suggestion. I will knit something for Kenny. It'll be my last present to him.'

11. NEW YEAR

The funeral ended up being a much larger affair than Peter (in his anxiety over Gavin's dislike of ceremony and being in the public eye) had hoped for, but perhaps not quite as grandiose as he had feared. They had followed Jonah's suggestion of holding it in the church that hosted Kenny's scout troop – a large building in the traditional cruciform shape, capable of accommodating the large numbers of police and public that could be expected to attend – and had finally fixed on cremation in preference to burial.

'We've been talking to the Council and the Woodland Trust, and we're going to plant a tree in Shotover Country Park,' Chrissie had confided to Peter the day before. 'We can bury his ashes with it and put up a plaque with his name on. I think Kenny would like that more than flowers on a grave.'

Gavin had held out successfully against suggestions that the coffin should be draped with a union jack. It entered the church on the shoulders of six uniformed officers, adorned only with a wreath of white lilies and a police helmet. Peter wondered idly whether there had been any arguments over whether the helmet or a scout hat were the most appropriate headgear to be displayed – and then was immediately angry with himself for having such flippant thoughts.

Gavin, too, arrived in uniform – probably to save himself the bother of deciding on suitable attire for the occasion – with Chrissie in a purple coat beside him. Press cameras clicked as they got out of the funeral car accompanied by Chrissie's sister, Michele, who had arranged for a neighbour to look after their mother so that she could make the long journey from Cornwall. A second car brought Lorraine, Dennis and their three children, while Gavin's brother, Clive, and his family arrived from their hotel on foot and slipped inconspicuously inside under cover of the distraction caused by the entry of the scout troop, all smartly turned out in clean uniforms.

The only place where Jonah's wheelchair could be accommodated was the south transept, which gave him a close – if sideways – view of the area at the front of the church where the main action would take place. He and his friends took their places alongside another wheelchair user, whom Peter recognised as Mary from the nativity play. It seemed that one, at least, of Chrissie's class had insisted on being present.

'Hello!' A woman in a light green hijab leaned forward to speak to them from the other side of the wheelchair. 'My name's Basmah. Rakiya was so keen to come, but I was afraid she'd be the only wheelchair user and it would be difficult. She's in Mrs Hughes's class at school and she's been watching the news stories like a hawk. We recognised you at once,' she added, looking at Jonah. 'You're the detective who tracked down the men who did it, aren't you?'

'Well, I was part of a big team of people,' Jonah smiled back.

'Mrs Hughes came to see us and suggested that it might be a bit much for Raki,' her mother went on, 'but she can be very stubborn when she puts her mind to it.'

'Mum!' Rakiya protested, waving her arm jerkily towards her mother.

'So Mrs Hughes very kindly explained the whole service to us, and she let Rakiya choose one of the songs.'

'I've never been in a church before,' Rakiya told them in slightly slurred speech. 'It's very big.'

'It has to be, because so many people wanted to come,' Jonah told her seriously. 'We're lucky. We've got the best seats. All the other police officers are stuck at the back.'

Peter gazed round, leaving the talking to Jonah. From their

vantage point he had a good view of Gavin and Chrissie as they sat, white-faced and nervous, on the front pew, waiting for the service to begin. The organ played softly. Then the music became quieter and faded into a final cadence. After a few moments of silence the solemn opening of Handel's Largo signalled the arrival of the deceased, and the congregation stood as the coffin made its way slowly down the aisle followed by two scouts carrying flags.

Watching Gavin's anguished face and visibly shaking shoulders, Peter was glad that he had cautioned him against joining the procession. Chrissie, standing next to him, appeared more composed – you might almost say serene – but Peter suspected that this was a massive act of will brought on by her determination to be strong for Gavin and composed enough for the reading that she had chosen as her contribution to this public recognition of Kenny's life.

The coffin was placed on trestles in the crossing between the main body of the church and the transepts. The pall bearers stood briefly to attention, then turned in unison and walked smartly to seats reserved for them at the back of the church, in pews occupied by other officers, all in their best formal uniforms. Chrissie got to her feet and placed the police teddy on top of the coffin where it would be visible to the whole congregation.

The vicar – a small dumpy woman wearing a black cassock and purple stole – asked the congregation to sit. Gavin slumped into his seat as if he would have found it hard to stay on his feet much longer. Chrissie, by contrast, sat unnaturally upright staring straight ahead, as if she were studying some distant object behind the priest's left shoulder.

After some words of welcome and a short prayer, the vicar announced the first hymn: *The Lord's My Shepherd*. Peter remembered that Gavin had chosen this because it had been sung at both of his parents' funerals.

Stella stepped nervously forward and delivered the Bible reading in a clear voice, only faltering a little at the end. It was a short passage from the Gospel of John promising eternal life to all who believe. Peter hoped that Gavin and Chrissie would not dwell too deeply on what level of faith might be required to qualify for this promise. As far as he knew, Kenny's religious observance had been limited to attending church parade occasionally with his scouts.

A senior officer, whom Peter did not recognise, spoke briefly about Kenny's exemplary career and said that he would be sorely missed among his colleagues. Chrissie read a short extract from *Charlotte's Web*, in which Charlotte speaks of the transience of a spider's life and the importance of friendship. Then she looked round at the congregation before announcing the next hymn.

'We chose this song because the children all enjoy singing it in assembly at school,' she said, glancing towards Rakiya, 'and I can remember Kenny singing it when he was at school too. It's about keeping going even when things aren't how we'd like them to be.'

She returned to her place next to Gavin as the introduction to *One more step along the world I go* started up. Peter noticed for the first time, that there was a piano positioned on the opposite side of the church, close to the pulpit, and he recognised Mrs Perkins, the pianist who had accompanied the nativity play, sitting at it.

The vicar gave a short address, in which she urged the congregation not to allow indignation at the way in which Kenny's life had been cut short to devalue that life or to cloud their memories of him.

'We will never know why we were not allowed to have him here with us for longer,' she concluded, 'but we can all be grateful for having been given the privilege of knowing him during that all-too-brief time.'

More prayers followed and then the final hymn, which was *Abide with Me* – another safe hymn, Peter reflected, for an occasion where most of the congregation only came to church for weddings and funerals. The vicar pronounced the benediction. Then the congregation remained standing as the organ began playing again and the pall bearers came forward to lift the coffin and carry Kenny's body back to the waiting hearse. The scouts got up from their seats near the back and hurried outside, ready to form a guard of honour.

Gavin and Chrissie held hands as they followed the coffin up the aisle. Other family members joined the procession. The vicar came last, pausing at the back of the church to invite everyone to a buffet lunch, which the scouts would serve in the church hall while the family attended the short committal service at the crematorium.

As soon as the organ started playing again after the vicar's short speech, Peter got to his feet and hastened up the aisle, keen to be the first to reach the door. He shook hands briefly with the vicar, muttering a few meaningless phrases and then slipped out into the porch. He positioned himself at one side, where he could scrutinise everyone as they came out without blocking the way.

First to leave were two young men with notebooks in their hands – journalists, he assumed. Then, keeping close together and with their heads bowed, he recognised Doug Finney, Mike Lambert and Dave Gillis. He stepped forward to intercept them.

'Gavin asked me to tell you that he particularly wants you to stay for the refreshments,' he told them. 'He wants to speak to you all. So please stay until they get back from the crem.'

Dave and Doug exchanged doubtful glances. Mike pushed past and slipped out, muttering as he went, 'No thanks. Too many cops around for me!'

'Please!' Peter repeated, looking at the other two, who continued to look uncomfortable. 'For Gavin. He wants to thank you for helping to find the guy who killed Kenny.'

The guests were coming out more quickly now. Peter stepped back to allow them through. The two men seemed to be about to follow Mike out into the weak January sunshine, but then Craig appeared and took charge.

'Where's Mike?' he asked sharply.

Doug and Dave shrugged.

'He wouldn't stay,' Peter informed him. 'He left a few

minutes ago.'

'Right!' Craig turned to Brendan, who had come out just behind him. 'You take these two through to this buffet lunch the padre talked about, while I go after him. I promised Gavin we'd all be there when he got back.' Then he swung round to address Peter. 'I spotted a couple more of the guys sitting with Mr Bannister. Do you mind waiting for them to see they get the message too?'

'No problem,' Peter nodded. 'That's what I'm standing here for.'

Most of the guests had finished lunch by the time Gavin, Chrissie and the other family members returned from the crematorium. The scout leader signalled to two of his troop, and they hurried out to the kitchen to replenish the plates of food ranged on long tables at the side of the room. The vicar, who had followed them in, went over to a group of police officers sitting round a table near the centre of the room and spoke to them in a low voice. They immediately got up and made room for the family to sit down.

This seemed to prompt a general movement among the guests. Some people started collecting plates together and returning them to the serving tables. Others responded to the announcement that there was more tea and coffee available, and took their cups for a re-fill. However, Peter felt that this activity was all just cover for watching for an opportunity to approach Gavin and Chrissie to offer condolences – or else to justify themselves in not doing so, for fear of saying the wrong thing.

'I must just pop over and have a word with Chrissie,' he heard a woman saying behind him. 'It's such a dreadful thing to have happened. He was so young!'

'Dreadful,' a man's voice agreed. 'But I suppose at least, with him being so young, he didn't leave a wife and kids behind. I was speaking to someone at work the other day-'

'You've got it all wrong there, son!'

Peter turned abruptly at the sound of Stan's familiar voice

– familiar and yet speaking in a tone that Peter had never heard him use before.

'Don't ever go telling a man who's lost his son that things could've been worse, because they couldn't! How is it better for Kenny never to have had the chance to marry or have kids? If you can't speak sense, you'd better keep your trap shut!'

Peter stared as Stan's face suddenly crumpled and tears started running down his cheeks. He blinked them back and leaned further back in his seat as he mumbled, 'I'm sorry. I didn't mean to …'

The man and woman stood up, muttering words to the effect that it didn't matter and everyone was upset at Kenny's death, before setting off on their mission to speak to Chrissie. Sylvia, sitting next to Stan, took hold of his hand in hers, while Bernie pushed chairs aside to get through to put her arm around him.

'Talk about insensitive!' Lucy exclaimed indignantly.

'No pet,' Sylvia said gently. 'He didn't mean any harm. People do that – try to make things feel better by thinking about how much worse they could be. We had it a lot when Stephen died. I remember one friend of mine – a good friend – saying that at least he was at peace now. She thought, because he killed himself, he must have been really miserable and – and …'

'And now he wasn't miserable any more,' Bernie finished for her. 'But he never *seemed* miserable. That's what none of us could understand! But you shouldn't make excuses for him,' she added, glaring in the direction of the man, who was now standing behind Gavin while his wife attempted to catch Chrissie's attention. She was not yet ready to forgive him for having upset one of her oldest and dearest friends. 'Just because lots of people do it, it doesn't make it OK.'

Peter, having decided that there was nothing useful that he could contribute to the discussion, turned his attention to the couple, who were now engaged in conversation with Chrissie. He was relieved to see that the man remained silent, contenting himself with nodding and smiling as his wife assured Chrissie, 'if there's anything – anything at all – that we can do, you only have to ask.'

They moved on and were replaced by Toby Hitchin, still full of energy and still keen to tell them what a great mate "Ken" had been. If Lucy wanted an example of what "insensitive" really looked like, Peter reflected, this was it. But perhaps he was being unfair. The lad was young and had probably never had someone he knew die before. Moreover, he was a police officer, and part of his behaviour might well be bravado designed to keep his mind from dwelling on the fact that he could easily face the situation that Kenny had been in himself one day.

There was a queue of guests forming in the centre of the room now as many of them prepared to leave and wanted to "have a few words with" Gavin and Chrissie as they did so. Peter cringed as he heard a young woman telling Chrissie earnestly, 'I do know something about how you're feeling ....' Then he mentally chastised himself as she went on, 'When my little boy was taken from me, I just cried and cried for weeks.' It just went to show how careful you ought to be before criticising people for the things they said and did.

'Come and sit down!' Lorraine called from the central table. 'Have something to eat. These sausage rolls are delicious.'

Chrissie slid into one of the chairs that her sister-in-law was gesturing towards, but Gavin shook his head. 'I'm not hungry,' he muttered. 'And there are people I want to talk to.'

He hurried over to a corner of the room, well away from the tables of family and friends, to greet the cluster of homeless men who were standing there, holding empty plates and talking in subdued voices.

'I'm glad you stayed. Thank you for coming and thank you for helping to track down the guys who were responsible.' He turned to Michael Bannister, the warden of the homeless shelter. 'If there's any of this left over,' he said, waving his arm to indicate the tables of food, 'I want you to take it. It'll only be thrown away otherwise, I expect. I'm sure some of your guests will be glad of it.'

'You're not wrong there,' Michael agreed in his gentle voice. 'I could think of several who could do with a few more square meals inside them than they're likely to get fending for themselves.'

'That's very generous of you.' Father Damien emerged from the back of the group and took Gavin by the hand. He gripped his arm with his other hand, smiling up briefly before letting go.

'Not really,' Gavin mumbled. 'It's the Scouts who made it all.'

'And I wanted to thank you for bringing Brendan to Mass on Christmas Eve,' Damien continued. 'I hope you and your wife didn't find my homily too boring. I'm told I sometimes go on a bit!'

'You said some lovely prayers. I liked that one about "those who have lost heart" – at least I think that's what you said,' Gavin added hurriedly, suddenly unsure of himself again.

'That's right,' Damien smiled, '"You give strength to the weary and courage to those who have lost heart." It's a prayer for anyone who's having a hard time. Let me know if you'd like me to come round and pray with you again – or if there's anything else I can do. Do you still have my card?'

'I think so. Chrissie will have put it somewhere safe.'

'Good. Well, as I say, don't hesitate to ring me if there's anything I can do. Now, if you'll excuse me,' the priest added, noticing a young man hovering at his side, evidently keen to speak to Gavin, 'I must just have a word with Peter before he goes.'

He moved off, making way for the earnest young man to say his piece.

'I don't suppose you remember me,' he said, putting out his arm and resting his hand on Gavin's shoulder, with some difficulty because he was considerably shorter than the burly police officer. 'I was at school with Kenny. We used to play football together. I'm Darren – Darren Bowden.'

'You're right, Gavin confessed, 'I don't remember you. I'm sorry.'

'Don't apologise! It must be thirteen years ago the last time I came round to your house. We got split up when we moved on to High School. Kenny was in a different class to me after that. But I remember you helping us to put up a tent in the garden, and your wife bringing out glasses of homemade lemonade. I never knew anyone made that anymore! It was just something we read about in Enid Blyton books. I used to tease Kenny that his mum was like one of those farmer's wives there always were – you know! They used to stuff the kids with food and the kids called them "a real brick"!'

'Yes,' Gavin smiled. 'I read those books when I was a kid too and then I remember Chrissie reading them to Kenny. And now I think I do remember you. Weren't you the one who kept putting on different disguises, like the fat boy in those stories?'

'Happy days!' Darren nodded. 'I was so sorry to hear what happened to Kenny. You must be devastated. I keep looking down at my own little boy and thinking ....' He took a sip from the glass of wine that he was holding. 'But I suppose there's a reason for everything.'

'Yes, I suppose you must be right,' Gavin mumbled politely, without conviction. 'Well, thank you for coming. And now I must go and speak to some more people.'

He crossed the room to where Damien was engaged in conversation with Peter and Jonah. At least they could both be trusted not to come out with meaningless platitudes; and he would like to know what would be happening next as far as the prosecution of Kenny's killers was concerned.

Bernie saw him coming and pulled out a chair.

'Come and sit down,' she called out softly. 'You look all-in.'

'Forensics finally came up with the goods,' Jonah was saying to Damien. 'The DNA under Harry's fingernails is Stuart's – just as we expected – and there were footwear marks in the hall that match the shoes that Shane was wearing when we arrested him.'

'And Terry's car was picked up on traffic cameras in the

area that morning,' Peter added.

'Being driven by a man with a beard and with a couple of passengers,' Jonah continued. 'So we're charging them all with Harry's murder.'

'Didn't you say that they all had alibis though?' queried Damien. 'What about them?'

'Shane and Stuart were each other's alibis,' Jonah told him, 'so we can ignore them. Terry's was a bit more elaborate. He sent Holly off to visit her aunt in Norwich the day before. She made a point of being seen at the Care Home where her aunt was living – with some story about her husband having developed a cold that morning and not wanting to risk infecting the old people – and slept in the room they'd booked, and even made friends with another traveller at a service station on the way home and got herself seen drinking coffee with him there as if they were together. She did a very professional job of creating the impression that they were both miles away when Harry was killed, but we managed to get to the truth in the end.'

'Are those the same guys you're charging with killing Kenny?' Gavin asked. 'I keep getting the names confused.'

'Well, it was Shane Butler who was actually driving the car,' Jonah explained patiently. 'He's admitted that, but claims that hitting Kenny was just an unfortunate accident, after which he panicked and drove off. I can't see the jury buying that story, so I reckon he'll go down for Life, with a minimum of at least thirty years. He's the younger of the two Butler brothers. We think it was *Terry* Butler who was running the show – or maybe Terry and his wife Holly together. Then Stuart Hatton is their enforcer who "persuades" the likes of Ross Pilling to pay their debts.'

'So it was all about drug gangs defending their business interests,' Gavin murmured sadly. 'All this killing just to make money out of the likes of Mike Lambert!'

'That's more or less what the Oxford Mail said this morning.' chipped in Lucy. 'They went to town a bit on demanding a police clamp down on illicit drugs.'

'And blaming the students for attracting the dealers to the city,' commented Bernie wryly, 'as if the problem was unique to university towns! Admittedly, Professor Mickelsen-Scott's letter to the Times won't have done anything to disabuse them of their image of academia as a hotbed of sex and drugs!'

'Oh?' queried Damien. 'I must have missed that.'

'He's an economist,' Bernie explained, 'He was advocating the legalisation of cannabis on the basis that then the bottom would drop out of the illegal trade and the gangs would stop resorting to violence to protect their business.'

'Which completely ignores the fact that criminals like the Butler brothers would simply look for an alternative way of exploiting the vulnerable to make money for themselves,' commented Peter.

'Precisely!' agreed Jonah. 'If you want to argue for legalising cannabis it ought to be on the grounds that there are now so many ordinary members of the public who can't see anything wrong with occasionally smoking a bit of weed that the law can't be enforced – like prohibition in the United States.'

The room was beginning to empty now. Michael Bannister was helping the scouts to clear away the food. The sea of blue uniforms had vanished.

'Do you think it'd be OK if Chrissie and I went home now?' Gavin asked anxiously. 'I don't want anyone to think … but …'

'Of course.' Peter got to his feet. 'Would you like me to drive you?'

'No. I'd rather walk. I'll just go and find Chrissie.'

He looked round trying to locate her. She was standing by the door, greeting people as they went out.

'Goodbye then,' he murmured over his shoulder as he hurried over to join her.

She was talking to a dark-haired woman in a black coat. They seemed to have a lot to say to one another. When Gavin got closer he recognised Bella. He hadn't seen her in the church, but presumably she must have been there. Thank goodness she had approached Chrissie and not him. He wouldn't have had any idea what to say to her, but Chrissie and she seemed to be getting on like a house on fire. Sensing his approach, Chrissie looked up and smiled.

'Do you mind if we go now?' she asked when he reached them. 'I've invited Bella to come round and choose something of Kenny's to remember him by, and she needs to get away soon. The vicar says she'll see everyone out, and Lorraine says she'll take care of the family.'

'I was just coming over to suggest exactly the same thing,' Gavin smiled back, relieved that his ordeal was almost over. He turned to Bella. 'Do you mind walking? I feel I need some fresh air.'

'Me too,' Bella smiled back. 'And thank you. Are you really sure you don't mind me taking something? I don't feel I've got a right – especially after …'

'If you pick something we don't want to let go, we'll tell you,' Chrissie assured her. 'I'm sure Kenny would want you to have something. He really was very fond of you. I never understood why you split up.'

They stepped out into the cool January air and set off on the short walk home.

'It was all my fault,' Bella said in a low voice. 'I can see that now, although I blamed it all on Kenny at the time. I wish I hadn't said all those things to him now. I knew deep down that it was just his work and he couldn't help it, but I told myself he mustn't care about me if he couldn't be there for me when I'd lost my job and everything was so awful!'

Chrissie slipped her hand through Bella's arm.

'And that poor police woman! I said such dreadful things about her!' Bella continued. 'I'm so ashamed! They won't tell her about it, will they? I'm not a racist, really I'm not!'

'No. They won't tell her,' Gavin said, making a mental note to speak to Jonah about ensuring that Stella did not gain access to the tapes of his interview with Bella.

'And Kenny would be so upset if he knew!' Bella sobbed. 'I've just made such a mess of everything!'

Gavin hurried on ahead to open the door. Trust Chrissie

to take pity on what she evidently saw as a damsel in distress, but they already had enough of their own emotions to deal with, without bringing in this young woman who might well simply be an attention-seeker. If Kenny had ended their relationship because he found her too demanding, surely he would not want them to be burdened with her now?

Chrissie led the way up to the spare bedroom. Gavin was about to retreat to the lounge when it occurred to him that, in her generosity, Chrissie might allow Bella to take away some treasured possession that he would not be able to bear losing. He hurried after them, taking the stairs two at a time.

'A friend of ours helped us to pack everything into boxes,' Chrissie was explaining. Kenny's clothes are in that case there, and that box has the stuff from his desk. There are loads of CDs in that box over there. I'm not sure about the rest. Where would you like to start?'

'There was this sort of little hand-painted bowl we got when we were in Ibiza. I bought one for him and he bought one for me. He had it on his desk with paperclips in it.'

'Yes. I remember dusting it.' Chrissie reached over and opened the flaps of a large cardboard box. 'It'll be in here. Go ahead – have a look!'

Bella soon retrieved the bowl and stood clasping it in both hands.

'Thanks. I – I suppose I'd better go now.'

* * *

'May perpetual light shine on him for ever, and may he rest in peace,' Father Damien concluded as he stood looking down at the sapling, which Gavin had just finished planting over Kenny's ashes. He crossed himself and added, 'Amen.'

'Amen,' repeated Gavin and Chrissie.

They stood in silence for several minutes. Then Chrissie bent down and wiped the brass plaque, which they had fixed on a small wooden post in front of the tree, with her scarf. She stood up again and put her arm around Gavin's waist. He placed his around her shoulders and hugged her to him. Damien waited patiently, his hands clasped together in front of him and his head bowed.

Chrissie was the first to move, applying gentle pressure to prompt Gavin to turn round to look down the hillside, across the tops of the trees to Oxford.

'It'll be lovely coming up here in the summer,' Chrissie murmured. 'I'm glad we thought of this, instead of burying him in some old graveyard.'

'Yes,' Gavin agreed.

They stood for a while longer, contemplating the view. Then Chrissie shivered as the wind blew across the hillside and ruffled her hair.

'Time to be going, I think,' she said, starting off across the grass towards the path that led back to the car park. 'Those lesson plans won't write themselves!'

'It was kind of you to let Craig stay in Kenny's room,' Damien said as they made their way back to where Chrissie had parked the car. 'There aren't many people who would do that.'

'I've got all Kenny's things in the spare room where I can go through them when I feel up to it,' Chrissie answered, 'and it'll be nice knowing there's someone else in the house besides the two of us.'

'Craig deserves a chance to get himself back on his feet again,' Gavin added, 'and we owe him a lot for finding the man who killed Kenny.'

'You're not worried that people will think you're trying to replace Kenny?'

'If they do, they need their heads examined,' Gavin declared.

'No one could ever do that,' Chrissie said firmly. 'It's just a sensible, practical arrangement. I just couldn't face going in that room any more – not yet, anyway. It doesn't help me remember Kenny; it just reminds me that he isn't there anymore. We're going to get a nice display cabinet for the front room and put some photos of Kenny and some of his things

– his swimming medals and scout badges and that sort of thing – in there, where we can see them; and Craig's going to sleep in his room and keep it clean for me until he finds a proper place.'

'Kenny doesn't need his room any more,' Gavin added sombrely, 'and Craig does.'

'And when we want to think about Kenny, we'll come up here, where he used to be happy,' Chrissie concluded. 'Now let's get back and have a cup of something to warm us up. And I've made tiffin. You must try some, Father. I used to make it with Kenny when he was little. It's so simple, even pre-school children can do it. Shall I give you the recipe?'

RECIPES

You can try some of the food described in this book for yourself using the following recipes. You can also download individual recipes in PDF format here:

https://sites.google.com/view/bernie-fazakerley/recipes

CHRISSIE'S GINGER CAKE

Ingredients

7 ounces plain flour
3 teaspoons ground ginger
½ teaspoon bicarbonate of soda
3 ounces margarine
2 ounces brown sugar

2 tablespoons golden syrup
2 tablespoons black treacle
1 egg
Milk to mix

Method

1. Line a 6" square baking tin with baking parchment.
2. Set the oven to 160°C /325°F / Gas mark 3.
3. Sift the dry ingredients into a mixing bowl.
4. Melt the margarine, golden syrup and treacle gently in a saucepan or in a bowl in a microwave oven.
5. In a measuring jug, beat the egg and add enough milk to make up to 4 fluid ounces.
6. Add the melted mixture and milk-and-egg mixture to the dry ingredients and stir well.
7. Pour the mixture into the tin.
8. Bake for 75 - 90 minutes, until firm to the touch.
9. Cool on a wire rack before cutting into squares.

CHRISSIE'S CHOCOLATE GINGER BROWNIES

Ingredients

8 ounces margarine

13 ounces sugar

4 eggs

4 ounces self-raising flour

3 ounces cocoa

2 ounces crystallised ginger (chopped)

Method

1. Line a rectangular baking tin (7" by 11" by 1½" deep) with baking parchment.
2. Set the oven to 180°C /350°F / Gas mark 4.
3. Melt the margarine and pour into a large mixing basin.
4. Add the sugar and stir well.
5. Beat the eggs and add them to the mixture.
6. Sift the flour and cocoa into the basin.
7. Mix well.
8. Pour the mixture into the tin.
9. Bake for 40 minutes.
10. Cut into squares while still in the tin and leave to cool before turning it out.

CHRISSIE'S CHEESE STRAWS

Ingredients
4 ounces plain flour (or wholemeal, if preferred)
4 ounces margarine
3 ounces strong cheese (Cheddar, Cheshire or similar)
A little water

Method
1. Grease a baking tray.
2. Set the oven to 200°C /400°F /Gas Mark 6
3. Grate the cheese into a small bowl
4. Sift the flour into a large bowl
5. Rub in the margarine
6. Add the grated cheese
7. Mix together with a knife, adding a little water if necessary to make it stick together
8. Roll out and cut into strips.
9. Put the strips on the baking tray and bake for 15 minutes or until golden brown.

CHRISSIE'S CHERRY ALMOND PUFFS

Ingredients

500g Puff Pastry
75g glacé cherries (chopped)
50g sultanas

200g marzipan
Milk and sugar for the glaze.

Method

1.   Grease a baking tray.
2.   Set the oven to 240°C /400°F /Gas Mark 8
3.   Roll out the pastry to a thickness of about 2mm.
4.   Cut into rounds about 10cm in diameter.
5.   Roll the marzipan into a strip about 3cm wide and 6cm times the number of pastry rounds in length. Cut it in half.
6.   Distribute the cherries and sultanas along one of the strips of marzipan.
7.   Lay the other strip on top and squeeze them together.
8.   Cut the marzipan sandwich up into squares and put one square on each round of pastry.
9.   Moisten the edges of the pastry with milk.
10. Bring the pastry up round the marzipan and seal the edges together.

11. Turn the rounds over and mark the top with a cross using a sharp knife.
12. Brush the top with milk and sprinkle sugar on to make the glaze.
13. Bake in the oven for about 20 minutes or until they are golden brown.
14. Cool on a wire tray and store in an airtight tin

CHRISSIE'S TEA LOAF

Ingredients

8 fluid ounces cold tea
4 ounces brown sugar
1 beaten egg
8 ounces self-raising flour

5 ounces sultanas
4 ounces currants
5 ounces seedless raisins
(Or use 14 ounces of mixed dried fruit)

Method

1. Soak the brown sugar and dried fruit in the tea overnight.
2. Grease a small (7" by 4" by 3½" deep) loaf tin.
3. Set the oven to 160°C /325°F / Gas mark 3.
4. Mix the egg and flour into the sugar, fruit and tea mixture.
5. Bake for 1 hour. Then turn the oven down to 150°C /300°F / Gas mark 2 and bake for a further 30 minutes.
6. Cool on a wire rack.
7. Serve cut into slices and spread with butter.

PETER'S WINTER SALAD

Ingredients

2 ounces long grain brown rice	1 tablespoon olive oil
	1 tablespoon malt vinegar
1 carrot	Sprinkle of cayenne pepper
1 onion	Sprinkle of paprika

A few leaves of kale or cabbage (red, white or a mixture)

Method

1. Cook the rice and allow it to cool.
2. Put the oil and vinegar in a large bowl and beat together.
3. Add a little cayenne pepper and paprika (or omit these for a less spicy dish).
4. Wash the vegetables.
5. Chop the onion and cabbage/kale.
6. Peel and grate the carrot.
7. Toss the rice and vegetables together in the oil-and-vinegar dressing.

BERNIE'S APPLE PIE

Ingredients

8 ounces plain flour   A little milk
2 ounces lard or vegetable lard   Cooking apples
2 ounces margarine or butter   Sugar to taste
Water to mix

Method

1. Stew the apples with as much sugar as necessary according to taste.
2. Set the oven to 200°C /400°F /Gas Mark 6
3. Weigh out the flour, lard and margarine into a food processor.
4. Process the mixture until it has a "breadcrumbs" appearance. (Alternatively, rub in the fat to the flour with the fingers in a mixing bowl.)
5. Add enough cold water to make the mixture stick together in a stiff dough.
6. Roll out a little more than half of the pastry and line a pie dish with it.
7. Fill the pastry case with stewed apple.
8. Roll out the remainder of the pastry to a disc large enough to cover the pie.
9. Moisten the edge of the pie with milk and put on the top, pressing it down firmly all round. Use a knife to

score a pattern round the edge, as in the picture, and to make a cross in the centre to let out the steam.

10. Brush milk over the top and sprinkle with sugar to make a glaze.

11. Bake for 20 – 30 minutes until the crust is golden brown.

CHRISSIE'S CHOCOLATE FUDGE

Ingredients

2 cups white sugar

1 cup brown sugar

Knob of butter

1 cup milk

4 ounces dark chocolate

Vanilla essence

Method

1. Prepare a shallow baking tin by greasing it with margarine.
2. Put all the ingredients together in a large, thick pan.
3. Bring to the boil, stirring until all the sugar is dissolved.
4. Boil vigorously for about 20 minutes, until the "soft ball" stage is reached. (If you have a sugar thermometer, boil to 115°C /235°F. If not, test by dropping a small amount into a cup of cold water.)
5. Remove from the heat and add a teaspoonful of cold milk and a few drops of vanilla essence.
6. Beat vigorously until sugar crystals start to form (about 10 minutes).
7. Quickly pour out into the tray. If it is ready, it will start to set immediately.
8. Mark into squares with a sharp knife, then leave to cool before breaking it up and storing in an airtight container.

MINCE PIES

Ingredients

8 ounces plain flour
2 ounces lard or hard vegetable fat
2 ounces butter or margarine
mincemeat

Method

1. Set the oven to 200°C /400°F /Gas Mark 6
2. Grease a bun tin.
3. Put the flour and fat in a food processor and process until the mixture resembles fine breadcrumbs.
4. Add about 2 tablespoons of cold water.
5. Process until the mixture holds together to form a stiff dough, adding a little more water if necessary.
6. Roll out the dough thinly.
7. Cut rounds to line the indents in the bun tin.
8. Put a teaspoonful of mincemeat in each round.
9. Cut slightly smaller pastry rounds to cover the pies. Stick them on using a little milk.
10. Make a hole in the top of each pie to allow steam to escape.
11. Brush the tops with milk and sprinkle sugar on them to make a glaze.
12. Bake for 15-20 minutes, until they are golden brown.

DEIRDRE'S RAISIN COOKIES

Ingredients

6 ounces margarine
¾ cup white sugar
¾ cup brown sugar
2 eggs

2 cups self-raising flour
2 cups oats
1 cup raisins
1 teaspoon vanilla
essence

Method

1. Set the oven to 180°C /350°F / Gas mark 4
2. Grease two baking trays.
3. Cream together the margarine and sugar in a large bowl.
4. Add the eggs and beat well.
5. Add the flour, oats and raisins, and mix thoroughly
6. Drop dessertspoons of the mixture on to the greased baking trays leaving room for them to spread during baking.
7. Bake for 15-20 minutes, until they are golden brown.

SYLVIA'S CHRISTMAS PUDDING

Ingredients

6 ounces currants
6 sultanas
12 ounces raisins
3 ounces mixed peel
4 ounces self-raising flour
8 ounces suet

8 ounces breadcrumbs
1 teaspoon mixed spice
1 large carrot, grated
4 eggs, beaten
Milk to mix

Method

1. Put all the ingredients in a bowl and mix well, adding enough milk to make the whole mixture moist, but not runny.
2. Grease two two-pint pudding basins.
3. Pour the mixture into the basins and cover with greaseproof paper.
4. Steam for 8 hours.
5. Store in a cool place.

CHRISSIE'S TIFFIN

Ingredients

8 ounces plain biscuits
4 ounces margarine
Glacé cherries

1 heaped tablespoon cocoa
1 tablespoon golden syrup
Dried fruit

Method

1. Melt margarine, syrup and cocoa together in a large bowl in the microwave oven or over a pan of boiling water.
2. Grind the biscuits to fine crumbs in a food processor or by crushing with a rolling pin.
3. Mix the crumbs and fruit into the melted mixture.
4. Press into a baking tray and leave in the fridge to set.
5. Cut into squares.

THANK YOU

Thank you for taking the time to read Weed Killers. If you enjoyed it, please consider telling your friends or posting a short review. Word of mouth is an author's best friend and much appreciated. Thank you,

Judy

ACKNOWLEDGEMENTS

I would like to thank all the Facebook friends who contributed suggestions during the planning stages of this book. In particular: Marion West came up with the title; Liz Parkinson suggested some useful background to the Hughes family including the idea that PC Hughes Junior should be called Kenneth and that his mother should be a Special Needs teacher. Sarah Tyson's idea that Mrs Hughes might be keen on baking developed into a plan to include a recipe in every chapter.

I am particularly indebted to Heather Rotherham, who advised me on how Kenny's parents could be expected to behave after his death. She also read sections of the book and advised me on how to make them more true to life. I hope that that it has turned out in the end as a fitting tribute to her son, Luke, to whom it is dedicated.

"Because I knew you I have been changed for good." (quoted in the dedication) is a line from the song *For Good*, by Stephen Schwartz (from the musical *Wicked*), which was performed at the service of thanksgiving for Luke's life.

The Apostrophe Protection Society Facebook Group provided valuable advice on punctuation, in particular regarding the vexed question of the correct use of apostrophes in the word "ha'p'orth".

As with previous books, I am grateful to Gillian Gilbert for reading the manuscript, giving helpful comments and pointing out typographical errors.

I am indebted to the authors of a wide range of internet

resources, which have been invaluable for researching the background to this book. In particular, *Care for the Family*'s personal stories provided insight into the different ways in which parents may be affected by the death of a grown-up child (https://www.careforthefamily.org.uk/). Other sources include:

- Wikipedia (https://en.wikipedia.org/)

- Google Maps (www.google.co.uk/maps)

- Oxford Homeless Movement (oxfordhomelessmovement.org.uk)

- The Crown Prosecution Service (www.cps.gov.uk)

- Tweets from the many police officers (human and canine) with Twitter accounts

The following books were invaluable in helping me to appreciate the different ways in which parents may grieve the loss of a child, and, I hope, enabled me to portray Gavin's and Chrissie's different reactions in a realistic way:

- *A Grief Observed,* C S Lewis, Faber & Faber, 1966;

- *When Bad Things Happen to Good People*, Harold S Kushner, Pan Books, 2002 (previously published in America in 1981);

- *Lament for a Son*, Nicholas Wolterstorff, Eerdmans Publishing Co., 1987;

- *A song for Jenny,* Julie Nicholson, Harper Collins, 2008.

Some books suitable for talking with children about death are mentioned in the text:

- *Badger's parting gift*, Susan Varley, Harper Collins, 1984

- *The Velveteen Rabbit*, Margery Williams, first published 1922

DISCLAIMER

This book is a work of fiction. Any references to real people, events, establishments, organisations or locales are intended only to provide a sense of authenticity and are used fictitiously. All of the characters and events are entirely invented by the author. Any resemblances to persons living or dead are purely coincidental.

Many of the locations and institutions that feature in this book are real. Their inhabitants and employees, however, are purely fictional. In particular:

- The Special School where Chrissie Hughes works does not exist and is not based on any school in Oxfordshire or elsewhere;

- You will search in vain for Gladstone Road, Palmerstone Crescent, Ridley Avenue or Chichester Road;

- The Norham Lodge Hotel is a figment of the author's imagination;

- The Oxford Mail is a real newspaper, but any of its opinions reported here are entirely made up;

- Professor Mickelsen-Scott does not exist and does not resemble any real member of the academic staff at the University of Oxford or any other university.

MORE ABOUT BERNIE AND HER FRIENDS

There are now thirteen **Bernie Fazakerley Mysteries**:

1. **Two Little Dickie Birds**: a murder mystery for DI Peter Johns and his Sergeant, Paul Godwin.

2. **Murder of a Martian**: Peter and Jonah solve a double murder and Peter meets Martin Reiss for the first time.

3. **Grave Offence**: Peter investigates an assault and a suspicious death, while Jonah is in rehab in the spinal injuries centre.

4. **Awayday**: a traditional detective story set among the dons of Lichfield College.

5. **Death on the Algarve:** a mystery for Bernie and her friends to tackle while on holiday in Portugal.

6. **Mystery over the Mersey**: a murder mystery set in Liverpool.

7. **Sorrowful Mystery**: Jonah investigates a child abduction and Peter embarks on a new journey of faith.

8. **In my Liverpool Home**: Bernie and her friends return to Liverpool to investigate a suspicious death in Aunty Dot's Care Home.

9. **Organ Failure**: a body is discovered under the organ in St Cyprian's Church and Jonah is called in to investigate.

10. **Rainbow Warrior**: One of their friends is injured in a hit-and-run incident and Jonah is convinced that this is attempted murder.

11. **Admission of Innocence**: Father Damien calls Peter and Jonah out of retirement to solve a murder case and prevent a miscarriage of justice.

12. **Lethal Mix**: Three of Lucy's student friends are injured in an anti-Muslim hate crime in Liverpool. Jonah, Peter and Bernie assist Merseyside Police to bring their attacker to justice.

13. **A Secret Gardener?** Bernie's friend Martin discovers a body in the Fellows' Garden of his Oxford College.

PC Gavin Hughes has featured in several of these, but "Weed Killers" is the first novel in which he is a central character. Look out for future books in this new series.

Bernie also appears in two other novels:
- **Changing Scenes of Life**: Jonah Porter's life story, told through the medium of his favourite hymns.

- **Despise not your Mother**: the story of Bernie's quest to learn about her dead husband's past.

There is also a book of short stories, in which Peter narrates his side of the story:
- **My Life of Crime**: the collected memoirs of DI Peter Johns. This includes some episodes that appear in other books, but told from a new perspective, as well as some completely new stories.

You can find them all on Judy Ford's Amazon Author page: www.amazon.co.uk/-/e/B019315B1M

Read more about Bernie Fazakerley and her friends and family at https://sites.google.com/site/llanwrdafamily/

Visit the Bernie Fazakerley Publications Facebook page here: www.facebook.com/Bernie.Fazakerley.Publications.

Follow Bernie on Twitter: https://twitter.com/BernieFaz.

GLOSSARY OF UK POLICE RANKS

Uniformed police

Chief Constable (CC) – Has overall charge of a regional police force, such as Thames Valley Police, which covers Oxford and a large surrounding area.

Deputy Chief Constable (DCC) – The senior discipline authority for each force. 2nd in command to the CC.

Assistant Chief Constable (ACC) – 4 in the Thames Valley Police Service, each responsible for a policy area.

Chief Superintendent ('Chief Super') – Head of a policing area or department.

Police Superintendent – Responsible for a local area within a police force.

Chief Inspector (CI) – Responsible for overseeing a team in a local area.

Police Inspector – Senior operational officer overseeing officers on duty 24/7.

Police Sergeant – Supervises a team of officers.

Police Constable (PC) – 'Bobby on the beat'. Likely to be the first to arrive in response to an emergency call.

Police Community Support Officer (PCSO) – A uniformed civilian member of the police service.

Crime Investigation Department (CID) – Plain clothes officers

Detective Superintendent (DS) – Responsible for crime

investigation in a local area.

Detective Chief Inspector (DCI) – Responsible for overseeing a crime investigation team in a local area. May be the Senior Investigating Officer heading up a criminal investigation.

Detective Inspector (DI) – Oversees crime investigation 24/7. May be the Senior Investigating Officer heading up a criminal investigation.

Detective Sergeant (DS) – Supervises a team of CID officers.

Detective Constable (DC) – One of a team of officers investigating crimes.

These descriptions are based on information from the following sources:

[1] Mental Health Cop blog, by Inspector Michael Brown, Mental Health co-ordinator, College of Policing. mentalhealthcop.wordpress.com/, accessed 31st March 2017.

[2] Thames Valley Police website, www.thamesvalley.police.uk , accessed 31st March 2017.

BERNIE'S "FAMILY"

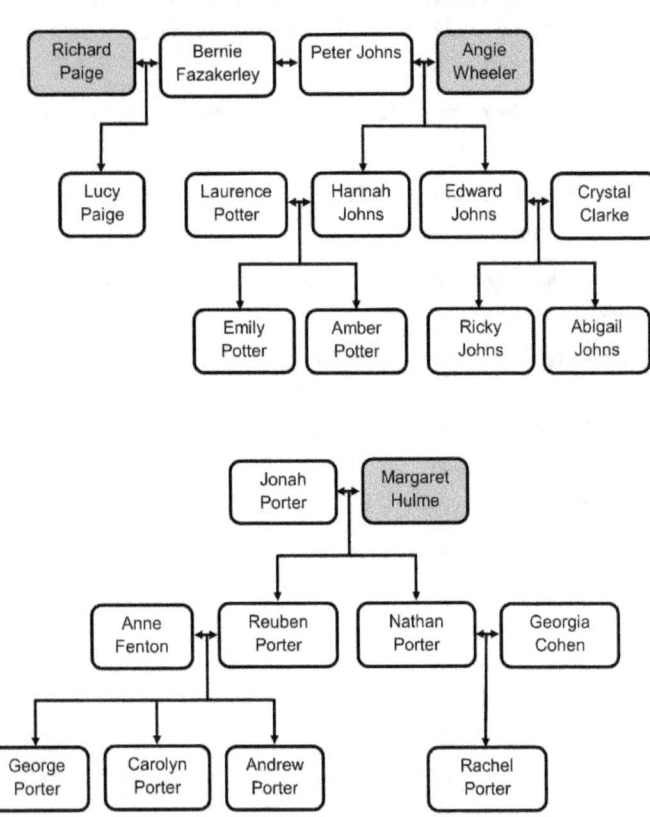

WHO'S WHO

Victims

PC Kenneth (Kenny) Hughes (24)

Harry Whittle (16)

Hughes Family

PC Gavin Hughes (50)	Kenny's father.
Christine Hughes (51)	Kenny's mother.
Clive Hughes (62)	Gavin's brother. Lives in Inverurie.
Irene Hughes (62)	Married to Clive
Flora Hughes (31)	Clive's daughter. Lives with Irene in Inverurie.
Lynsey Hughes (34	Clive's daughter. Lives with her husband and children in Aberdeen.
Russell Hughes (60)	Gavin's brother. Emigrated to Australia 1983.
Annette Hughes (60)	Married to Russell
Lorraine Rowbottom (55)	Gavin's sister. Lives in Hull.
Dennis Rowbottom (57)	Married to Lorraine.
Gloria Sinclair (78)	Pauline's mother. Retired to Cornwall in 1995. Suffering from dementia.
Arthur Sinclair 1935-1998	Christine's father.
Michele Sinclair (55)	Christine's sister. Moved to Cornwall to look after Gloria in 2015.

Whittle Family

Yvonne Whittle (45)   Harry's mother. Cleaner.

Trevor Whittle (48)   Harry's father. Taxi driver.

Leo Whittle (12)   Harry's brother

Members of the homeless community

Craig Manson (35)   Rough sleeper. Ex-military.

Douglas Finney (44)   Rough sleeper.

Dave Gillis (68)   Rough sleeper.

Brendan Connolly (53)   One-time member of St Cyprian's Boys Club. Recently released on licence from a sentence for manslaughter.

Mike Lambert (38)   Cannabis user. Lives in homeless hostel.

Michael Bannister (70)   Assistant Priest at St Cyprian's 1975 – 1978. Left the priesthood in 1980. Now manager of a homeless shelter in Rose Hill.

Bernie's "Family"

Bernie Fazakerley (61)   Married to Peter. Formerly Fellow in Applied Mathematics at St Luke's College. Jonah's Personal Assistant.

DS Richard Paige 1939-99   Married to Bernie. Lucy's father.

Lucy Paige (19)   Bernie's daughter.

DI Peter Johns (68)   Married to Bernie. Retired from police.

Angela Johns 1954- 2003   Married to Peter.

Hannah Potter (39)   Peter's daughter. Married to Laurence.

Laurence Potter (43)   Married to Hannah.

Edward (Eddie) Johns (37) Peter's son. Married to Crystal.

Crystal Johns (39)   Eddie's wife.

Ricky Johns (3)   Eddie's son & Peter's grandson.

Abigail Johns (2)   Eddie's daughter & Peter's granddaughter.

Emily Potter (9)   Hannah's daughter & Peter's granddaughter.

Amber Potter (6)   Hannah's daughter & Peter's granddaughter.

DCI Jonah Porter (61)   Married to Margaret.

Margaret Porter 1955-2014   Married to Jonah.

Reuben Porter (35)   Jonah's son.

Nathan Porter (29)   Jonah's son.

Friends of the family

Deirdre Carr (73)   Widow. Member of St Cyprian's congregation. Constantly supplies Father Damien with food.

Stan Corbridge (80)   Married to Sylvia.

Sylvia Corbridge (79)   Married to Stan.

Fr Damien Rowland (41)   Priest at St Cyprian's Church.

Celeste Gilbert (74)   Grandmother to Leroy, Daniel and Stella

Grace Gilbert 1973-2004   Celeste's daughter. Mother to Leroy, Daniel and Stella

Leroy Gilbert (30)   Celeste's grandson, Stella's half-brother.

Daniel Gilbert (23)   Celeste's grandson, Stella's half-brother.

PC Stella Gilbert (20)   Celeste's granddaughter. Trainee police constable.

Police Personnel (listed alphabetically)

DI Rupert Andrews (44)

Sgt Malcolm Appleton (32)

Chief Superintendent Alison Brown (59)

Inspector Tracy Burton (43)

Dr Michael Carson (59)   Pathologist.

DCI Anna Davenport (42)

PC Stella Gilbert (20)

PC Toby Hitchin (24)

Inspector Jordan Fox (39)

Sgt Pamela Gregson (39)   Custody Officer

DS Andrew Lepage (35)

DC Alice Ray (28)

DC Joshua Pitchfork (26)

DCI Jonah Porter (61)

PC Callum McLaughlin (23)

Jennifer Moorehouse (43)   Civilian staff member.

PC Louise Otterbourne (24)

PD Q (7)   General Purpose Police Dog.

PC Melanie Stanton (33)   Dog Handler

PC Ben Timpson (27)

Others (listed alphabetically)

Janet Beddoes (52)   Head of lower school at Chrissie's school

Holly Butler (36)   Terry's wife.

Shane Butler (37)   Brother to Terry.

Terence (Terry) Butler (41) Brother to Shane. Married to Holly.

Davina Greenslade (46)   Consultant trauma surgeon

Stuart Hatton (35)   works for Terry and Shane.

Belinda Kennedy (54)   Bella's mother

Bella Kennedy (27)   Kenny's ex-girlfriend.

John Kennedy (56)   Bella's father

Ross Pilling (31)   Sells drugs on the streets.

Shirley Prentice (67)   Neighbour to the Whittles

Alfie Simmons 2006-2018   Member of Kenny's scout troop. Died in an accident in summer 2018.

Emerald Simmons (12)   Alfie's sister

ABOUT THE AUTHOR

Like her main character, Bernie Fazakerley, Judy Ford is an Oxford graduate and a mathematician. Unlike Bernie, Judy grew up in a middle-class family in the South London stockbroker belt. After moving to the North West and working in Liverpool, Judy fell in love with the Scouse people and created Bernie to reflect their unique qualities. She has worked in academia and in the NHS.

As a Methodist Local Preacher, Judy often tells her congregation, "I see my role as asking the questions and leaving you to think out your own answers." She carries this philosophy forward into her writing and she hopes that readers will find themselves challenged to think as well as being entertained.